INFINITE GROUND

INFIN ITE GROUND

A NOVEL

MARTIN MacINNES

ASHLAND PUBLIC LIBRARY
66 FRONT STREET
ASHLAND, MA 01721

MELVILLE HOUSE
BROOKLYN • LONDON

INFINITE GROUND

Copyright © 2016 by Martin MacInnes
First published by Atlantic Books in the United Kingdom, August 2016
First Melville House Printing: August 2017

Melville House Publishing
46 John Street
Brooklyn, NY 11201
and
8 Blackstock Mews
Islington
London N4 2BT

mhpbooks.com
facebook.com/mhpbooks
@melvillehouse

Library of Congress Cataloging-in-Publication Data

Names: MacInnes, Martin, author.
Title: Infinite ground / Martin McInnes.
Description: First American edition. | Brooklyn : Melville House, 2017.
Identifiers: LCCN 2017012247 | ISBN 9781612196855 (hardcover)
Subjects: LCSH: Missing persons--Investigation--Fiction. | South
   America--Fiction. | BISAC: FICTION / Mystery & Detective / Police
   Procedural. | FICTION / Psychological. | FICTION / Literary. | GSAFD:
   Mystery fiction.
Classification: LCC PR6113.A2628 I54 2017 | DDC 823/.92--dc23
LC record available at https://lccn.loc.gov/2017012247

ISBN: 978-1-61219-685-5

Designed by Betty Lew

Printed in the United States of America

10 9 8 7 6 5 4 3 2 1

'Why should I be disgusted by the mass that came out of the cockroach?'

—CLARICE LISPECTOR,
THE PASSION ACCORDING TO G.H.

PART ONE

CORPORATION

I.

Walking is something perfected by children, the people who learn it and who have nowhere else to go. Walking is a special pleasure of children and they see it springing up in others. They learn it quite similarly, watching each other move. Children are the ones who learn to move for the first time, and not simply by growing but by moving themselves. Children don't need to tell themselves to continue moving, once it's all started, and adults are grateful for this process having been enabled. Once it's been established, walking commands the community area as people move around and pick up pieces and drop them elsewhere. In addition to transporting body-weight and facilitating social interaction, walking maintains air-diversity in trailing multiple breaths across and over each other, and this in turn supports the growth of vegetable, fungal and animal life.

TRIBES OF THE SOUTHERN INTERIOR, P. 17

HE GOT THE CALL in the night, for some reason. His help would be appreciated going over a case. How recent was unusual—the man had been gone only three weeks. He was to put everything aside and concentrate, for a spell, exclusively on this. Resources would be made available. He would be given all the support they could provide.

He explained his doubts and received the necessary assurances: he would have authority and resources; he could work independently or in league; though he had officially retired, to all intents and purposes it would be just as if he remained a senior investigating officer.

CARLOS, THE MISSING PERSON, was twenty-nine years old, single, and lived in a small apartment under an informal rent agreement that afforded him little security. He had joined his workplace—a financial institution in the process of a large and complex merger, leaving it for the moment without a name—six years ago, straight from college. He was devoted to his job, known to forego holidays.

He had recently moved into his own office, with a personal secretary: a considerable forward step. His work demands were said to have increased threefold, but remained nothing out of the ordinary. Reception records showed he was arriving earlier and leaving later every day.

Carlos took a metro and two buses to and from his work. To enter the corporation building he would wait for a vehicle to approach the basement parking lot entrance and jog or walk briskly in behind before the barriers closed. He phoned his mother, Maria, every second Sunday. Maria had been planning the meal at La Cueva for some time. It took around thirty-five minutes, after Carlos had got up from the table, for the party to establish that something had gone wrong. His cousin, Gabriela, had insisted they continue their meal, the price of which meant it was considered a treat.

Maria first reported her son missing the following morning, but he couldn't be registered as such for another thirty-two hours. By this stage not only had all possibly significant forensic information been dispersed from the restaurant, but Carlos's flat had also been reoccupied, his possessions, among which was either a telescope or a microscope, dumped in two black refuse sacks left out on the street.

The original investigating officers monitored his phone records, bank accounts and email addresses; all activity had ceased on the 24th. They interviewed his family, reconstructed the night in question and promised they would do all they could to find him. Most likely, one officer had said, your son left of his own volition, and he will walk back in through this door just any day now.

THE INSPECTOR FOUND IT a little confusing to begin with, going over his questions with the people concerned—family, friends, the staff at La Cueva, adjacent diners on the evening Carlos disappeared—as their answers seemed laboured, artificial. People responded to his enquiries without any evidence of thinking. They spoke, almost to a person, in the manner of a performance. Of course they did—they had been through all this before, he realized, several times at least. He was not the first to put these questions to them. And now, bringing them back, all he was doing was dredging up remembered, polished versions of the things they'd said some time before.

'IT IS JUST,' SHE said, 'that I haven't been back here since. Maybe none of it happened. Is that possible, Inspector? Is that ourselves, there, at the table?'

'Just tell me, Maria, exactly what you remember.'

'Well we hadn't all been together like that in years. A reunion of sorts, and it was all my doing. I sent the invitations, made the phone calls, the reservation. The thing about the meal—it wasn't to celebrate a particular occasion like a birthday or an anniversary or something, it was simply for the good of us all seeing each other. Many years, I'm ashamed to say. It was a beautiful night—because of the atmosphere, the light. The storm had cleared; it had just stopped raining.

'As you know, my son Carlos pushed back his chair, excused himself from the table and went to visit the bathroom. We had eaten our starters and we were enjoying our main courses. It is a little surprising Carlos got up while we were eating. He is normally such an attentive and thoughtful man, though I imagine you never believe a mother when she says these things, and why would you? And he had already gone earlier—I assume that that was where he went, the bathroom—which is also unusual, because he had not drunk more than three glasses of wine.

'Should I really carry on with these details? I'd thought they were only important to me, because of what happened later, what was about to happen, in the restaurant I mean. I wish I could remember everything. It was remiss of me not to have started from the very beginning and recorded everything my child did, moment by moment, so I could always have it—of course I never expected him to go, to experience losing him, which is unnatural, a mother having to confront this in the case of her child. Not that I am giving up hope, either. For one thing I have brought you here, to the scene.

'I began making lists. I've been doing so ever since he disappeared. There is so much I don't know of his life and I wouldn't even want to speculate, it's his own private area, it's not a mother's business, but at least at the start, when he was small, I had complete knowledge of things such as where he slept, and so I have begun making lists of my impressions from his early years. Here, I will show you one.'

The inspector scanned the pages, the locations written in brief descriptions as items numbered from the margin: 'folds of assistant midwife's lower arms'; 'sand on cove'; 'forest-patterned blankets'. The list went on. He nodded for her to continue.

'Well, we recorded significant moments like birthdays and his first day at school, we have an album of photographs of those sorts of things, but it is all the uncountable, absent pictures between them that are difficult now. I'm not saying it's possible to record everything, I know it's not, but we could have done more, we could have held on to more of these details.

'He pushed his chair back a little, careful not to let it screech on the tiled floor, and he smiled at his cousin, Gabriela, sitting to his left in a beautiful soft yellow gown that might have been thought too much for a routine family gathering, only this wasn't routine at all, as I've explained, and I'm sure we would all have remembered it even if Carlos hadn't disappeared. As he was pushing the chair back several inches in order to give himself room to stand, he stopped, aware just in time of the waiter about to pass between our table and the next; and it is just like Carlos to notice in time, he is very observant, and considerate, kind. He paused for a count of two, dragging out the motion, before finally standing up and walking to the bathroom. And that is the last I saw of him.'

She looked nervous. He thought she was waiting quite anxiously for his reaction. She looked away, then sharply back at him, as if trying to catch him out.

'I have a confession, Inspector. In reality, I didn't see him stand up from the table. I was aware of him doing it, from the corner of my eye. I didn't pay attention, but others later told me he had gone to visit the bathroom. This is merely how I have chosen to remember it, with more of the detail it deserves.

'I spend a lot of time imagining him pushing back his chair. I spend days doing only this, Inspector. I could speak about this for as long as you have to listen, which I know you will advise me is contrary to the interests of my health, but still, it helps, in some way.'

THE HEAT OBSTRUCTED HIM. It slowed down everything. Action took a little longer in this weather. Getting dressed, preparing food, going up and down a flight of stairs. You had to walk slowly as a caution against ruining clothes. He was late for appointments, yet frustrated when the other party arrived later still.

Transport suffered, one public strike after another. Walking wasn't much better: in dense pedestrian areas you could actually feel, live, the substance sloughing off the population. At the same time other life quickened. By afternoon there was the odour everywhere of product turned to pulp. The bins, even at a distance, appeared unstable, as if you could see the fruit inside expiring, liquefying and vanishing. It was getting worse. He longed for the inhalation of cold, fresh air, all but floored by the momentary consideration of standing on a dawn coastline, the sound of a slowly lapping tide, the hint of new colour to the east.

The inspector lived in the north of the city, a significant distance from the station. When he and his wife had first moved in it had been relatively cheap. Food outlets on street level, an assortment of unpretentious cafés. The area had an unjust reputation for high crime rates. It wasn't a quiet place, but that was okay. The calls, in various accents and languages, the crash, at all hours, of bottles tipped into industrial bins. Sirens, infants crying. They had got used to it all; they hadn't minded so much. She used to say she couldn't sleep in hotels. Something about the silence. She had been conditioned by the drone of accumulated outside sounds, louder in their evenings as they prepared to sleep. He, however, could and did sleep anywhere.

A commute of forty-five minutes minimum was required to get into the city, and he had enjoyed this journey, not just as a buffer, but as a productive time to think, encouraged by movement and transition. He had often had ideas, insights, breakthroughs in cases, even, as he walked with the hundreds of others down towards the subway tracks or emerged blinking out into the sunlight at the other end.

He liked to imagine the subway traced the route of the river, the Rio Paraná, passing from the east, where the hills on the city edge gave way to the sculpted landscape of the financial district. The river itself changed according to context. From the corporate verandas the water could appear golden, the sunlight refracted off several thousand glass panes; from the river edge itself it was brown and fast, thick with the smell of copper.

La Cueva was set into a natural hillside out on the eastern limits, past the financial district, near the top of a climb. At capacity it seated two hundred diners with additional space for eighteen at the bar. The floor was finished black and was reflective for three hours late in the morning into early afternoon. Prices were considered moderate to expensive. The Rodriguez family running La Cueva specialized in steamed river fish; it was what Carlos was eating the night he disappeared, and so the inspector ordered it too, whenever he ate there.

He was always made to feel welcome by the owners, partly, he thought, because he was inconspicuous, slow, he never made a scene. It would not be evident to the other diners that a police official was there, regardless of whether or not he was present in a work capacity. And the owners seemed a little uncomfortable, almost apologetic, having hosted the scene of a crime, something inexplicable.

They barely cooked the river fish, were at the very least skilled in making it appear that way. Kept the head attached, even the eyes, though the flesh came away easily and softly with the fork.

The case was not clear cut. It interested him. As if it were not enough that the man had disappeared just like that, from the middle of the restaurant, without any warning whatsoever, and further that the mother, in relating the incident, had gone on for some time about what even he would consider insignificant details, it turned out, now, that this woman was not who she claimed to be. She was not related to the disappeared, had in fact never met him, was merely employed by the mother to speak on her behalf, she being— the real mother, that is—still too upset to return to the restaurant.

Maria—he had yet to find out the actor's name—had continued in her narration at the restaurant, reconstructing for him what had happened, or at least her idea of what had happened, along with some of her apparently inexhaustible supply of speculations. What it came down to, he thought, the fuel for this torrent of words, was her astonishment. What had happened, simply put, was impossible. Carlos had gone to the bathroom and then to all intents and purposes he had stopped existing. 'There is something awful about it,' she said, 'in the old sense.' She had the feeling she could have followed him directly, gone where he had gone, put each foot in the right place every time, and still been none the wiser. As well as being distraught, confused, she was afraid. It was almost as if she had been moved suddenly into a country whose rules and customs she had not mastered, yet she had gone on smiling, carefully choreographing her steps, talking in a slow and laboured translation full of clichés and idioms, ready-made blocks of speech that she could present in the hope it would not become obvious that she did not, in fact, know anything about this bewildering foreign place in which a man can simply be going about his day and then be cancelled. She was not in favour of investigating the occult, that was a dangerous path, she said, a tricky slope, but there was something dark and strange at work here, and often now, even in broadest daylight or while going about her shopping in the supermarket, say, she would watch her step, mindful of the ever-present possibility of going under, of falling, vanishing into a darkness.

HE LOCATED COPIES OF the local and national papers printed on the day of the disappearance and on those immediately preceding and following. He knew the weather—the last day, incidentally, of rain before the heatwave—the traffic levels; the sporting events; the political engagements. He recorded every crime, however unrelated or innocuous it seemed; took note of every traffic violation in the city in the hours after Carlos had gone missing.

A supplementary pull-out in one of the less reputable dailies had listed an anticipated astronomical event. The event, if that's what he was to call it—a passing astral arrangement—had been predicted to take place on the date of Carlos's disappearance, but he could find no further allusions in the subsequent press. Omega Centauri, a globular star cluster thousands of light years away: twelve billion years old and vast enough that from areas low in artificial light it resembles a full moon. However many times he read the article, he couldn't really understand what it described. He imagined eclipses, moon shadows, breaks in the line of vision. An arbitrary pattern, a geometry moving inconceivable distances away and Carlos, meaninglessly, hidden from view in a shadow line.

He knew the staff at La Cueva and he knew the regulars and he knew each room and every exit. He went out for cigarettes. He visited the bathroom. There was nothing unusual about the restaurant, nothing that seemed to present any opportunities for a sudden and comprehensive disappearance.

He visited morgues and looked through unidentified bodies and saw nothing. Speculating amnesia, he consulted the psychiatric wards and hospitals but got nowhere. The questions were familiar and the staff were sure they had given the police these answers before, some time ago.

He worked largely without thinking. It was the best way. He would fall into something, a discovery. He amassed notes, detailed transcriptions of his days' enquiries, the places he went to and the people he talked with. The more information that accumulated, the more likely something of significance would come up. Some detail, no matter how innocuous it might appear at first, would be the key to finding out where Carlos had got to on the night of the 24th.

II

Stretching out to full height, the standing body imparts feelings of control, potential and pleasant awareness of violent reserves. Getting up from the chair at day's end recapitulates a version of evolution in which the human rises to a more powerful position, at an increased distance from the ground. The sensation of abrupt elevation, at 5 or 5.30, is surpassingly pleasurable and leads to a real sense of warmth and job satisfaction. None of this exists in the interior.

TRIBES OF THE SOUTHERN INTERIOR, P. 29

SUCH WAS THE PROTRACTED nature of merger negotiations, the corporation Carlos worked for had been nameless for years. The inspector believed this was deliberate, designed to exploit loopholes, circumvent various responsibilities. The corporation's legal team as well as its administrators, its marketing department and its front desk staff, had to adapt their language to account for the fact that the body they worked for had no name. It was difficult for the inspector to make external enquiries, because he could not immediately identify the word for the entity to which he was referring. This delayed his progress; he came across as vague, too general, as if he were not actually interested in retrieving the information. He had not forgotten the name, he said, it was simply that the institution, for the moment, did not have one. He had assumed that for tax, pension and payroll purposes the corporation would have an

13

interim name, even just a code, a long series of numbers that could be used in transactions and other official communications, but investigations suggested otherwise.

He learned that, unlike the apartment, which now housed a young, polished PR consultant, Carlos's office had not been reoccupied, and employees remained prohibited from entering. According to the original reports, anything of real substance had already been removed. Although it was detailed that the computer remained on the desk, it was a shell: the hard drive, containing all the reports Carlos had contributed to, the total record of his emails in and out, his work-time diary, the various projects he was working on at the time he disappeared, had gone. His login had been disabled—a reflex action that kicked in, the inspector was told, after seven days of unscheduled leave. Retrieving the hard drive, and the associated physical evidence of work—paper files, reports, folders—was proving inexplicably and confoundedly difficult. The secure storage facility used by the police department claimed no record of the items. Corporate representatives responded to his telephoned enquiries in automated tones, assuring him the necessary authority would investigate his requests and contact him at the earliest opportunity.

HE WONDERED WHETHER CARLOS had been involved in fraud. It would explain why the work records had vanished. It might offer a partial explanation for his disappearance: a desertion, a flight.

The inspector had little experience of this kind of duplicity and had kept his time in the financial district to a minimum, but he knew he had to follow wherever the case led. He borrowed an unmarked car from the station and joined an artery heading east.

The traffic was interminable and everything was made of glass. He failed to understand the thinking behind it. Was it as literal as wanting to appear transparent? A corporate confidence trick? The last thing you could do in daylight hours was look inside, the sunlight blasting back from the surfaces. Other glass was dark, tinted, frosted. It was difficult to think clearly. He continually adjusted his sunglasses, rubbing the infernal itch across the top of his thick black hair, wiping his forehead with a handkerchief, cursing under his breath, the damp spreading under his arms stopping him from removing his jacket.

At the front door of Registro Mercantil the caretaker had him show identification and complete a series of registration forms and an additional survey. He waited almost an hour for a clerk to appear, before being taken to a small basement room lined with rows of tall grey cabinets. The archives amounted to only a percentage of the transactions covering the years he had requested; for anything else he'd have to wait. Clearance could take a while, the clerk said, and left him to it.

The main indicator of large-scale fraud was records of unlikely purchases. According, at least, to his half-remembered training. The problem in identifying evidence was the impenetrable legalese. He could see himself spending hours fruitlessly scanning through the minimal paperwork. Were he to be rigorous, trace the nature of every significant outgoing payment, or, say, only those whose purpose remained unclear, he would have to leave aside virtually everything else in the investigation. At this early stage he couldn't justify limiting his remit to such an extent. Technically, nothing linked the disappearance to financial irregularities or even to the corporation at all; the process of requesting assistance, the loan of an officer better versed in fraud, for example, would itself be too time consuming and ultimately to the detriment of the case. So he really was, as he saw it, on his own. He would comb through the records as quickly as he could, not wasting longer than a single afternoon.

The corporation moved money around. That, at least, was clear.

He came across some highly unusual claims. A protest group had launched a civil action, claiming illegal occupation of land in the interior and the resettling of tribal communities. Information was scarce—much seemed to have been deleted or redacted and it had inevitably come to nothing, the parties arriving at a settlement. The individuals concerned were impossible to trace. Some of the original reports suggested violence on the part of the protestors, but the full extent of the allegations had subsequently been erased.

He had to leave the basement more than once in search of coffee and air, neither of which gave much relief. He went blindly, hopelessly, through the reams of printed information, drifting off only into the most indirectly related speculations, catching himself much later seeing the hands had still been working, the pages parsed, and he would resolve to focus more firmly on the task at hand, stay on track, but the same thing happened again, the pattern repeated, he'd go outside.

It might have been easier if he could append the pages, score through anything obviously irrelevant, highlight any patterns of potential interest, but the signature demanded by the clerk prohibited him from duplicating any records. The camera focused on him from the southwest corner of the room. He continued.

He found the corporation paid a significant monthly amount to a 'performance agency'. Considering the use of an actor to represent Carlos's mother, it was a lead of sorts. He pushed himself back from the desk, took out his mobile phone and began ringing around. Eventually, he sourced a number and was put through to one of the directors. She was disarmingly open, admitting they hired out 'performers' to fulfil various capacities at the corporation. They would prepare and send men and women to act as low-level employees; it was especially helpful, she said, when the corporation was entertaining prospective clients, engaged in a series of meetings and wishing to give the best possible impression, displaying an appearance of optimal efficiency and hard work. She admitted it seemed counter-intuitive at first.

'Trust me,' she said, 'they appear much more convincing in the role of hard-working, busy employees than such employees do themselves. It's more common than you'd think. Of course, some of the hired staff are working so hard at appearing to be working hard—filing, checking reports, making urgent phone calls and demanding to speak to so-and-so—that there's really nothing inauthentic about it at all.'

Staff weren't hired only to populate the office at such times, she went on; sometimes it's the opposite, hired so that they're not needed to populate the offices. 'Certain personal obligations, understandably, conflict with the necessary fulfilment of corporate duty. The corporation, and increasingly many other institutions, will pay for outside performers to stand in for their own staff's daily lives. This is easier to do if the obligation is based on viewing something—say a son's or daughter's participation in a concert or a sporting event—when the hired staff can be visible at a distance and report back with the required information. It's at the employee's own discretion, of course, but the majority are only too happy to brief outsiders on how best to stand in. We suspect some staff invent or exaggerate work, so they can hire performers to cover personal obligations. It is enough, most of the time, that you're represented; it doesn't have to be you. Caring for elderly parents becomes especially trying, so in addition to housing them in permanent leisure communities, performers from agencies such as ourselves stand in on visiting days. This is not immoral or duplicitous, Inspector. In almost all cases the relatives are not only quite aware of what is going on, but also relieved at how smoothly the encounter goes, how their son or daughter appears to really listen, to be genuinely interested. Besides, it naturally speaks very well of the parents that they have brought up children who have gone on to be so successful, working in the kinds of institutions that can pay for the courtesy of ersatz personal encounters.'

The longest-serving false employee had been with the corporation more than four years and had become so adept at appearing to be effective that the gap between this and actually being effective was invisible, arbitrary, and she was in fact deemed essential to the smooth running of the business. Seeing her so confidently and authoritatively appearing to do her job was instructive for the other office members, who could watch and learn from her and see how to do it themselves.

The limits of what the agency people could be expected to do were not clearly defined, but it appeared likely, the director said, that they had been used to build an aura of gentle festivity on workers' birthdays and to insert morale-boosting moments of ambiguous flirtation when certain team members appeared to be feeling down. It was even possible there was some truth in the rumours reported, including that one office member had been seen receiving detailed tuition from another, presumably an actor, on how to sneeze better, i.e., in a way considered more acceptable within the industry— quieter, more professional and controlled.

They sent employees out on public transport and in adjacent cafés on workday mornings, looking brisk and ready for the day ahead, helping others in the industry approach their work in an optimal frame of mind. They were deployed by the coffee room at typical low-sugar periods, ready with promising and uplifting slices of anecdote and gentle conversation, which employees could look forward to resuming and developing at a later date. They waited in the car park in the evening, so no one real was the last to go home; they took exactly two minutes forty seconds to return from bathroom visits and they produced particularly purposeful rhythms punching keys even on slow, midweek afternoons.

She insisted, however, that the corporation continued to legitimately function—it was unusual, for instance, on any given day to find the ratio of real to representative office workers fall in favour of the latter. The corporation maintained its operation and made money; it was a self-supporting, autonomous system, because if there ever came a point when the corporation ceased to be profitable there would be no funds left to pay the agency and the actors. The fact that they remained there was proof positive that things went well.

She had no record of Carlos. They had not, to her knowledge, engineered any performances in his professional or personal life. He thanked her and ended the call, before continuing his search of the files.

The door opened and the caretaker told him the time was up. He hadn't realized at all how late it was. Clearly he'd been talking on the phone much longer than he'd thought. He gathered his things and followed the dreary figure upstairs.

He had his bag searched, then sighed as he removed his jacket, put his arms out to be patted down.

'This weather, huh?' he said.

The caretaker said nothing.

HE THOUGHT THINGS OVER on the drive back. He'd need, of course, information from the corporation itself regarding the performance agency. It explained the mother—presumably a complimentary service offered in sympathy and support to the real Maria, who still couldn't bear to talk.

The easiest thing, of course, the inspector thought, the least disruptive and the cheapest, would have been to put someone from the agency in Carlos's seat the moment he'd gone. Colleagues were taking on his work and doubtless extra staff had been brought in to help, but they only replaced his product, not his presence. The vacated office remained off limits and it would continue to be so, treated as a site of potential evidence, until the inspector declared otherwise.

When the caretaker had interrupted him, he'd been cross-checking bulk orders of office supplies. A circuitous route towards locating Carlos, he would admit, should any updates from his seniors be demanded. It had been reasonably interesting, perhaps only because the items were listed plainly, and also, he supposed, because of the familiarity of the content. He could fool himself into thinking he was being efficient and capable, when really he was just relieved at having understood something.

The orders could be broadly categorized under worker and machine supplies. So in addition to ink cartridges, data sticks, copier toner, replacement hard drives and memory, there were five-kilogram coffee tubs, quantities of antibacterial gel, paper towels. What had seemed slightly odd, the only thing really, after the performance agency payments, was that in the last several years these costs were constant, despite the slow, steady expansion of the business. The growth of the corporation's estate failed to match its supplies.

Fairly minor, he imagined, but something to look into.

BACK AT HIS APARTMENT, the inspector found that the company's listings online contradicted the true nature of the estate as indicated in the records: between 10 and 20 per cent of property accounted for on paper led to nowhere real. Fundamentally, the corporation was smaller than reported. He was sure this would turn out to be an error on his part, financial naivety, something he had failed to understand.

After a substantial time trawling the Internet for clues to the discrepancy, he found a reference to 'corporate contingency' sites. It was common practice, he discovered, for larger corporations to rent additional office space in remote locations, typically on the outer edges of new towns. A single tall building catered for a dozen companies or more, lying empty most of the year. The offices were primed for work, fully furnished, connected and in some cases guarded by watchmen in booths and remotely surveilled.

Post-disaster, the theory went, a corporation could re-establish itself in one of these sites, continue as if nothing had happened. The assumption was that any attack would focus primarily on the city, so an alternative was needed, a contingency site. Several days each year a team was dispatched to prove it could be done. Before the taxi ride from the central hub, secretaries prepared packed lunches, coffee flasks and bottles of still water. The gates were opened, networks re-established and the team went in to work, careful not to look outside. In most cases, he read, staff hated it, couldn't wait to get back to the real office. Too quiet. The days going on and on. No one went there more than once.

He read it as an example of corporate anxiety. Their imagination of the apocalypse was limited and picturesque, affecting a distinct, geometrically precise land segment, allowing civilization to be transported elsewhere, uninterrupted.

For the practice to be as widespread as it was, it had in some sense to be profitable. He wondered what statistics would show over productivity: what the difference in daily output was between employees who believed that everything, no matter what, was going to be okay, and those with no alternative workspace.

He wondered if workers would go calmly about their daily work, more adept, in the knowledge of readied replicas. Idealize the unfilled places where, once settled, everything would run more smoothly. A microwave plate obstructed as it rotated; a door failing to close firmly on a first attempt; a suboptimal phrase used in a rare group-meeting interjection: all those things could be smoothed, corrected, perfected in the parallel office.

He was amazed and impressed by the colossal corporate arrogance, the stunning lack of imagination. The idea that all places—a forest, a desert, conceivably even seas—were really urban spaces in the preliminary stage.

He had been reading for hours. He hadn't eaten a thing since lunch. He took his wallet and went downstairs in search of food. Waiting for duck and rice in the Celeste Imperio he remembered something, a story told by a colleague at a bar—or was it, he thought, stretching on the red plastic chair, a detail he had read long ago, perhaps in an American novel? In the story an insurance worker had suddenly disappeared. Midthirties, married, father to two. No history of mental illness, no particular financial insecurities, no sign, his wife had said, of anything amiss. He had left for work at the usual time on that last morning, finishing his coffee as he pulled on his coat, kissing her on the left cheek as he stepped towards the door.

He had never come back. He had not reported to the office. Had made no attempts to contact anyone, left his bank account untouched. She swore he had been killed. He had suddenly been made inactive, something impersonal had struck him. No body was found. She pressed several months later for a funeral in absentia, a ceremony to encourage the transition. The missing man's brother arranged a detective to search. One day, six years later, the wife took the call. I have some news, the brother-in-law said. We have him. He's here. I'm watching him right now.

He's dead.

He's not.

He lived, they discovered, two towns down. He had switched across two letters of his Christian name. He had a wife, a son, a daughter. He was rising through the ranks of a local insurance firm. The detective had watched him for some time. He cooked the same meals in a regular routine carried over from the first life. Continued to swim in a pool twice weekly, just as before. He had quickly amassed a record collection near identical to his previous. The wife drove with the brother and the detective, insisting on seeing the life. She thought, she said later, that she was dreaming or watching her own life as if from outside. The new wife reproduced her hairstyle and her gait. The children, though younger, enjoyed a power balance identical to her own offspring. There was a languor, a carelessness expressed in the lay of objects on the new lawn exactly as there had been on their own six years before.

Could it be him? she said. It looks just like him, but it's not, it can't be. A twin? Removed at birth? You hear about these things, she said. You read about them. The amazing coincidences, the same choices, down to the smallest thing.

Nothing had ever been explained. The man, when confronted, said nothing, offered no reason for his actions. The marriage had not been formalized and it proved difficult to bring a case against him, all but impossible to put together any charge more significant than wasting police time.

The thing I don't understand, she said, is why would he leave me if only to build exactly the same life again? Sure, it would hurt if he'd run out on me, left me for someone else—but at least then I could understand it, I think. But he didn't do that. He did the same thing again, the same life twice.

The inspector searched for the exact words of the phrase. *He left and grew the same life again, a few miles on.*

He wondered now if this insurance company also used contingency sites. If the man had been encouraged, however indirectly, to build a duplicate of everything in his life, some blank and dull response to the possibility of ruin. More than once, everything again, towards a greater chance of preservation.

The server called his order number.

III

In other societies, sitting is the dominant body position. Sitting on furniture, the body is set into three straight lines of near equal length with right angles on the lap and beneath the knees. From here it is easily folded into its smallest possible shape, the knees pressed to the face and the heels to the posterior. In this folded position, the body is transportable and readily fits inside a small box. This encourages people to stay indoors and travel in vehicles. The mechanical formation of the body in a sitting posture, with minimal pressure, strain or curvature, the rods flatly expressed via the joints, matches the expectation of completed tasks, and its tiered expression resembles steps or stairs, most explicitly when viewed in profile, implicitly endorsing existing power structures and habits.

TRIBES OF THE SOUTHERN INTERIOR, P. 42

HE'D EXPECTED SOMETHING GRANDER. The use of acting staff, perhaps, had done it, suggesting a firm priding itself on innovation and experimentation, alert to the power of appearances.

From the outside there was nothing to distinguish the corporation's offices at all. One building appeared to drift into the next, a row of high, frosted-glass structures. At ground level it was almost empty, a holding room, a pre-corporate zone. Anyone, it seemed, could walk on in. It was no cooler here than outside, warmer if anything. Lack of entrance-level air con would count as a more unusual deterrent to walk-ins. He imagined the front doors rarely used, people coming in early, as Carlos had, via sublevel parking lots and elevators.

Up on the sixth floor, in the preliminary waiting room he'd been shown to, the surfaces gleamed. Wood panels and chrome finishes added to the pristine appearance, which he found very impressive. He was no longer aware of the temperature, which must have been perfect. Altogether, a very well-maintained operation, after all.

Entering the office zones, he'd naturally speculated on who, among the people he saw at the desks and by the copy room, entering and exiting the bathrooms, the kitchen area and the conference rooms, was real (i.e., a legitimate and authentic office worker) and who was simply paid to look that way. He'd imagined there would be something more fluid in the way real people went about their work, something natural, an ease from having practiced the same movements time and again. Obviously the performers would take their cue from the mannerisms displayed by the authentic office workers, but he remained confident he'd be able to tell them apart.

People who really looked like office workers, the ones who seemed distant, committed, perhaps exhibiting hints of stress and short temper—those, that is, who lived up to his general expectations of what an office worker is—they were the ones he would have to be wary of. Though perhaps the performers would be reluctant to exaggerate their actions for just that reason. They may have been the quiet ones, the ones he didn't notice, those in light shirts almost blending with the whitewashed walls.

He had been left waiting for some time now. He rubbed his eyes. He was tired, no longer used to the rhythms of a working day. He was able to excavate quantities of sleep from his tear ducts: golden, odorous, granulated matter. Hitting on a fertile area, he dug for more, picking out pieces between forefinger and thumb.

He needed some air.

Standing up, he went to the nearest window, but the latch was merely decorative; he couldn't get it open. To the right of the window, framed on the wall, was a series of photographs, figures in suits standing solemnly in rows. He absently went over the tiny faces. He might have recognized one. He isolated it, leaned in close, but was unable to identify it, to assign a name. Male, midthirties, dark hair firmly side-parted; nothing to make him stand out from the others. Trace of a smile? Each time he looked, he saw a slightly different expression. And though there was little to distinguish it, he was increasingly sure he had seen it before, and more than once.

'Excuse me,' he called as the door briefly opened and he caught sight of an arm. A moment later it reopened and the employee entered, asked if she could help.

'I think I know this man,' he said. 'I'm sure I've seen him before. Could you remind me of his name?'

She put on her glasses as she approached the photograph. 'I'm sorry, which one?'

He pointed slowly, careful not to blot the face with his finger. 'Right here.'

'I don't know. I mean I think I've met him, but I can't say for sure. He certainly didn't work here long, I can tell you that. Chances are he was a contractor, outsourced. Not a full affiliate. None of us would have known him, really.'

'Is there someone else, do you think, who could give me a name?'

She paused for a moment. 'I'm afraid not. I'm the longest serving of the current staff.'

'Okay. While I'm waiting, do you mind if I ask a couple of other things?'

'I didn't really know him, I mean . . . That is why you're here, right? To interview the others about Carlos?'

'Yes, but I have a few questions that aren't about him. I'd like to know more about company land. It's proving difficult, locating information. Particularly regarding land in interior regions.'

'We maintain various interests, of course, across the country and beyond. For a time we had holdings over the interior, but most of those have long since expired. You'll find little activity in any of them.'

'Where, precisely?'

'What do you mean?'

'The holdings, where were they?'

'The problem is that they weren't named places, rather forest sections, so I can't tell you, in so many words, where they were.'

'Well, how were they accessed? There must be roads, stations, outposts.'

'Of course, there were roads, single track; they're probably not usable any more. The company would fly wherever possible. I can fetch you the names of the nearest settlements, if you'd like. Though the concessions were such a distance away, and besides, I wouldn't imagine anyone lives there now.'

'Had he, perhaps, at any time, had any involvement with these holdings?'

'Carlos? Not to my knowledge.'

'Right.'

'Just give me a few minutes.'

She left the room. The inspector drifted back to peer at the face in the picture. He didn't forget significance and it was odd he couldn't place the detail. He was known for his attention to it, the quality of his memory. He had been successful, throughout his career, at entering people's homes either to plant surveillance equipment or to go through all their things, their cupboards, drawers, wardrobes, clothes, beds, the total contents of their premises, knowing, at the end of it, when he had got or done all that he wanted, that he could restore everything to its original state. Others couldn't do this, instead video-recording the disarrangement of the home contents, then slowly playing the video back; one operative, the most verbally confident of the team, describing the backward crawling of the action, piece by piece, directing the others so that they could negate everything they had done in the building, return each item to its resting state and make it as if they had never even been there, their presence, if it had been done competently, impossible for the layperson, at least, to detect.

'Okay, okay. São Vicente, Santa Lucía, those were the stations furthest east,' she said on returning. 'Anything else?'

He noted these down. 'One thing. Could you tell me about your contingency sites? Were these also located in the interior regions?'

'Our what?'

'I've read they're quite common. Prepared, empty offices built outside the cities. The idea being that the company reverts there in an emergency, say post-war.'

She really did, he thought, appear incredulous. For a moment he doubted himself. He remembered he had no real proof.

'I've heard nothing of those places. But even if we did have them, which I'm not saying we do—they are just a series of empty rooms, right? What could possibly be of interest there?'

IV.

KANDINSKI: Average. I don't know. How are you supposed to describe someone's voice? I guess he spoke quietly, but that's not what you mean, is it? Are you asking about pitch? Flat or musical, degrees of depth, that kind of thing? It's difficult to say. I didn't talk to him often. In fact . . . The best thing would be to talk to his clients, those whose meets he was involved with, though of course they remain off limits. The way he spoke—do you mean words or sound? The way he formed them, or just his choice or range of vocabulary? Average, as I say. Wouldn't stand out in a room.

DIAS: Yes, quite. There was never any question of a dip in his performance. If there had been, then, of course . . . But the work was exemplary, as always, never late, never in need of correction.

KANDINSKI: We noticed that he'd severely cut his hair and beard. Exposing, you know, that, on his forehead . . . I don't know how we hadn't noticed it before. It would have been indelicate to ask. It was unclear if it came from birth. Some of the women said there was no hair on his arms. They thought that was weird. Like he was a baby, born every day. Carlos did his own thing, we didn't want to get in the way. I thought this waxing and shaving might have been helping him in his work—we all have our odd habits, our continuation-ensuring techniques. I see now he was engaged in a different project. It's always easier to see the total form of the threads in retrospect. He was trying to expose himself, of course. That's what he was doing. He was trying to show us who he was, removing excess layers so that we could see him clearly.

DIAS: Liquid would pour from his eyes—I don't mean crying, he never cried, not that I saw. More than tears, sort of lines of water, almost fibrous, hanging. I used to wonder how the world would look that way, seen in water. But then, of course, it is already.

VASQUEZ: I saw him straining his fingers, examining his hands, pointing them out to himself. I didn't realize. I wasn't aware. You think I should have intervened? I just thought it was disgusting. And it was also mean. As if he was doing it to upset us. You see, he went, each time, to take away his mouth. That is what it amounted to, I'm telling you. He tried to dislocate his jaw, remove the mouth, throw it away like a used tissue. Isn't that strange? I mean, isn't that particularly strange? That horrible little O shape. When I saw that, I would do all I could to leave the room. I knew exactly what was coming.

KANDINSKI: His nails were cut extremely short. One day they were gone. I may have been mistaken. I called out to him; he turned away. Was he trimming himself? He became more slender. In dieting, lessening his body, perhaps he thought he could limit the influence and spread of whatever he believed it was. We're all trying to get to the bottom of this thing, right? To work out what happened. As I see it, his projects were some response to what a part of him saw was happening inside him. And these response-projects were crudely physical: dieting, manic shaving, hiccupping, hanging upside down, cracking his jaw and contorting his face, arms held wide, as if simulating flight.

KANDINSKI: I heard him sneeze—I had heard nothing else like it. It was extraordinary. You know Carlos is a slender man, not much of him anyway. Well that just made it all the stranger. The lack of noise when he landed. You'd expect a man, when he jumps like that, to make some sort of impact. He didn't. He just landed with his shoes on the tiles and barely a tap. I just saw this flash of dark and a sort of vertical jerking in one of the bathroom mirrors. It took me a while, still looking in the mirror, to place the sound that he had just made. I was fascinated by the grimace on his face. I still hadn't turned around; I'll admit it, I was a little afraid. He appeared to be stretching the orifices of his face. He cracked his head down and to the side in a diagonal thrust each time he jumped. He was launching himself into these sneezes, and, I'll tell you, he looked disappointed every time he landed.

KANDINSKI: He would wear earplugs at all times, even during meets. He had to strain, leaning forward, to interact. He murmured something about 'invasions'. About being 'inhabited'. And he was clicking his jaw. This was perhaps the most minor among his symptoms, but it was oddly noticeable and grew the more so. It was a mild irritant, then a source of disgust. The clicking increased in volume and severity. First he moved his mouth into a small O shape, so that he might speak nothing, elongating his jaw. Then he would affect his bones somehow—from some centre—so as to arch upwards either side of his lower face. This gave a fleeting impression of imbalance and asymmetry, making him appear, not like two separate people welded to each other, but as two different expressions of the same identity or two postures from different moments over each other. It unsettled all of us. And then he cracked the shape, dropping that part of his face that was raised, so that it actually overtook the other half, affecting a dry, rapid wrenching sound as the bones moved past each other. He didn't seem to feel a thing. He did it resting, playing with his features, grinding his mouth and its architecture into a constantly shifting variety. Straining forward, apparently trying to concentrate, but as if unable somehow to hear himself. The thing was—and this was the embarrassing bit, this is the thing we're having to account for now—he continued to perform his job, to do so, indeed, with competence, and for some considerable time.

V

Ceremonies performed to mark transitional stages in individuals' lives often involve the ingestion of toxic secretions gathered from plant-aphid symbioses, subsequently ejected from the mouth, along with bile and other stomach contents. The noise created during these expulsions is listened to by experienced tribe linguists, able to divine the hundreds of thousands of words compacted inside. In drier periods of the year, linguists express these stories day and night, and the community listens. Content in these stories varies greatly, and attempts to draw common tropes have largely failed. A slightly less than statistically significant proportion include references to seas, volcanoes and other natural phenomena not present in the community's own environment.

TRIBES OF THE SOUTHERN INTERIOR, P. 57

THE INSPECTOR HAD TAKEN the same subway train for twenty-five years. On the rare times he was late and on the 8.40 he was aware of the difference in the air. More of these people had cooked: it was on their massed breath. They'd spent longer on breakfasts. He'd learned to trust his nose. He remembered investigating the disappearance of a soon-to-be-married couple. Their flat was unusually clean, but this was contradicted by the air. Microwave stains suggested at least one of them worked late. The bathroom retained the faint lemon scent of shampoo. This was the closest, he knew, he would get to their skin. They had decided to leave together and cleaned their evidence, but they couldn't get rid of the smell. He pictured them together on a yacht in the Pacific or heaped, broken, at the bottom of a disused quarry.

Each inhabited room had its own ecology. He'd insisted, every time, on being the first officer on site and on entering alone. When the teams came in they broke the purity. There was a limited amount of time to gauge the air and it began expiring when he opened the door. From the effects of damp in the bathroom he could make a reasonable guess at how long the occupant spent looking in the mirror. More interesting, and more substantial, were the personal ecologies of cohabitants—couples, flatmates, families. The longer they spent, the stronger each ecology grew. There was a pattern to the way they ate, slept, washed. The amount of time spent in the place affected air fabric. He knew there were problems in a place that was fresh; people who worked so hard at it, cleaning, hiding, wanted out. More than once such freshness in a building had been an indication of murder.

A clotted interior, by contrast, was healthy. Even after all these years he could appreciate a place that had been walked in. Each example was different. He would state that air is exceptional in a building that contained quick walkers. All manner of reasons. More efficient digestive system, so more adventurous meals. A more varied spread of mites and spores from the draught made by the swish of moving feet. Kitchen objects returned to cupboards briskly, vibrating the surfaces of the worktops below. These people showered more, made love faster. They spent longer outside and came back frequently and briefly, opening doors at a higher daily rate.

He remembered things from his own place. The smell of the yellowing pages in books piled high against the walls. Tea herbs fused inside from endless nights by the lamp. The mixing of tangerine skin and the sediment of oversleep, traces of each other retained under fingernails. The passing of time that led to the very particular stage favoured in the life cycle of fruit: ripe, heavy, almost bursting, bruised and fly-begun. Just the way they had liked it.

He could estimate how much language had been made in rooms. It was intuitive, but he tended to be right. A room would be more hectic after language. Perhaps people who spoke more moved differently, and that was all. He used to think he could see language where it fell. The loads amassed at a particularly conducive right angle. It was one of the things that made a bathroom different— its dearth of words. Rooms affected more by language were softer, warmer. It was cold where no one had spoken for some time. All these tiny clues were significant when a person had gone. Everything previously invisible became amplified, enlarged. Each detail was there to be decoded; the key to understanding a collapsed civilization. And any one might bring them back.

He remembered the little things. The asymmetrical accumulation of dirt in a vestibule, only six days after a vanishing. The new damp on the right angle where the cupboard met the wall, from all the water boiled in grief etiquette. The refuse left out. The mildew gathering on clothes left wet. The dank air of a room where sleep had repeatedly failed. A disrupted, broken ecology.

WHEN A PERSON GOES, that habitat never comes back. An occupied room is a great diversity of life. The inspector would have limited time in Carlos's office. It was the place to start. He was working against extinction.

When his wife had died, it wasn't just her body that had gone. She had been an incalculable volume, and there was nothing unusual about that. She didn't stop at the edge; she had a field of life around her. Her scent, her appearance, her effect would have been wholly different if even one day of her biography were omitted. There was a frame around her, a hive, a community created by the kind of thoughts she had and the way she spun her hands and moved her feet. It wasn't just that she had gone; more than her had been devastated.

Sometimes it could seem, in quieter evenings and especially, for some reason, after he had accidentally fallen asleep and woken, alert to and surprised by the dark, that her past animation was the most remarkable thing in the world. He would stare, stunned, still in the dark, at bare, still areas of the apartment that had once been hers. Across which she had moved with humour and purpose. He would be convinced, suddenly, that the whole thing was impossible; equally, that she could have been there and that now she could be gone.

There was a time when he worried their apartment might literally be poisonous without her; that the only thing keeping him alive in this space was the balance made by their accumulated behaviour. Removing her breath, her words, the manner and selection of the food she prepared with him was of potentially grave significance—he was shocked, appalled that the possibility had not been further investigated. They had actually patronized him; someone had given him a card bearing a number. As far as he saw it, it was a perfectly valid concern: it might be toxic here, now, without her, he had thought. Everything's different. My health will go to pot, he had said—just you wait and see.

It was only later that he thought of further evidence for his theory, wishing he'd presented it at the time. In long-established couples, especially the elderly, who are very sensitive to change, the death of one frequently leads to the death of the other. It is not a romantic thing, not a death of the heart, he had thought, and neither is it simply a matter of grief-induced stress weakening the immune system and leaving the widowed more vulnerable to infection; no, it is about a home space undergoing a sudden violent extraction, disordering a balance that had been slowly and painstakingly built up over many years. It is about a new toxicity entering the home. Without her being there he was more exposed: her contribution to climate and atmosphere was significant, and now it was all shot to pieces. How could he trust the air in a room that was his alone? The idea was ridiculous. There was no evidence to say that his routines and behaviours were fit and able, any longer, to make a viable living space—such things ought to be checked, he thought, as soon as someone leaves, rather than simply trusting them to get on with it, just as if nothing had happened. It was the same way with a birth, particularly a firstborn child, when the couple is simply sent home with the baby after a day or two, if they're lucky, and expected to get on with living with this addition, although nobody has told them the first thing about how to manage it. It was outrageous—the thing breathing, crying, eating, defecating, completely changing everything, without any preparations put in place or routine safety checks being made. He didn't know how any of them managed.

They had talked about it several times, at a very premature stage. One of the rules they had agreed was that they would be a unit as much as was possible, largely to minimize the risk of arbitrary rupture. Travelling distances, optimally, should be done together. That two rather than three of them might go was out of the question. Those kinds of things would have to be affirmed on a daily basis. New equipment installed in the home area would be tested before use, and then quarterly, by an electrician. There would be smoke alarms and carbon monoxide sensors and they were to sleep, always, for the first few years, in the same room. They would alternate sleep duty—one of them, reluctantly, would have to try to sleep, while the other would listen for evidence of the child's continued breath. This was how it would have been.

VI

HE WAS MISSING SOMETHING. He made a simple vacuum pump from rubber tubing and a cylindrical cassette. He walked into the empty office, held the vacuum directly above Carlos's chair and took a sample of the air. He was sceptical, seeing Isabella, at first, and prior to speaking with her. She was less than half his age. She couldn't have had much, if any, legitimate experience analysing crimes and other scenes of potential significance. Straight out of college, she was to work with him on the empty office, overseeing the forensic reading. He had no say in the matter. She was the only staff available, and so he should let it go, get on with it.

Eighteen hours later she showed him what had been revealed under a high-intensity microscope: a scale fragment from the wing of a dragonfly; several dirt molecules bearing high iron content; detached strands of cotton-polyester composite; part of a drifting human hair; several orders of living fungal spores; yeast; jet fuel; black carbon.

He wanted more. The desk, the keyboard, he said. Pick up what's on the floor. The walls, the panes, the edges of the windows. There is always something.

———

REPORT EXTRACT

The subject leaned in as he worked. He is exhibited in the office: in areas of his chair previously warmed and wet by the body; in the marks and indents showing how powerfully or otherwise he hit his keys, and at what angle; in the dust and dirt patterns on the monitor which are the expressions of his breath, revealing the positions in which his head and neck were hung.

One of the abundant materials taken from the carpet is scalp hair. Hair is elastic, cornified tissue made of threaded epithelial fibres comprising a root, a shaft, and growing according to a strict cyclical pattern of action, degradation and rest. An unusually high proportion of the fallen strands were of the anagen and catagen growth stages at the time of separation. Detached unnaturally, they were cut in the office.

His hairs are coarser than average and faster to grow, reaching, if unchecked, a minimum extension of 2.2 mm weekly. But he limited his hair and nails with unusual vigilance, unnerved by autonomic recovery. Parts kept coming back at him blindly; he watched and cut at them.

There is marked evidence of exogenous deposition on the recovered strands of his scalp and body hair.

Episodes of high anxiety and continuous stress led the body to source further extrinsic material as desperate repair. Tonal difference on the back and seat of the chair indicate he sweated. As well as cooling the skin and lowering excitation, heavy sweating may cause environmental particles to adhere directly to the hair shaft, and hence to be chemically incorporated into the body. Strontium, zinc, silver, cobalt, nickel and other ambient metal toxins are sourced in higher than average quantities [Mn: 15.2–26.3 ppm; Zn: 78–108 ppm], secondary losses to the body's essential nutrient store having led to aggressive absorption of airborne mineral particles. These levels of deposition are highly atypical and should be detected only in sub-adults, when adolescent growth demands increased vulnerability and lowered resistance to the outside world.

ISABELLA FED HIM REPORTS and told him more were coming. He briefed her about what he already knew, what he had heard. Various testimonies from colleagues of Carlos being ill, something unspecified, altering his appearance and behaviour. The suggestion and denial, at once, of Carlos contracting an infection. He hadn't been able to pin down the claims; their answers were long, evasive, rhetorical. Though he worried how unlikely it all sounded, the report seemed to give them some weight. What he needed from Isabella now, he said, was something concrete. If Carlos was ill, then he wanted a diagnosis, a precise identification from an analysis of his remaining things.

OTHER THAN THE FLOOR and the chair, the surface Carlos had made most contact with was the keyboard. Even at a resting state, before he'd thought what to say, his hands lay flat on it. The condition of the keys gave a hint of his language, greater wear indicating higher use. With this he fell into line, matching almost exactly to Zipf's law. Deposition indicated words with the highest use had a frequency twice that which followed, and so on down. The uneven spread of foreign objects—pollen, skin cells, microbiota, foodstuffs—confirmed the general content of his language.

But they could do more with this. The inspector wanted the specimens analysed, particularly the microorganisms sourced from the body. Isabella surprised him. She was prepared. She would swab the keys, locate the life present at the edge, identify, through gene sequencing, the many species living in his skin.

'Good, good,' he said, shutting the car door as they stepped out onto the street. Even after several visits he continued to look up; Isabella barely seemed to register the tall glass buildings.

Though Carlos had been gone weeks already she was confident the edge-life would remain, impervious to environmental stresses—temperature, moisture, natural levels of UV radiation. There would be a persistence.

But the skin, Isabella said, walking while she spoke, moving quicker than he was accustomed to, would be just the beginning. He made a noise, somewhere between a gasp and a snort. He embarrassed himself; it's my condition, he said, I ought to exercise more, but this heat . . .

'This is it,' he said.

They entered, took the elevator up.

Isabella surveyed the interior walls and floors. Though she had analysed materials previously gathered there, this was her first time present in the building. The inspector followed as they passed into the atrium, through the corridors and offices of the sixth floor, noticing that the photograph with the rows of faces had been removed from the wall. Staff seemed to look at him differently. With Isabella he walked at a brisker pace and with purpose. They carried cases and equipment. Perhaps he could organize another round of interviews, accompanied this time.

He removed the tape and the barrier and opened the door to the vacated office. Well, he said, here we are. She knelt before the desk in mask and gloves. He paused by it, too, at the threshold. She unwrapped the first swab stick, coated in fluid, and brought it down on the centre key.

THEY TOOK COFFEE IN her small, ground-floor office at the university hospital. Books lined the walls, erratically ordered. George

Eliot was a surprise. She had folders open on her desk and kept picking them up, placing them back down as she talked. She was alert, energized. The heat didn't seem to affect her. It was clear she had something to tell him.

'Firstly, I can establish beyond any doubt this man was not well. Microbiota I've found corroborate results from scalp and body hair.'

'What was it? What was wrong with him?'

She held up her hands, telling him to slow down.

'To begin with he was malnourished. I'm guessing you already know that from talking to friends and colleagues. But did you know his skin was infected?'

He leaned in, urged her on.

'Inflamed.'

The inspector blinked several times and imagined a red body bursting apart.

Isabella's brown hair was held in a bun. She wore a lab coat over a skirt and vest top. She had perhaps noted he was uncomfortable with prolonged eye contact; she got up, walked while speaking, Bic in her left hand, looking occasionally to the window and the courtyard with its well-maintained grass quadrants and flowerbeds.

'His skin held an unusual variety of microorganisms. The combinations are interesting. I'm certain acne rosacea affected his face, particularly his forehead. Imagine, Inspector, blotches across him, a constant source of irritation. This partly accounts for the high yield of skin cells across the keyboard.'

'Okay,' he said, writing furiously. 'And can you tell me what it is? What the name of the illness is?'

'I'm running tests, cross-checking the information.'

The scribbling stopped.

'What I find interesting,' she said, 'is the nature of the microorganisms, because I can tell you Carlos was not held together well, and I'm not just talking about the skin. The communities living there indicate an inflamed gut, and the presence of certain other organisms. We can infer some of what happened in his gut, the particular microbiota present there, from his skin: we can move backwards, sketch the centre from the edge.

'An axis: skin, gut and brain. With a second move we can make assertions regarding the mental state. Simply from what we've now learned about his gut.'

She opened her mouth, but delayed.

'The diversity inside him, the particular ecology? It's strongly linked to psychological disorders.'

'What was the illness?' he repeated.

'Slow down,' she replied. He thought he saw traces of a smile.

'I won't be coarse. Won't be pushed.

'There was a unity to the physical and psychological symptoms—I won't say one caused the other.' She looked right at him, drew breath. 'Let me describe his condition in more detail. Several of the species I found work against him, preventing him from digesting food. They secrete small compounds that break barriers and act as chemical signals that damage cell function. Some organisms may have reached his brain. The enteric nervous system—which lines the intestines with neurons, hundreds of millions of them—communicates directly with his brain. And in this case, with these microbes, it is sending distress.'

He realized the day's cloud cover was unusual only when he saw the light move across the room and Isabella momentarily shield her eyes. The flickering shadow patches and broken light looked, he thought, just like a swarm on her, an infestation of bees.

'The organisms may have entered his brain,' she repeated. 'Step back from the investigation. Doesn't it strike you as extraordinary? His gut fermented anxiety, paranoia. Other likely side effects: hallucination, hypergraphia. I think he indulged in fantasies, wrote long arbitrary notes until his hand hurt. This isn't metaphor, Inspector. I'm not saying he became distressed because of how a stomach illness changed his life. While that may be true, it's secondary. The microbes, in some sense, activate change in his thoughts. Think of it like a factory producing the elements of feeling—chemistry.'

'Go back,' he said. 'So he did pick up an infection. That's what happened? Then where did it start?'

She moved her hands again, frustrated, annoyed. 'No, I can't identify the source.'

'No, no.' He leaned forward. 'Keep . . . This breakdown you're describing, it was a physical event. Meaning that there might be something—some source—still present in the office, right? Isn't that dangerous?'

Did she know, he wondered, that he had gone into the office days ago, bringing in his vacuum, with nothing covering his face?

'I don't think that's the case. The masks were purely a precaution. If I thought anyone in that building was in any kind of danger don't you think I would have acted?'

She moved to the window again. He speculated whether the plants in the beds immediately outside were her doing. He wondered if the ashtray on her desk was a courtesy, finding the explanation as unlikely as the alternative. He didn't know a thing about her.

'The plants will look good in this light,' she said, turning back to him. 'Let's see the gardens.'

REPORT EXTRACT

His windows are east-facing and the heavy volume of lashes detected on his keyboard and on his desk is higher than would be expected from the limited time spent directly facing the sun. One possibility is a rapid blinking reflex instilled through long exposure to light-reflective surfaces such as seawater. His exposed skin had prematurely aged, wrinkles growing in areas adjacent to the eyes, which contracted, pushing out his cheeks into a smile or a grimace.

His stationing almost exclusively within the bounds of his office during the day and his home by evening and through the night led to muscle atrophy more typically seen in the decreased muscle mass of persons between 60 and 70 years of age. Muscle strength has lessened anywhere between 30 and 40 per cent. By these and other means his decay was accelerated, the onset of his final disappearance beginning perhaps with his first day present in the office.

———◁◦▷———

'PUT IT DOWN,' SHE said. 'Listen. You don't need notes. I'll reproduce anything you need. But I want to get back to it. Because we haven't got to the matter yet. I haven't described what happened to Carlos.'

They went slowly, more at his pace, making a circuit of the hospital gardens. He used to visit often, before, but hadn't been in many years.

She gestured while speaking, still wearing the lab coat, guiding him through the botanics. He needed a bit of help, clearly, she must have thought; it wasn't subtle. Light, plants, animals. The larger environment a learning aid.

'What I swabbed from the keyboard is part of a chain moving through him. There wasn't a secret and pure Carlos kept sealed from all this, you know, watching. Whatever happened cut through everything like—like an acid.'

She kept stopping her speech, as if she expected him to say something, bring his own perspective on the analysis. After a couple of seconds she would smile and move on again, he thought, in a kind of disappointment.

'I'm going to go with this, Inspector. Because I want you to have an understanding of what it was like to be Carlos. What may have happened to Carlos.

48

'There is no clear distinction between him and his room, inside and out. Likewise no neat separation of physical and mental parts. There was nothing he could do about that—he couldn't decide, say, to no longer have anything to do with the life of the room; *he would be thinking via the life of the room*. It's harder to see his shape, harder to locate him. There isn't a free-standing identity surveying its environment, Inspector. I think he'd seen that.

'Definition was his problem. None of him was solidly drawn. His skin came loose, rich and fertile in microbiota. He sloughed off. His immunity was weak, no longer doing its job to any reasonable standard—a common effect of depression and anxiety. It wasn't sealing him, wasn't asserting his identity, so he was vulnerable, exposed, wide open to the world. This happened to all of him. You can imagine how terrified he was of the city. He was forever ill. He was a segment of environment. He was almost nothing. Take a cup, scoop some air, that's what he was. How are you going to find that?

'Are you surprised he disappeared? Think of the image most people carry of themselves, in the front-facing third person. A man and a landscape clearly defined. But he couldn't think like that any more.'

The inspector tried not to be distracted by the passing vegetation, nor to reveal his interest in the marsh pitcher plants, which she would doubtless consider populist, vulgar. Later, perhaps, they could tour the glasshouses.

'Isabella—is this a Ph.D. topic of yours? Listen, I wonder . . . Can you be clearer? What exactly are we talking about? You said this wasn't metaphor, then you say he disappeared in his office. What do you mean? Because it really happened, he disappeared. We have a bereft family and an empty bed. He's no longer there, distracted on a bus in traffic or queuing for his coffee. This is real. We're dealing with a person reported missing from a restaurant. He got up, he moved, walked through the office doors, got out. So what are we talking about?'

'If I'm being difficult, Inspector, it's because it's a discussion I usually have only with myself. I'm not saying he literally disappeared, into the room, into the desk, into the walls; of course I'm not. I'm saying it's the kind of thing he thought about, that he imagined happening. I'm saying he forgot who he was partly as a symptom of his illness, partly as a reflection of that illness. There is a chance this affected what he did later, even at the restaurant. But . . .'

'What?' He turned to her, stopped. 'What else?'

'Well . . . He also, in a sense, well he was disappearing. I said he was malnourished. I said he was losing the capacity to digest food.'

'In theory, could someone wholly disappear this way? Be so corrupted and disturbed they become smaller and smaller, until there is nothing left?'

'Forgive my frankness, but that's a pretty stupid question. You've heard the expression "waste away".'

'Let's go back a little, again. I want to at least establish something and move on. Two things, even. You are saying his illness, a physical thing, had a strong psychological element?'

She began walking again, he followed. He kept having to shield his eyes.

'I am.'

'Therefore, isn't it possible that the source was also psychological, even behavioural?'

'Well, it is possible, but I wouldn't class that as any kind of breakthrough.'

'Secondly, that the illness broke his identity. That he lost himself. And this was strongly linked to an attack on his immune system.'

'Yes.'

'And how much of this is speculation?'

'I am equally certain about the corruption of his skin and mind. That is my professional opinion.'

'And we are getting this from a keyboard?'

'From what's left on it. The only slight novelty is the specificity of the second move, into the brain. It's old news, though most people would still consider it alien, that individuals can be identified by fragments of microbiota—DNA that isn't technically their own. That isn't even human.

'To begin with he would have claimed, you know, that it wasn't him, that it was an illness, a parasite, a disease. That's what I think. But you can't get anywhere with it. I feel bad for Carlos. Even when he doubted it, even when he worried—"This anxiety isn't me, this is an illness." That doubting, cynical voice? That was affected, too. He couldn't get outside.'

'In some sense, I think, you admire what's happened.' He turned, at the edge of the gardens. They could see, over the green, the traffic lines, the rows of accommodation, the beginnings of the market.

'I wouldn't say that. I just see something neat in it. Two disappearances: internal and social. He stopped believing he was real and then nobody could see him. Inspector, I have another appointment. I really should go. But you will keep me updated on the investigation? I would like to find out where he's gone.'

VII

VASQUEZ: We never went there. But he never invited us. He was devoted to his office. He spent whole nights at his desk. Do you think that's it? That did it? I'm not suggesting the office itself is dangerous. I didn't say that. I'm still working here, aren't I? I was—I am—his secretary. I'm not at risk, Inspector. Do I appear ill to you? And it's evident that you'd say the same yourself. You're here.

KANDINSKI: Let me clear this up. Carlos was an isolated individual in every respect. Whatever happened to Carlos happened to him alone. In everyday behaviour we, his colleagues, have our guard up. We're safe. We're not liable to lose ourselves. You're not going to embarrass yourself, are you? Are you going to give us those masks you wear?

DIAS: The cleaning of the ground was a rhetorical measure. Though we couldn't touch his office it was important still that we felt we could be getting on, moving on. The contractors did a good and thorough job. The entire sixth floor—we lifted the contents of our desks outside, opened the windows and spent the afternoon in an adjacent hotel suite while they cleaned. We came back, to all appearances—so long as we averted our eyes from his place—to a new day. Thing about him, see, he was his own man. Kept himself to himself. And you could trust him; he was reliable. He wouldn't spill out secrets. Information was secure. He was solid, as I say. Dependable. Nothing got to him. Nothing. His work was exemplary. Almost exceptionally, he never made a single request for stress leave. Why would I consider that suspicious? A man doing his job? Carlos was at peace in this place. As I say, you should have seen him at his chair.

VASQUEZ: Yes, he had everything arranged there. As his secretary it's one of my roles to maintain the quality and utility of my employer's instruments. I mean everything—from the security systems protecting his hard drive to the brightness of his monitor. He had a tendency to sit close to the screen, and, of course, this meant that his constant breathing generated a clouding effect. It was unfortunate. I would attend to this on his breaks. I would polish. His seat would sink—though he wasn't a large man, as you know, in fact he was slender, some would say he was barely there. We used to say he failed to activate automatic doors. Still the chair would sink after a time, typically 7 mm every two months. So I would attend to that, so that his eyes would face the optimum height for receiving images. I'd replace his keyboard every thirteen weeks. That was standard. His pressing fingers would erode the most common letters, leaving everything askew. The surface becoming imperfect, unlevel. Some of the workers go lightly on the keys, they skim the plastic, write more quickly—'ghosters', we call them. Their keyboards are replaced annually. I ensured the wires and leads webbing together all of his electronic equipment did not tangle and vermiculate the way these things can do. This is a surprisingly common source of pent-up aggression. I gathered and stocked the black fountain pens he wrote with and the crisp yellow legal pads, narrow ruled and without margin. I provided him with his refreshments at appointed times, performed all the essential functions of a secretary, primarily based around his meets. It's only in the past two months he prohibited my entering his office. Until that time I managed his environment to the best of my abilities, doing all I could so that he would fit in seamlessly on arrival every day—I wanted him to ignore all peripherals, attend only to his central tasks. Ideally, he should not even notice my presence, he should glide. He should be completely alone, the better to concentrate on his tasks.

———◄o►———

KANDINSKI: You're very quiet, Inspector. You haven't said a word in quite some time. Nothing. Is this some new style of interrogation? I wish I knew what happened. I can't appreciate—can't accept—the change. I read about an experiment—perhaps it was an installation. The subject is given a sleep-depriving substance and put in a small, locked room, well lit, with just a chair, desk and a bottle of water. The walls painted white. And on the desk there is a plant, an ordinary house plant, the kind you never really notice in another person's room. Just there, always there. These plants, despite appearances, are about to decay. It happens suddenly, the wilting. Chemically manipulated to fall, just like that. And you have to watch. The ceiling bulb is caged. And you can close your eyes or lean down with your head resting on your folded arms. But you will not tire. You are stimulated. You will always reopen your eyes. In twelve hours everything is gone. You watch the thing—the life— become smaller and smaller, until there is no life. The leaves fold in on themselves, withdraw. But the thing is, technically you watch it. This encroaching nothing. This erasing. It is something that is happening, a positive thing. How can going away be a positive thing? The soil becomes fuller. Larger than before. The door locked, the life present. The door opened, the life, the thing, gone.

KANDINSKI: I saw him once, through frosted glass, suspended from his feet, hanging vertically. I assumed, I think, that it was an illusion, his shoes hanging upside down, his suit. But even through the glass you could see they were embodied. Someone was inside. It makes sense, fits the pattern. I'd guess now he was trying to drip out what he thought with. Catch it in a bucket! Pour it all away! I saw a blurry shadow stumbling, falling. I imagine that was him getting up, righting himself, getting to his feet. But, poor man, pouring out his head like that, straining all the thought away, out, as he desired. He fell! Evidently there was a stranger living with us for ten months. Not that we really knew Carlos anyway, to begin with. The original Carlos, in his office, before he had left the building. I'm curious what remains . . . Apparently, we're still not allowed in. Absurd. Why can't we walk in another man's office, a fellow man, a colleague? Though I suppose we never did before, bar Señora Vasquez, who knows nothing.

VASQUEZ: I am not Señora Vasquez, I only pretend.

KANDINSKI: You do realize the door is on upside down? Removed at the hinges and reapplied oppositely. Why? It won't open naturally this way. Who did this? What does Vasquez have to say?

DIAS: What happened to Carlos? Is that rhetorical?

KANDINSKI: The first day he didn't arrive—which would be the day after he disappeared, the first morning we worked without him—there was a pile of sticks by the sixth-floor copier. Vasquez reported it and saw that it was cleaned up almost immediately, I mean almost immediately the first of us had noticed it; it could have been there all night for all we knew. No one noticed any bigger trail leading in, just this one deposit of short, broken sticks rather neatly placed together, almost folded or arranged, like a bird had made it, Vasquez said.

VASQUEZ: It is a minor detail, but you said to include everything, right, no matter how insignificant it might seem? Everything we remember around the time of his disappearance, anything at all out of the ordinary—that's what you said, isn't it? Well the only thing I have is the sticks—around fourteen of them, the largest no more than 4 cm long and 2 wide. It might have been a joke, a game somebody was playing, only I can't think of anyone who fits the bill. We have a very strict policy here regarding the outdoors. Technically, you are supposed to change footwear upon entering the basement, though security are likely to turn a blind eye, so long as you've been indoors all the way, entering your car via a garage annex, etc. But whoever trailed in the sticks must have walked outside, over woodland I imagine, which is quite unorthodox. Any vestibule areas are designated 'mud rooms'—they're explicitly thresholds, where anyone coming from outside can fix themselves, change outfit and adapt to being indoors again.

VASQUEZ: I've often wondered exactly what he was trying to tell us. I never mentioned this to anyone, but before they cleared the sticks away I inspected them, I looked for signs. There was this change, this atmosphere—it was 10.00, which meant that Carlos was late, unprecedented, as you know, and maybe we all just sensed that something had gone wrong. Nothing had been communicated at that stage, he'd been gone only a matter of hours. But I swear something was different. The sticks landing there suddenly. I don't see how they could have been brought in or who could have done it. We couldn't all have missed the pile, could we? No one had entered since 8.47.

KANDINSKI: I thought they looked prepared, built—that they weren't an accident. That's how it looked. I don't know if it was a part of something bigger, some clue or other. Where they were placed, it looked like what had been there before—carpet—was gone. That this stick pile had replaced it. I know that doesn't make sense. We're not, as a rule, superstitious on the sixth floor—someone might occasionally send round the horoscopes, but that's as far as it will go. So it means something, it's notable, when I say that we were spooked.

VASQUEZ: I know that he went missing from the restaurant the previous night, and that there was no question of him returning here in the interim, but several of us had the feeling he'd been here again, he'd visited, that the office was the real place he'd vanished from. Isn't it a little suspicious it happened at a restaurant? The ideal place for a vanishing, right? Because presumably everything there would be covered up almost instantly—all the cooking, the cleaning—and there would be nothing left to recover, no evidence. I shouldn't say this. It's nonsense, I know. I'm just saying what it felt like and I want to tell you everything.

KANDINSKI: Someone said they smelled burning.

DIAS: The sticks were a curse. They came as he went missing. That day was a write-off. You might think it's crass to talk this way, but I don't care. I'm telling you everything. It was our lowest daily yield that quarter. It was really poor. We were distracted. The sticks got in the way.

KANDINSKI: They weren't supposed to be there and they changed everything. I know we had them cleared away the moment the first of us noticed anything, but by that stage it was too late, the damage had been done. They had contradicted the office. It should have been unfathomable, the sticks, and I gather that's how it was for some of the others. But for me, that day, I had the terrible feeling that it had been entirely natural and correct that the sticks were there. And that around them and over them was something else, and that stuff was us.

DIAS: I don't want to feel that myself, my staff, my office are intruding.

KANDINSKI: I imagined the sticks multiplying, covering the floor, the walls, the drawers, then piling up in layers, drowning us slowly. We kept climbing, there was less air to breathe, then the sticks were inside us, pressed against our orifices, until finally they swallowed us. I got that from a small pile of sticks innocuously trailed on the office floor. How on earth can you account for that? The sticks were provocative, they changed us.

DIAS: Vasquez tried his number repeatedly on the hour. The family hadn't yet got in touch, nor the police. It was too soon for anything to be made official. I know you have your reasons, I know there has to be some line drawn, but those first forty-eight hours, when someone has gone but is not yet considered missing, they strike me as very strange. What kind of suspension are they supposed to be in? So we, or rather Señora Vasquez, kept trying his number; we'd have to get through eventually, wouldn't we? Someone would pick up. What's the alternative—nothing? We were annoyed rather than alarmed, because we were counting on Carlos, we needed his input and by the time I arranged appropriate cover it would be getting to the end of the working day.

VASQUEZ: The sticks meant something. Someone had put them there that way, in that particular formation. We shouldn't have ordered their removal, we should have given them more of our attention, offered them a more considered response. The individual sticks were very delicately placed over each other. There was a sort of symmetry to it, a pattern repeated either side of the centre. Each stick appeared to have a contrived relationship to all the others. We should have measured them; it might have told us something. There may have been a message kept inside. But maybe it's best we didn't find out, that we didn't read it.

DIAS: You think there's something else going on now, around us in the office, something awful, something we don't want you to know about, and that's why we are keeping you in here and spinning stories about the sticks? Something that also happens to be the answer to the question of what ultimately happened to Carlos. Am I right? Have I caught your trail? Why don't we go out this moment and see what's happening? No one is expecting us to emerge for at least an hour. If we go now, into the foyer and towards the other doors, what we would see would be completely natural and unscripted. We would go out into the middle of it and if there was anything happening then we'd see it right away, it'd be all around us. Shall we do that? Shall we go out right now? Are you sure, Inspector? You're ready?

VIII.

Marks in the ground assert the person has unquestionably been alive. He has made contact with the earth. Whatever else may be in question, this is not. He has walked thousands of miles. The deep marks cut in earth in tribute to the departed imply the cumulative erosion caused by a single pair of feet. If done continuously and in the one place, this causes fire and breaks the skin. Friends, family, others who had known the person may cover the hole in the earth as they pass it during the course of their day. When the holes are filled with water, and then the water drains, the life of the absent person is shown developing and evaporating mysteriously, and not once but many times, until eventually there is no hole there, no mark even, and the rainwater rushes by. The person is gone.

TRIBES OF THE SOUTHERN INTERIOR, P. 114

'I'LL HAVE A FULLER report for you soon,' Isabella told him over the phone. 'I'm still identifying some of the flora.'

'It's taking longer than you expected. Aren't you leaving soon? I don't mean that it's taking long, I—'

'I have found something interesting, though perhaps not significant. Several of the species usually exist in symbiosis with the fluke *Dicrocoelium dendriticum*. But you won't see that in humans.'

'Ever?'

'Only extremely rarely. It'd be difficult to consume it. You'd basically have to swallow an infected ant. *Dendriticum* is a parasite. It moves up through the food chain. The interesting thing is that it actually changes the behaviour of the animal hosting it—it puts it in danger by engineering opportunities for predation.'

'Really?'

'Several species do it. I can show you some reports. And we're finding new ones all the time. One species, we think, actually leads the insect to the sea and bursts open the head there.'

'So, wait, he might have had this in him? Carlos might have had some parasite? Because there was something his colleagues kept saying, something developing in him . . .'

'As I just said, humans don't get infected by *dendriticum*. It just doesn't happen, statistically. But say he did somehow have *dendriticum* or a related species—it would be largely incidental. On a macro level he wouldn't appear different. The intestinal disturbances I've discovered are various and local. It's not a case of a creature moving around in his head, Inspector—you haven't really thought that, have you? And besides, I didn't find *dendriticum*—just traces of it. I'm seeing microbiota that appear new to me. It's likely an identification problem. As I said, give me a day or two.'

'But I was thinking,' the inspector said, 'couldn't someone manipulate these organisms? You know, alter them. What's the word you used? *Engineer* what they do?'

'Yes, I'm working on one right now. It inhibits naive reductionism in laypeople . . . What do you think? I mean, sure, you could play with the genome, given enough money, but could you do anything meaningful? No. We're looking, with Carlos, at something else. If the evidence I'm seeing in his office relates to a contagion—and I'm not saying it does—then the source is something wider. Causally, we'd be looking at an environment, not an organism.'

ENDROHPERIUM ENDILICITIN

A species of microscopic parasite recently discovered in diners at an exclusive restaurant serving wild hog in Jakarta, Indonesia. The parasite dug through the intestinal tract and explored the host body. Diners reported symptoms including nausea, desperation, severe headache, a sense of hopelessness and a dry throat. The illness was quickly traced to infected pork, the restaurant being the first link common to each of the patients.

Biological discovery was late due to several statistically unlikely behaviours eventually leading to mammalian infection. The sequence of hosts in the parasite's life cycle is as follows: salamander faeces—ant—fish—salamander liver. It is disseminated across each predator's body as its ex-host, the prey, enters the digestive tract. In a standard life cycle *E. endilicitin* develops from egg to maturity, but in the case of the human infection the developmental process was extended.

E. endilicitin appears as a different organism according to its respective host environment. The first stage in the prelife sequence is in salamander faeces deposited in mangroves. The ant relies on this as a regular protein source. Once settled, the egg begins to grow, drawing on internal glucose to develop in size and break into the nervous system. This stage is coterminous with a change in the ant's behaviour. The infected ant, at dusk, deviates from its normal path: instead of returning to the colony it goes to the water's edge. This is the stage at which *E. endilicitin* most frequently ceases; the anatomy of almost all of the ant's predators is not conducive to the parasite's continued growth.

The vast quantity of ants originally infected, however, means that at least some parasites are able to reach maturity in being eaten by fish with a favourable internal environment. These fish, under the influence of *E. endilicitin*, become increasingly slow and sluggish, spending uncommon amounts of time visibly on the water surface, leaving them particularly vulnerable to predation.

In turn, large salamanders—omnivorous and amphibious—consume the fish. The parasite is now 10,000 times its original size. In almost all cases this is the fullest extent of *E. endilicitin*'s life, eggs being released into the salamander faeces. Remarkably, however, on several Indonesian islands, and due to a geographical quirk, salamanders, rarely preyed upon, are consumed by forest hogs at a stage in which *E. endilicitin* remains alive. Forest terrain is the typical habitat of both salamander and hog, although the former favours coastal edges; normally, therefore, the two species do not cross. But the inland rivers identified have unusually high saline content, caused by mineral deposits; effectively, the area simulates the sea edge, theatrically misleading the salamander.

Following consumption of the salamander, the hog harbours *E. endilicitin*, prolonging its mature status. This unlikely series of events facilitates rare growth in *E. endilicitin*, leading to the emergence of a highly developed, outsize adult creature, and, in at least one case, to a raft of infected adult humans.

THE INSPECTOR BEGAN TO suffer from increasingly vivid visions of an office worker destroyed at a desk. He had read a short newspaper report on a middle-aged employee rotting behind a partition for three days. Heart attack. According to the line manager, 'due reports were automatically submitted via prompts set up in his account. We had no reason to believe he was not present and well; as far as we were concerned the work was being completed, and to a reasonable standard. There was no reason to query anything.'

He kept thinking about this. He forgot the name. He couldn't help but see the man as Carlos. He imagined how it could have happened, and dreamed, over several disturbed nights, of the details of the process.

The employees taking naps of five to seven minutes, heads nestled in one of the loops of their crossed arms. The deceased ordinarily the first to get in and last to leave. The quip going, off-record, that he was in line for a promotion.

The worker, dead at his desk, having felt unwell for some time. A manic form of claustrophobia. The land edge frustrating him. What, from a distance, seemed a smooth line being a mass of inlets whose true course he could never chart. Nauseous, he considered the folds of brain-maximizing surface area, the similarly fractal organization of the respiratory, lymphatic, nervous and circulatory systems.

The worker had wanted out. Only a total tracing of the world edge would compensate for work's effect. Then he would be neutral, like when he was born. He would sleep on beaches, parking lots and gardens, and he would register atmospheric changes and anomalies in the world's axis caused by the close appearance of an asteroid, and as he slept the sky would not be a fixture or a limit but a shimmering transparency.

His calves thrummed a walking impulse that was suppressed by the desk. Every time he got up, his coastal expedition was frustrated by a mundane task: filing or faxing over a new copy of a contract. He made the same twenty metres' progress only, infinitely.

He had tied his laces in a different rope knot every morning. He inserted paragraphs into reports where the initial letter of each word combined to form the Latin names of extinct sea species. His productivity rose and fell in approximate accordance with the nearest tide. The changing pace and confidence in his cafeteria and bathroom walks were consistent with the force of lapping sea-water. He sweated more, and it smelled like crab.

The deceased worker made amendments to the office structure. He surveyed the strength of the walls and measured the amount of sunlight that filtered through the east-facing window in the morning. He could taste salt on his tongue. His anxiety was a shell secreted like calcium carbonate.

The full quantity of his blood—a gallon—passed through his heart in under a minute. He lifted his left arm and put the heel of his hand against his forehead, supporting himself as he always did, holding himself up. A fixture of blood totally conveyed sixty times an hour. It kept setting himself up to be doing something, he thought—all that work, all that preparation. He drummed his fingers along the desk edge, looked to the floor.

He continued filing and reporting. His skin began to decompose. The air filter was turned up. His colour was put down to an unusual effect of the internal lighting. His voice was no longer capable of emitting anything other than a single long note, which was perfectly sufficient for the completion of his tasks.

He declined extra-corporate invitations. Air moved through him, but not breath. The light sent and reflected from the monitor screen bypassed his head chasm.

Significant floral and faunal interaction was established. He remained present in nearby trees, traces of his hair and skin found in nineteen birds' nests of various sizes. Faeces from newborn birds implied his digestive ecosystem. He was partly consumed in the course of his walks, and there was evidence of his defleshing in the grasses.

He tucked in his shirt and tied his sleeve ends with rope to stop organs dripping out while shaking hands with prospective clients. He kept his mouth closed to contain fly clouds. Larvae ate his bloated, purple gums, sculpted his tooth enamel.

A drawn-out process first of marbling, maceration and finally putrefaction took place, while he maintained a consistent level of activity at his desk. Self-produced corrosive enzymes slowly digested the gastrointestinal tract. He postponed indefinitely weekend plans. First the skin was imbibed in water, then the blood vessels turned dark. The skin organ was a loose sheet capable of slipping on or off and he found it harder to meet deadlines. Inside was a set of organs deflating and a system of billowing gas. Being the chamber below the neck and above the abdomen, containing the heart and the lungs and acting with regards to the latter as a bellows for air filling, the obliteration of the thorax definitively removed any lingering fantasies of reanimation. The office remained active and open for business all through the night. Only bone, cartilage and desiccated soft tissue remained, all edible material having been consumed.

The inspector, finally, woke up.

IX

The substance ingested is believed to evoke secrets contained within the individual. During the ejection, surprising meanings emerge. Detailed descriptions of ancient life are recounted. There is much laughter, partly as a technique used to relieve awkwardness felt from being around something so intimate, and partly because many of the details are absurd. Predictions are made regarding future events and, subsequent to what is revealed, the community may be lifted from its current site and moved to a safer location.

TRIBES OF THE SOUTHERN INTERIOR, P. 119

WASH YOUR EYES, INSPECTOR. Was that what she had said? He should wash his eyes?

He had not previously realized that eyes are a common infection route. Hands on an unclean surface rubbing against them and bringing in a strain. A speaker, he imagined, might transmit an infection directly to the listening eye. Was it better, safer, living looking at the ground, maintaining distance in conversation and spending a disproportionate amount of time alone?

He was uncomfortable with the idea that his eyes had taken on an infection. That every time he blinked he might be pasting it more firmly to his body, pushing in deeper whatever it was. His vision, which he had always thought of as an isolated thing, turning against him.

He didn't feel any different, wasn't noticeably infected by anything new. But then there were the recent disturbed nights, the strange dreams. He thought back to the amount of time he had spent in the sealed office. This could be an incubation stage. He wouldn't necessarily feel it. More likely he had misunderstood the nature of her warning, Isabella in fact talking figuratively. Telling him he wasn't seeing things clearly. He could pick up the phone and ask her—she had been thoughtful enough and suffciently interested in the case to offer him her home number. But he wasn't quite sure how he would boil down his unease into a direct question. And anyway, she was working on something else now and it was late and, what was it, Friday? She would be busy, his call would not be well received. There would be plenty of opportunities to clarify the matter at a later point in time.

SHE HAD GIVEN HIM an idea, though. She might not have appreciated the credit, but he was energized. What she had demonstrated was an impossibility: results from a desert office. Out of invisible microbiota decaying on a keyboard he was presented with an identity in crisis. Together, extrapolating from the data—combining the lab results with information gleaned from family, friends and colleague interviews—they were in the early stages of reconstructing Carlos. The inspector's imagination had been so affected by the environment that he saw the whole project biologically: they were attempting now to regrow Carlos. Not Carlos himself, but a replica: a clone of the missing person. The more comprehensive the replica became, the more susceptible it would be to interrogation. Discovering Carlos, discovering at least what had happened to Carlos, may come down to their ability or otherwise to establish a reasonably complex and faithful simulacrum.

The thing with clones, especially in popular entertainment, was that they missed out on the maturation process and went straight to a fully formed identity. Really you had to start earlier, the new identity had to be born, then age in the world. Strictly, then, in cloning Carlos they might have to wait twenty-nine years to find out what had happened . . . He was both frightened by and attracted to the idea that a clone maintained absolute fidelity to the original life. They could watch the individual from birth, a team of them, from a distance, conducting the experiment under approximately natural conditions, only the clone unaware of his origin. They would monitor him growing, record reams of apparently innocuous data hoping that a code might be expressed, clues preceding his ultimate disappearance from the family gathering that night at La Cueva.

But that was fantasy. Science fiction. His idea, a legitimate, practical idea, was to rebuild Carlos's office. He would find a suitable space and begin reconstructing it; the walls, the floor, the desk. He would render the simulacrum as faithfully as possible. In duplicating the office he hoped something might emerge. Nothing fantastical—he didn't expect the man to rematerialize out of posthumously coated walls. It boiled down to traditional and routine police work: he was trying to develop an insight into the identity through a closer understanding of the environment. He would go into the office every morning and leave in the evening at matching times. Something might come through. Whether, in regrowing the original office, the same illness might bloom—the illness that seemed to have dismantled Carlos—was a thought he quietly ignored.

HE FOUND A GARAGE to let in the dry-field industrial estate just out of town, one with the right approximate dimensions and an east-facing window. It took him three days to gather what he needed. He installed blinds, cut and laid a carpet, painted the walls. He brought in a desk the right height from Office Supplies and a monitor, a keyboard, an extra set of shoes and a suit. He played a recording of work-day sounds made at the corporation and played it on a loop.

The other lots were used for storage or by artists. He came in carrying a briefcase and a coffee and walked briskly, greeting anyone he met with a curt 'Hello' or 'Good morning'. He sat at the desk and tried to forget who he was and to live as Carlos had. Each time, to begin with, he broke off quickly and turned his attention back to the construction of the room. He believed the problem was fabric; the room wasn't built right yet. Once the duplicated space had been correctly established he could run an accurate simulation of the working day. To make the room feel used he rolled in it and ate lots and spoke nonsense monologues, anything really, the thing was just to get words out. The keyboard was new; that was a problem, but there was nothing he could do other than just be at it: there was no way of speeding that up.

The garage was damp and poorly lit. The noise coming in from outside was unreasonable. The harsh heat made him sweat at his desk. He couldn't imagine what it was the other occupants were doing in the places they rented. He heard people pacing, talking aloud to themselves. To block this out he turned up the office audio. He had arranged for the agency to send over several performers in the guise of colleagues and prospective clients. This was to help him feel the place really was a working office. He wasn't sure what the performers had been told. He gave his name as Carlos and no one said a thing, although chance had it that at least one was involved in an interaction at the corporation.

The possibilities afforded by the use of the performers were impressive. There was nothing, for instance—except money—stopping him from hiring a full cast who could then perform a successful resolution to Carlos's disappearance. It would be something very special indeed to be privy to the scene where Carlos walked back in. They'd all benefit from it. That kind of positive mental reinforcement was said to be tremendously advantageous.

He barely had time to consider one possibility when another burst in. Imagine a full reconstruction of the evening in question at La Cueva—they could script all of it, based on thorough interrogations of the extended family, the staff, the other diners, leaving to chance only the moment Carlos left the bathroom. Perhaps the actor, living for that night exactly as Carlos had, would begin automatically reconstructing his actions, intuiting them, that is, without even needing to be told. Watching him closely enough, for once—and wishing, too late, that they had done so on the night in question—they would at last find out what had happened.

They could re-enact the dinner scene with perfect fidelity, only when Carlos got up to leave something innocuous would change his mind and he would resume his seat at the table. They could repeat this particular, crucial scene over and over, until it seemed perfectly fluid and natural and bore itself into the hillside, into the earth.

He could direct the cast in reverse, beginning from the moment they first realized Carlos hadn't come back. It would be therapeutic. If done well enough a sufficient number of times it could even establish itself as a viable alternative to history.

So far it was all going well. He arranged the meeting in the night, so he could lead the client through in the dark and they wouldn't have to observe the dirt, the decay, the ruin on the edges of the estate. He illuminated the office and everything seemed up to scratch. They exchanged long blocks of corporate information, nodded and drank their coffee. Getting up to offer a parting handshake, the inspector froze—a rat had moved diagonally across the garage, clear in the light against the fresh blue carpet. He winced and moved into the handshake, imparting a compensatory firmness against the obvious fact that the set had fallen down. The performer smiled, didn't miss a beat; but the inspector had been humiliated. The frailty of the set had been made all too apparent and he knew he had to work harder.

He drew further plans of the original office. They'd taken detailed photographs of the desk surface, additionally using thermography in darkness and recording what came up. Fine carbon powder, poured over certain areas of the desk, also brought out artificial textures. This was where Carlos had rested his elbows and lay down his one coffee mug. A trace of a circle represented a pause in activity, the beginning of a period of reflection—the setting down of the mug.

Each faint ring left on the desk had a direct mental correlative. He knew the significance of the artefacts. What seemed erratic and inchoate contained its own routine and order inside. Carlos would drink and think differently as the working week progressed. The coffee rings were testament to this. The mug was covered, sealed, theoretically keeping heat throughout the day. What Carlos did with it, how and when he lifted, sipped and set it down was an indication of his changing state of mind. It provided an opportunity for the inspector to authentically reproduce his character in the duplicated office. It was an exciting moment.

HE WENT TO GRASP and lift the mug with both hands and thought, as Carlos had, how strange the simplest things were. He slowly but firmly took it and drew it in towards his lips, sometimes placing it down again without having drawn liquid.

These days, when he happened to be outside, the inspector wore a surgical mask. He was seeing little of his friends. Isabella had been calling. Others from the department, too; messages about leads, developments in the case. The inspector thought, sitting at the desk, that he might as well get on with it, drink the coffee. He placed the mug down, looked at it, considered the size and limitations of the room, a perspective on himself from outside—by the doorway, from the ceiling, from outside the warehouse via the window—and tried to apprehend it, get on with it, but it was difficult, and so it took him some time, particularly on Mondays.

On Tuesdays there was a greater degree of regularity, there was the reflexive training of the prior day's actions, his better preparation in the task of being there, at his desk, even if much of that time was spent fruitlessly trying to apprehend the day, attempting and all but failing to get on with it. He had doubtless suffered on the Monday from the emptiness behind it, the two-day lull and quiet, the weird ill-discipline of a body given no direction, sitting back with less than optimal posture and looking at screens.

Tuesdays were easier. By Tuesday he had been given at least a little of what to expect, what to do without thinking that he was doing it, just doing it, working. On Tuesdays he would be almost working. He would not catch himself doing what he was doing as often on Tuesdays as he would on Mondays, and so this was easier, and so he would drink the coffee at a slower rate, and not cause further anxiety in the course of trying to alleviate it, as he had done and would do again on Mondays. Tuesdays were easier.

Still, things were problematic.

Moving, getting up from a sitting or reclining position, waking oneself with the aid of a set alarm and a resolve to heed its noise (though 'waking oneself' was an odd way to phrase it, he always thought, being impossible really), channeling oneself about a room or through corridors and halls and out on to streets and roads and past other buildings, was, he supposed, something that you had to start and stop, and so you were sort of making it happen, although often during it, it would be the last thing on his mind, filled rather with incidental things such as passing shop-front signs, the speed of other pedestrians (an irritation or a challenge), expressions, musical refrains, rudimentary numerological patterns that he scanned and played out silently and had done deep into childhood, as far back as he could remember—must have been, he assumed, some nervous tic or other—constantly drafting the list of things he needed to do: food shopping to last him at least the next several days, appointments to keep, books he had always been meaning to read, etc., and not actually thinking about what he was doing at all; certainly he had never included 'walk' in the list of things that he must do.

He at least, if he concentrated, could condition how he walked, go slower or faster, softer or harder as he chose, and he could stop it entirely—although always temporarily—whenever he wanted. Breathing wasn't quite so clear.

Again it was something he could modify and, with an effort, condition, and again it was something best performed without thinking. It always unsettled him when he became aware briefly of how he did it; he would immediately be convinced the inhalations were too shallow, the chest too tight and that now, in his misguided attempt to watch himself, he was inevitably changing what was happening, somehow intaking only malodorous, dead air, insufficient to support his metabolism, his heart contractions and the circulating of his blood, and he would wish he had never started on this, throw up his hands and wonder how on earth he was going to turn off all this watching and let it all just happen again.

He longed, every day, for the end of the day. The meaning of his work was concentrated in its finishing. What he was doing he was doing so that it could no longer be done. When it was absent it was at its best, when there was nothing left of it—that was when it had been perfected. When you couldn't see it, when there was nothing left of it—that's when you saw how important it was. It was all about not being there, he saw. The work was there so that it could be destroyed; he was there so he could be somewhere else, in theory.

He was used to the days, used to not even counting on having days, used to there just being days always, because what else could there be if not days? But he was also used to the idea that days were about reversing them into nothing, making, so to speak, non-days of them, about running them out of themselves. That this was the thing to do, then, running the days out. That was his work. Turning the day seamlessly into another day. Which was a notable achievement, of course, there being so many things to attend to, and all at the same time—it was a marvel, he thought, that any of them managed to do it at all, to get from one day into another, to keep everything going just like that.

WAS IT REALLY POSSIBLE that this was what had happened to Carlos? That as he had made the days into nothing, so he had made himself into nothing? That some agent present in his office had accelerated the process, that in the weeks, even the months preceding his ultimate disappearance, Carlos had steadily diminished, maintaining only the coarser processes of living and working, but with less of him available in every passing moment? And nobody had noticed?

He looked up, back out over the duplicated office, and felt a lurch of panic. The structure of the room, the nondescript, identikit furnishings—everything took on a sinister character. The room appeared carnivorous. A person—an employee—consumed here? Absorbed by immediate habitat? He pictured Carlos sitting where he sat now, the mouth opening and beginning a long exhalation, delivering over everything inside him and finally the surface too—the skin, nails and hair, the eyes—until the process was complete, he was gone. Silently, anonymously engulfed by the world.

His short lease expired. He wasn't sure how the exposure to Carlos's situation, the details present in the office, had affected him. He wondered what would happen next. It was difficult to think about, to consider in any way that wasn't grossly reductive. It wasn't just metaphor, not necessarily. He had researched Isabella's speculations, the reports in journals linking bacteria and obsessive trains of thought. It was possible that the origin of the thought—an infection, something picked up in the office—became what the thought was about. Material into symbol. Substance. You were driven in circles. The brain was stuck, running up against its limits. Tidying the desk. Checking the lock on the door again and again. He read about a girl consuming her house, literally eating it, beginning with the walls. What was Carlos's single thought? The transmission of a strain. Infection. Invasion. The single idea dominating, returning again and again.

Carlos had done nothing so stark, so brilliant as consume his own walls. Although walls had been important to him: they had found prints on the entire office perimeter, every centimetre. He pictured Carlos running his hands along the walls, sceptical of the room's integrity, repeatedly checking the boards that maintained, for the moment, his private space. Even the inspector could see the parallels between the wall-like organs of his body and the places where he lived. Their analysis of the empty office was the ultimate intrusion: it was as if Carlos had seen it coming all along.

X

In time, the missing outgrow their houses and become part of the wider environment. This is one of the reasons the community is respectful to animals during hunts, and why it rations the amount of materials taken from any one part of the forest, not wanting to destroy matter indirectly related to the person they had loved.

Following signs of a vanishing, loved ones examine light for imperfections. It is far more likely that light has only subtly changed, concealing the missing person, than that this person has been voided. Objects too will be found to have disappeared, and plants, animals, fresh skin. The afflicted individual, the one whom no one, for the moment, is able to locate, will be amused and unable to affect people, other than through atmospheric impressions.

Light readings are made daily, variations noted; on some days, usually close to darkness, sudden changes in light momentarily reveal a full feature of the missing person, such as a limb or a facial expression. One such sighting is sufficient to rejuvenate the family concerned for several months.

TRIBES OF THE SOUTHERN INTERIOR, P. 148

HIS HEAD STARTED TO hurt. He felt a young man's pain in his gums and teeth. The whole lower part of his face, in the restless periods between night and morning, seemed in flux. He wanted to retreat into a more secure and solid area and rest there, but was unable to detach himself from the ongoing physical process. In these liquid periods he dreaded facing his new appearance in the morning, his altered proportions, the higher or lower setting of his jaw.

He was presently the least qualified person imaginable to solve and bring about a conclusion to the case. He was too tired—the years, this heat—to think much, to give shape to his theories, to notice anything he had not noticed before. He was looking straight ahead out of habit, seeing nothing at the edges.

If Carlos were the subject of an unusually virulent infection, something connected to his position in the corporation, then he couldn't be the only one. Where were the other missing persons?

That there was no indication of any connected spread of missing workers should have been enough to put the inspector's mind at ease, professionally and personally. This wasn't an epidemic. He wasn't, himself, at risk. Any symptoms he imagined were just that. They weren't real, they were inventions, possibly stress related. *Wash your eyes, Inspector.*

He started again. Opened a file at random: 17337. Carlos's employee number. He began doodling with his pen, cross-referencing, seeing what he could find. The number equalled the approximate net salary of the caretaker in the corporation building. It was a little under five hours in seconds, half their corporate working day. The typical number of steps taken daily by a non-sedentary worker. The number of heartbeats in a healthy, middle-aged male in four comfortable or three anxious hours. Close to the distance in light years to Omega Centauri.

The number, if converted into the Latin alphabet, read AGCCG. This, he saw, was biologically meaningful as a DNA strand: adenine, guanine, cytosine, cytosine, guanine. It repeated in nucleotide transcription errors in organisms making transitions from land habitation to sea. The mutations were coincident with seaward movement and remained present in all mammalian descendants.

He was perpetually half-asleep at his desk at home, dulled but kept awake by the thick and all but stale odour of filter coffee. Transcripts, testimonies from Carlos's friends, relatives; phone numbers, printouts of closed-circuit television frames, distant public-transport schedules beginning the moment of the disappearance and stretching on a day, a thick bundle of technical reports on the office; drawings, lines, ideas, many of which he looked at now and could think of no referent; theories, a nonsense logic he turned to occasionally in weaker moments; restaurant receipts, books, several coffee-stained mugs, pistachio shells, a tangerine peel. The contents of his desk flickered in the otherwise ineffective fan breeze. The heat only made it harder to stay awake.

He slumped forward, nestled his head in the figure eight of his arms.

He dreamed Carlos had been consumed. Dreamed of meeting a large man, three hundred pounds, on the thirty-fourth floor of a glass building. The man had just finished eating when the inspector arrived. His shirt collar was open, his tie folded and hung over the back of the metal chair, a white cloth handkerchief spread over his lap.

He woke and immediately realized something was different. Something had developed. He was being converted, no longer himself—self-rejecting, turning inside out. He ran, humiliated and urgent; he burst out over the bathroom floor. He sat on the bowl, head in hands, the room solid with the smell of his excretions. As his stomach moved, he fell in and out of appalling dreams.

Hours later he showered, did what he could to remove the smell, all trace, drank quantities of water and ice, lay down on top of his bed and tried to sleep.

He couldn't. He held the stomach, tried to still the shuddering cramps, delay it a while longer. Something nagged at him, although it was absurd that a thought, an insight, might come from this. He wanted to sleep, disappear. Still he couldn't; something insisted. He grimaced, pressed the heels of his hands against the damp mattress, lifted up his frail carriage and looked ahead at nothing, a wall. He smiled pathetically, waited. White space, a wall. The wall in the offices, the corporation. The photograph. He knew where he had seen that face before.

It was an August, too, and almost as bad as this one. Garbage collections delayed, rotting in the heat. In the poorer neighbourhoods windows stayed open. Barbecues in parks and gardens.

The smell of food lingered. Animal imprinted on clothes and skin. His wife washed down in evenings, too. He would join her, the cut of cold water like blades on his back.

The odd thing he had noticed on entering the building all those years ago was the sudden and dramatic escalation of the smell; a stench, the air clotted and difficult to breathe. He had taken a moment to right himself at the bottom of the stairs. The palm of his hand had covered his mouth and he knew it would be difficult to go on.

It was unusual he had been called. It didn't sound significant. Just a smell. But he knew something was wrong the minute he passed through into the stairwell. This was not food. The murmur of a hive noise. Something rancid in the building. He couldn't call for others yet. He would first identify the source. The apartment was on the third floor. The neighbours wouldn't come out, not even the resident who had made the call. The smell was thick and heavy, taking over the stone stairwell. He had an idea what it was, but he couldn't do anything until he saw.

He rapped on the door. No sounds from inside. He expected radio or a too-loud television. Some background noise, at least. Quiet footsteps approached and then a smiling, healthy-looking man appeared in faded cords and an immaculate white T-shirt. 'Come in,' he said with a smile, and the inspector followed.

Inside it was difficult to breathe. He remembered how clean the white shirt was, and how compactly the man carried himself. The sound of the insects vast. A city's power. He said it was an honour to receive him, a man of law. He was smiling, but not ironic. He asked the inspector if he would like some iced tea and he almost said yes.

He was not manic. He didn't chatter ceaselessly or jerk angularly or wave his arms like a man who feels a great energy, having difficulty containing himself. He just seemed pleased to have the company.

'Would you mind if I took a look around?' the inspector asked. 'It's just routine.' He tried to smile briefly. 'Nothing to worry about.'

'Of course, of course. It's nothing special, I'm afraid, just an ordinary apartment. If I'd known you were coming I would have cleaned up.'

'It's better this way.'

'Okay.'

'I'm just going to walk around. Nothing to worry about. I'll be a moment.'

'Wouldn't you like me to escort you through the rooms?'

'It's not necessary, thank you. I'll be gone before you know it. I'll be out of your hair in no time. Thank you, though.'

'You're welcome.'

They were still standing in the narrow corridor. There was little natural light, the apartment placed off from the street and the windows western facing. The carpet was a dark brown colour. Nothing hung on the walls. Draped on the back of a wooden chair was a pair of formal trousers and an expensive white shirt.

He opened the door. Bathroom. Well maintained. Damp towel

hanging on the shower rail. It would stay damp for days in the humidity. You couldn't get anything done, everybody said.

He opened the next door. He was familiar with the layout of the building, the symmetry either side of the stairs, and so he knew this room was most likely the kitchen. He could have gone here first.

When he heard the roar of the insects, he had the idea that he was inside a computer, something neutral and artificial whose sustenance he didn't understand. It was difficult to identify the contents of the room. The insects distorted things, lent blur and motion. Blood lapped in ground pools, a lot of blood, the deceptive volume of approximately one individual. He tried not to step through it. It was blood only on the linoleum floor, nothing else had come through. On the worktop was a scalped adult head. The blowflies covered the brain, blue-black currants. The head was male. The eyes were brown and wet hair lined the length of the neck. On the table the torso was in the process of being stripped; he had interrupted the man. A navy blue and white apron hung from the bar that ran along the top of the cooker. Parts of the torso had been sliced, sheets two or three inches deep. These slices made him think of an orange cut down the middle, the fraying and the juice.

He had been trained to act logically and to prioritize. He phoned it in, quietly stating only three numbers, then continued surveying the room. Some of the parts were wrapped in foil.

He heard the floor splash.

'Don't worry,' the man said. 'I should have warned you, but really there is no cause for alarm.'

'What do you mean?'

'There is nothing to concern you here, that's all.'

'What do you mean?'

'This is not a human. Was it not apparent to you? I really hope I

84

didn't give you a fright. Easy mistake to make, I suppose, at least if you're not paying attention.'

'This is a man,' he said.

'It isn't. It's an Indian.'

'I see,' the inspector said. 'I see.'

'I'm sorry this has taken up your time, when really there was no need. I hope you can resume your work soon. You people provide a great service, I always think.'

The inspector had yet to identify the knife. From the look of the cuts, the blade would be a foot long. The parts had come away easily. He thought of wire and cheese, the freeing of the arms and shoulders. He had moved quickly and with only a minimal number of incisions. He had sheared the head off in one, hacked through the neck-stalk.

'There is a lot,' the inspector said, searching the room without a flicker.

'It was big.'

'I'm sorry?'

'Just what I say. It was big. You're right, there is a lot. Can I ask you something?' the man said, still standing in the doorway.

'Of course you can.'

'Why are your colleagues coming?'

'It's nothing to worry about,' the inspector said. 'I'm just meeting them here and then we are leaving. It's fine.'

'Okay,' he said.

'Yeah, it's nothing.'

'Are you sure you would not like some iced tea?'

'Yes, I'm sure, thank you.'

'But it's so warm.'

'It's rather embarrassing to admit,' the inspector said, 'only, I have a weak bladder.'

'Ah.' He smiled and laughed a little. 'That explains it.'

The inspector noticed a greying flap, four inches long with a slightly uneven surface. It lay flopped on to the counter by the kettle. Looked like a small fish. It was open at one end, where it had been detached. He saw that there were innumerable strings running through it, that the whole thing was rather a mass of strings with a strip of cover on top.

He watched the man speak. He was saying dull things and he was not moving from the doorway. It was six minutes since the inspector had phoned it in and still nothing, and no indication of the sign.

He watched the man speak and he said the right things in response and couldn't help watching his mouth, observing the wet inside, the automatic lathering of the tongue along the teeth-tops, the just detectable excess sound of the lips' contact.

He knew where it was now. The man had lost his concentration and given it away. He would have to reach for it. It would take the man almost a whole second to cover the knife with his hand and about half that time to seize it. The inspector asked a question about iced tea, about what brand he used, because he really was a connoisseur of teas. He was very sorry, but he couldn't take a glass just now, and as he finished asking the question the inspector reached for his belt and his gun and brought the man down before he had time to complete the arc of his arm towards the top of the fridge. It was over.

HE NEEDED TO ESTABLISH information, confirm possible links. He pushed up from the bed. His head was full and he leant heavily for a moment on the sill of the bedroom window. The evening light seemed too thick, too heavy, as if ready to burst. He pulled the curtains together.

The links, he thought. The killer, here—was it possible he had worked, however briefly, for the corporation? He didn't know if the timelines matched. For how long, even, had the corporation been active? He knew, exasperated, exactly what they would say: that the question was not straightforward. That he would need to clarify, be more specific. Which particular incarnation, they would ask, did he refer to? The corporation had undergone a series of mergers and subsequent divisions. It endured, they would tell him, via transition. So what did he mean, when he spoke of the corporation? What single thing, precisely, did he imagine?

His instinct was that the timelines didn't fit, the killer being too old for the photograph in the offices. Most likely he had been mistaken in sensing a connection. It was an uncommonly similar face, simply a coincidence.

But it wouldn't leave him. He needed to rule it out. Apprehending the criminal was the last he had seen of him. After armed backup arrived the man had been taken to hospital, then a holding cell, transferred on to a high-security unit, trialled and swiftly sentenced. The inspector's colleagues, particularly the senior officers in his department, had been unusually accommodating, granting him a short period of leave; his boss had then insisted he undergo a minimum three sessions with a staff counsellor—only appropriate, she had said, given the unusual trauma involved in the arrest. The perpetrator, by all accounts, had made no effort to conceal his actions; this was evident from the start, and meant things could move forward quickly. The inspector's presence had not been required in court and he was simply asked to participate in a comprehensive debriefing, detailing exactly what had happened that August afternoon.

He wouldn't try to work out the connections. Recalling the scene, even just thinking about the killer, caused his stomach to cramp, his temperature to rise, and he thought, moving ambitiously to his desk, he might vomit again, he might faint.

He wasn't sure what he had eaten, what precisely had given him the poison, but he had some idea. He pushed away a dull, distant thought. He'd start preparing his own food again. He'd live a simple diet now, fluids, carbohydrates and vegetables. He could purify himself. Hopefully he'd ejected most of what it was and the thing had passed. The timing was poor, he had work to do. But the timing was necessary. He had remembered the scene, placed the face in the course of vomiting across his bathroom floor. His illness had bred the realization.

He tried to circle around the thoughts rather than confront them. The connections: the corporation, the killer, Carlos. It should have been enough that he had felt it, known it. The killer would have information. There were the records, the archives: holdings in the interior, illegal practices and missing communities. The killer, insane, destroying an indigenous person. But what did it have to do with Carlos? What was he pushing for?

He speculated again on what had happened to Carlos. Isabella had not contradicted him when he asked if the source of the illness could be psychological, prompted by something Carlos had seen, something he had learned. This 'information', then, this source, whatever it was, causing the illness—could it be related to something within the corporation? Something in its history? Could it be related to the killer?

He didn't know what Carlos had found out. What kind of pressure he had been under. But if he could interview the killer, learn about his employment, the nature of his role in the corporation, then perhaps he could get a little closer.

HE MADE THE NECESSARY enquiries. Public information was minimal, the case having been omitted from the media by request. He was referred to several different departments, each clerk assuring him the following number would give him all the information he required. He remained at his desk, on hold, doing his best to resist the eruption of his rage. He spoke to someone else. He was transferred again. He was put on hold.

Eventually he got somewhere—a holding cell in the south. Montero sounded a little young for a sergeant. He seemed to be eating and to be addressing at least one other person in the room, the line coming in and going out, as if obstructed by an object. He did not have long, Montero explained—it was another very busy evening—but he would give the inspector what he could.

He remembered the case, of course. How could he not? The inspector had worked with him only briefly. It wasn't unusual that he couldn't place the name, the voice. People often told the story. Montero congratulated the inspector on his work. Who knew, he said, how many others that monster would have taken?

The inspector cut in. 'I'd simply like to know where he is. Which facility he's held in.'

'Yes, yes,' Montero said, apparently in full agreement. 'Why?'

The inspector asked him to repeat himself.

'Why do you want to see him?' he said. 'Are you sure it's for the best? Isn't it true the events had quite an effect on you, at the time?'

'Listen, just give me the name of the relevant facility and I'll be getting on.'

Montero made a noise, perhaps striking a match. He paused.

'I'm afraid we're going to have a problem.'

At any moment, he thought, the scene would correct itself.

Everything would be clarified and the manner of the officer—his colleague—would soften.

Montero explained the situation as best he understood it. It appeared, he said, to all intents and purposes, that the killer had been lost.

He clarified: obviously he remained in a secure facility—he would never be released, that went without saying. It's just that we are having some temporary difficulty, he explained, establishing precisely where he is.

The beginning of the problem, he told the inspector, was the killer's insanity.

'He struck me as lucid.'

'Quite,' Montero agreed. 'But did you ask him his name? He had no identification. Nothing especially unusual in that. But that's not what we're talking about. He claimed he didn't have a name. Kept up the claim for quite some time. The problem was there was nothing to identify him in the apartment. No passport, credit cards. No mail. Neighbours on nodding terms only—he hadn't been there long. The apartment was sublet or sub-sublet, paid weekly in cash, no contract. He worked independently, freelance, he said. Naturally, he would give us no more details.

'You would not believe,' he said, 'the trouble we have had administering this man.

'We assigned him the temporary moniker Juan Pérez. It would have been better, we agreed, if he had, in fact, been a real Juan Pérez, dead like the others. As this man had no bank account, you can imagine our surprise when his full legal team arrived.

'The defence was rhetorical. They said—I remember the words—that we had "no one we could legitimately charge". The onus was on us to identify him, they claimed. Until that point we could proceed no further.'

The inspector waited. Several seconds of silence.

'Well, that's it, effectively. We were at an impasse. He remained held indefinitely, awaiting trial. He was imprisoned, that wasn't going to change. There were other, more pressing matters. I won't deny it was frustrating. But we had our man, that was the main thing. Besides, what could we do? You should have heard the defence. The young lawyer said that given the limited information gathered, we'd no way to prove this was a living man. There was no laughter, Inspector. They said he didn't pay tax and he didn't procreate. He was nameless, had no known relatives. He didn't seem to have come from anywhere. What exactly were we dealing with? They used the word "suspect", as if none of it had really happened, as if you hadn't really seen it for yourself.

'The young lawyer said the suspect did not live anywhere. Nothing definitive placed him in that apartment for any length of time. By this stage the neighbours were refusing point-blank to cooperate with enquiries. The lawyer, with some relish—I wish I could remember the name—said the suspect, prior to arrest, had been continuously moving, never ultimately settling down in any one place. These were games, obviously. They were playing for time. They said he didn't live anywhere, said he wasn't, effectively, alive.'

The inspector was incredulous. He waited for the reveal, the truth explaining that this was a joke, it wasn't real. Nothing. It couldn't go on like this. 'In the trial, in interviews, was there anything to suggest Pérez worked for a financial institution?'

'We told you, we learned nothing about his job. He claimed he worked independently, that was all. Why?

'But he's there, Inspector—we have him, don't worry about that. For the moment, however, we're unable to pinpoint the particular facility he's held in. Inmates are transferred regularly and Pérez's location has become confused. And . . . well, he seems to have coerced some of the other prisoners. Whenever we look for Pérez, more than one of them claims the name. Groups of them, they copy each other in the way they carry themselves, the way they walk. You could say Pérez, in a manner, flows through the cells. If we thought there was any chance of a positive identification, then, really, we'd bring you in, Inspector. But it's been many years. And it would take some time—we're talking a minimum of six facilities. If you think it's worth it, then by all means, fill out an application and we'll have it processed just as soon as we can.'

XI

A chair makes an average man half as tall. The office employee spends around two-thirds of his life at this height or lower (asleep, childhood). Sitting in the one position for extended periods may have a quite different effect from that intended. After a period of two to three hours in a single seated position, the redundant legs become insensate. Obscured from view beneath the desk, he loses awareness of them.

The feeling, once he stands, is novel. He slaps the trouser legs to spark sensation and feels transparent charge in the momentum of his blood. The legs, having effectively been in storage, are returned to him in the manner of a prosthesis, an addition with which he has to familiarize himself again in order to activate. The loss of muscle strength in calves, quads, forelegs and thighs increases the likelihood of significant injury later in life, the decades-long disuse perhaps being returned to in the provision of a wheelchair.

TRIBES OF THE SOUTHERN INTERIOR, P. 43

HE WOKE TO THE insistent, shrill sound, sat up from the sofa in his front room, smoothed his shirt. It had been going on for some time. The sound had entered his sleep, into whatever he had been dreaming. He felt uncertain, not quite in his place, a little reluctant to pick up.

'Hello?'

'We have him.'

Carlos?

It took him several moments to realize the voice on the other end was referring to Pérez.

They had located him in the prison system. He was willing to talk, so the inspector acted quickly, arranging delivery of his service vehicle and washing and readying himself while he waited.

The hotel—which had a reputation for being unfeasibly lavish—was a distance away, past the city in the east.

His headlamps lit up demolition sites, fenced off, abandoned land and two last remaining tower blocks. It wasn't clear if anyone still lived there. He passed on, through rows of black-window bars, pawn shops and anonymous takeaways. He drove more purposefully through the night streets unimpeded. Why hadn't he thought of this before, the relief of night driving? The ease of getting somewhere, the reassurance of autonomy.

It was quite a peculiar arrangement, but he was in no position to turn it down. Several lawyers would be present and the terms insisted on a neutral location, taking the man out of prison grounds. Pérez had a story to tell, and he wanted to speak to the inspector and no one else.

He joined the Rio Paraná again, wide, enormous looking, extending into the clouded sky. For a while he drove in parallel. He could hear its rush through the open windows. The road was thin, with no edge-lights, no barriers in place on the riverside. He was out in dark farmland, in sheets of soft green, with the silhouettes of sleeping animals cut out of the land.

He had the feeling he had to get there quickly, that it was important. Potentially crucial. If he had been correct in identifying a link between Pérez and the corporation, then what he was driving towards could well be a revelation. The lawyers would push for leniency, finally giving up the identity of their client, along with the information he had to give, on condition of favourable treatment. Transfer to a low-security prison, perhaps. A comfortable place; somewhere he could live out the rest of his life quietly. The thought disgusted the inspector, but he should wait and see what the man had to give them before ruling anything out.

The ground-floor lobby was deserted. His shoes made a tapping sound on the bright, hard floor. Outside was sheer dark, the interior baldly reflected on the glass.

His instructions were to wait in the foyer until he was collected by officials, who would then escort him to the room where Pérez was held. Now he had stopped, had a moment to think, it seemed outrageous. That Pérez could be there, locked in a room. Presumably he would be shackled. There would be guards as well as lawyers, armed men. Pérez should pose no threat. Still . . . He would have preferred a meeting on prison grounds, with separating bars. He pictured the face from the photograph, blank, unremarkable. The man he had met at the doorway and apprehended in the apartment. The glazed, distant, vacant expression. The cool, unaffected way he had stood around an obliterated individual.

Pérez had frightened him more than anyone he had ever met. He pictured a box in the room upstairs. A cage, the man kept in metal. It all reminded him of a film he'd seen once, the name long forgotten. And something there: an identity switch?

He waited a moment more, then introduced himself at reception. 'They'll be expecting me,' he said.

He sat at the long bar, ordered a whisky to settle his nerves. His ears were ringing. His hands shook. He again reminded himself that there was no forensic evidence of a contagion in Carlos's office. He was simply tired, getting over the food poisoning. Too old to be taking cases like this.

He heard deep, thick laughter from further down the bar, followed by detailed descriptions of anatomy and intercourse. The barmaid kept her head down, mouth closed, alternating purposefully between wiping the glasses and the bar counter. To his left two handsome, well-dressed young men raised their shot glasses and smiled. He found himself nodding back. He ordered another whisky.

One thing that irritated him was the mysterious ability, as it seemed, of everyone else to remain composed. The interview subjects at the corporation, Vasquez, Dias and Kandinski, for instance, especially Dias—they never seemed to register the heat, whereas he always appeared flustered wherever he arrived. This sometimes aided him, lending an impression of a lack of care. He often seemed to be struggling to catch up with something, and this could give an opponent an unmerited sense of control.

But still, he would have liked it if at least one of the employees had shown the faintest sign of physical unease.

He downed his drink.

'Mengano,' the younger man said, offering his hand.

'Beltrano,' went the other, appearing irritated.

'Caballero,' the inspector offered, playing along.

'We thought you weren't coming,' Mengano said.

The inspector took his coat from his stool.

'He's here, don't worry. There's no rush, is there? We can sit. It's better we wait a moment. Have you prepared yourself, Inspector? Perhaps you should order another drink?'

'Who exactly—?' the inspector began, before Beltrano, still refusing to make eye contact, raised his hand to silence him.

A young woman, dressed in a black gown, walked past the bar and disappeared into the adjoining room.

'Isabella?' the inspector called, stunned. 'Isabella!'

'Let's go, we need to hurry,' the other one said, contradicting Mengano.

'But—'

'Come on. Finish your drink. We don't have much time.'

Mengano led them on, past the elevator to the stairs. 'He's up there.'

'Did you know, Inspector,' Beltrano said, as they began briskly ascending the first steps, 'that every single person has an appointed killer, someone who, upon seeing them, suddenly recognizing who they are, has no option other than to do it, usually with their bare hands?'

'What joke is this?' the inspector asked, struggling to match the pace of the two younger men. '*No option?* Are you Pérez's lawyers? I was under the impression . . .'

'You've got us wrong! We're on your side, Inspector. But humour us, won't you? Can't you think of examples from your experience in the force? Motiveless murders. Haven't you ever wondered?'

'I should explain,' Beltrano continued, 'the meeting, the recognition—whatever you want to call it—it hardly ever happens. World's a big place. People die other ways.'

'I like to dress darkly, discreetly, just in case.'

They suddenly branched off the staircase, turning sharply down a corridor of identical doors, then another, and another. They were moving so fast now that the inspector almost had to run to keep up.

'When it does happen,' Beltrano pressed on, without breaking his stride, 'when the killer meets the appointed target—remember he or she knows nothing about it. They're not bad people, necessarily. They don't—that is to say—choose to kill this person.

'It's just the way things are—'

'Where is this room?' the inspector cut in. 'Haven't we made a full circuit of the third floor?'

'Third floor? What are we doing on the third floor?'

'Isn't it on the fourth floor? Isn't that where he's held?'

'That's where we're supposed to be.'

'Mengano? Okay. But first I should come clean. The reason I know about this is . . . I've actually seen it happen. I've witnessed a real case. And it was quite something.'

They stopped by the staircase. The inspector wiped his head, relieved at the break.

'Some water?' Beltrano said, smiling and taking a bottle from his briefcase. 'Apologies, I was sure there was something in it.'

The men were smiling, watching him. He wanted to say to them, 'Listen, can't we just stop this? I don't want to hear this shit,' but he hadn't caught his breath.

Beltrano corrected his waxed side-parting in the mirror-wall.

'Let's go.'

They let the inspector start back up the staircase before them, as if he knew where to go, and they followed. He went along with it. He just wanted it over with, wanted to get there. They climbed another flight, two steps at a time, and started a loop of the fourth floor. It was a straightforward enough task, simply walking past every door. They didn't see a single person. Mengano continued. The inspector heard him from behind like an insistent voice in his head.

'Last year, September, late at night. Amazing. Raining hard. I couldn't believe he was able to make an identification. Wouldn't have thought he'd even be able to see clearly. I heard this voice: "Where are you going?" Not too loudly. Again. Then he reached out and grabbed the neck and wrenched—and it was amazing, because up until that point he had just been a pedestrian. He hadn't been the kind of person who could do something like that. Thing is the guy under his hand somehow got away. Ran.

'Like I say, amazing!

'He ran all through the city. People were afraid of him.'

'How did you—?'

'They thought that he was dangerous, because of the way he was running; he was desperate, he wasn't going to move out of the way to avoid hitting someone. They couldn't see that he was running from someone. He must have been going twenty, thirty minutes . . .'

'Inspector, I don't mean to be rude, only you're going to have to walk faster. Otherwise, well, we're just going to walk right through you. You do want to get there, don't you?'

'If they were running,' he managed, 'then you were too—you chased this poor man.'

'I had to find out what happened, didn't I?'

He heard Beltrano quietly behind him. 'Just this door here, any one, very soon now. It's around the corner, I'm sure of it.'

He was beginning to feel nauseous. He had drunk too much at the bar. His stomach curdled. When had he been sick in his apartment? One day ago? Two? A week? He had lost track, and now he was charging along a corridor with two strangers. He realized he hadn't yet established who exactly these men were, which body they represented. The official on the phone had led him to believe he would be met by police. But were they the lawyers, part of a team acting on Pérez's behalf? Were they more directly involved with the corporation?

Additionally, he wanted to ask for clarification on the illogical details in their story—was he supposed to believe Mengano had been present for the whole duration of the chase, running through the city at night in the rain? The way it was told it seemed Mengano had overtaken the pursuer, that he had, in fact, become him. If he was running, which must have been the case if the story were to have any credence, then the victim, the man being chased for no reason, would have seen him, leading to a confrontation when they both stopped, surely? And it became Mengano he feared.

'Can you imagine what he's thinking, waiting at the bus stop?'

'Almost there, Inspector.'

It was unpleasant hearing the words coming from behind, their footsteps, the quickness increasing, threatening to meet him, go through him. His instinct was to turn around now, but if he did, he knew he would vomit—that's all it would take. In any case, they wouldn't stop for him. He was positive that if he turned around there would be a collision, head-on. By this stage he had lost all hope of seeing Pérez. He doubted Pérez had ever been there.

'There were a few people at the scene—someone in uniform having just finished a late shift; a young couple who'd been drinking for hours—and they didn't like the look of the guy who'd just shown up. There was something not right about him. His pupils, nostrils—the whole face wild. He was leaning against the shelter, doubled over, retching, wheezing. Just like you, in fact, Inspector. He was wild and exhilarated. Terrified, but exhilarated—that's the thing, that's what I remember. He'd got away. He knew how lucky he was. He was living at his greatest capacity. And then he closed his eyes.

'So now he's on the bus, single deck, half-full, sitting at the back. He's still terrified, paranoid, thinking stupid things. He's even looking out the window at the back of the bus—that must've been why he chose the seat. But the bus pulls away. I'm thinking the guy must be imagining another scenario, say the bus suddenly stopping, a rapping on the door, a new passenger coming on—the same man, the hunter, walking the aisle towards the back of the bus. I mean, what would the guy do?'

His head spun. He didn't have control of himself. He was acting absurdly, moving up and down the corridor at the behest of these strangers, these sinister young men with false names. He knew how stupid he looked. He hated them. He heard himself snorting, panting. He felt sweat on his back and forehead, sensed the red spreading across his face. He heard them right behind him—not just the sound of their expensive shoes, but the swish of their shirts and jackets, the metronomic rhythm of their breath, the assurance of their ease and absolute control. How long would they keep going like this, chasing him? he wondered.

'Would he shout—for the other passengers, for the driver? What would he say? And what if the man, the attacker—and it's not his fault, remember, none of it is—what if he doesn't go all the way to the back of the bus? What if he simply takes a seat near the front, waiting, presumably, for the victim to get up and leave? What is he supposed to say to the driver then? Because this other man—the hunter—is only sitting in his seat, quietly; he hasn't done anything wrong as far as anyone can tell. The victim can't stay on the bus forever. At some point he has to get up, walk down to the front, past him. And he has to do it sooner rather than later; he doesn't want it to be just the two of them left as the bus comes into the terminus. But he also knows that, if he does get up to leave, he'll be followed. You see? That's what's so funny about it! It's impossible! It doesn't mean anything. It's a game and there's no way out.

'The guy sitting at the back, he's feeling all right now. His adrenalin's seeping away. His heart rate's returning to normal. He's starting to wonder if maybe he imagined some of it. It's so strange, surely it's not real. And this is the point when he opens his eyes.'

The inspector knew neither for how much longer he could continue like this nor why he was even trying. He wanted to confront Mengano: 'Are you saying you are a murderer? Are you saying you have killed someone, is that it?' That must have been the reason he was still with them—he needed to ask. But he had his hand clasped to his chest, his lungs struggling for air.

It wasn't particularly rare, this kind of bravado. People, especially young people, liked to try that around police, mocking them, hinting at crimes, while remaining careful not to state anything that might count as an admission of guilt.

'Are you ready, Inspector?' One of them put a hand on his shoulder. They'd stopped.

'This is it. We're here. This is the room. Everything you need to know is on the other side.'

He leaned on the corridor wall, put his other hand out, wheezed.

'Perfectly all right, Inspector. Gives me time to tell the part of the story I forgot. The beginning.'

'The most important part,' Beltrano continued. 'It could even come in useful, who knows?'

'True. What I meant to say, right at the start, Inspector, is that no meeting happens that is not preceded by a sign. An error. Something gone wrong—a single white flower placed on an otherwise clear path; an old woman walking backwards through a crowded street; a clock suddenly leaping several hours.'

'Gather yourself, Inspector. You don't want to be humiliated in front of your peers, do you? This is a big opportunity. Come on.'

Beltrano opened the door and the inspector pushed himself in. He hit a rush of air and was immediately refreshed. He breathed in deeply. He couldn't hear them behind him any longer. He wanted to go out further into wherever that air came from. It was completely dark in the room. He couldn't see anyone. Some game, some experiment, he thought. He wanted to enjoy the oxygen, but as he walked out into the room he felt a different surface under his feet—a thin mesh metal floor. A cage. The noise echoed out against something. A light turned on, dazzling him a moment before illuminating the space—it was the rear of the hotel, the refuse stored and collected below. Beyond that, the roaring wide river and a flash of forest.

He turned around, stepped back into the corridor. The men were out of view.

XII

Comparisons to burial and grave memorials in other societies are inevitable. The six-foot depth cut into earth is a similar practice, scaled up. There is the same belief, often, that the vanished person may return. In cutting six feet in, the approximate height of the figure is inscribed, the length cut also. The born person has been cut out of the earth, made of its materials; preparing burial re-enacts the life-giving, as if in bringing up turf, topsoil, rock, animal, the others are collecting substances with which to make the deceased living again, or to make another of him.

TRIBES OF THE SOUTHERN INTERIOR, P. 117

'HELLO?'

'Isabella? I'm sorry to be calling. Is it late? Of course it is, yes. It's just that I was wondering. I know it's been a while, but could we maybe go over one or two things? I mean, I wanted to run something by you. Is that okay?'

'Inspector?'

He thought he heard something on the line, an object being moved, perhaps a door being closed. Laughter, hushing, another voice.

'Yes, well actually—but no, now's fine, we can talk, of course. How are you?'

'Well, you know, one or two things . . . I thought I was on to something for a while, the case—I really did. But I must have been mistaken. Things got confusing. I don't know. I think it's this heat. I can never really see clearly, outside. Anyway. Not to worry.' He paused. 'How are you? You know, didn't I see you the other week at the hotel, I . . .'

'A hotel? Me? No, no, you're mistaken. But I've been meaning to call you.'

'You have?'

'Regarding Carlos. He'd been reporting to a physician for several months—you did know that? I don't have the records, but access shouldn't be a problem. Naturally, I'll be curious to see them myself.'

'That's really helpful. That's interesting. May I take the name, the details? I'll share what's inside just as soon as I have the file.'

'Already sent. Well? You wanted to ask something?'

'Yes, well, I've been playing everything over, so to speak, the theories, what happened to Carlos. Honestly, I think I may have to start questioning my judgement. Some of the ideas . . . I mean, there was a time when I was genuinely considering the possibility that Carlos broke apart, that something happened to him, molecularly, so to speak. Beginning in the office, I mean. The form finally giving way that night in the restaurant. It's absurd. But did we really discuss that? I mean, I can see now you were being figurative, it's just I haven't been feeling so well myself recently, there have been certain worries . . .'

'Worries?'

'Obsessive trains of thought, the same thing again and again, and it really isn't like me. And then, just the other week, a bout of mild poisoning, something I ate, resulting in some flux, sweating, vomiting. Nothing unusual, I shouldn't think.'

'Inspector, see a doctor. As a precaution.'

'Really? I will. But I would like to ask . . . what I would like to ask regards the outbreak of illness. In Indonesia—the parasite—'

'*E. endilicitin.*'

'Yes. The article you gave me.'

'Listen, clearly that was a mistake. I want to be quite firm about this: there was no trace of a parasite anywhere in Carlos's office. The microbial disturbances uncovered there are of a different order, a different scale entirely.'

'Okay. Of course. I was just thinking, I haven't perhaps been quite myself recently. I mean, I wasn't well and then I got really sick. Not that I really believed it, but . . . but I wasn't myself for a time. Could I have been exposed to something in the office? Some strain, some transmission aided by the heat? And I wondered if you weren't suggesting a parasite, actually, in bringing the article to my attention.'

'Firstly, you're doing too much. And I'm concerned. You're working this, as far as I can tell, completely on your own. Are you even seeing any other people? You're putting too much pressure on yourself. It can't be helping. I'm going to insist you see a doctor, for the food poisoning. It can't do any harm. And the article, Indonesia? I thought you'd be interested, after the reports, the sequencing. You seemed interested, but I'll admit my enthusiasm can sometimes get out of control. Did you know that other kinds of bacteria—green algae, for instance—have eyespots? That they can discern light and move towards it? So you can understand if I get carried away. Anyway, I thought you might have an academic interest in the article, that you might be curious. If I implied a direct link to the case, then I'm sorry, that wasn't my intention. I hope I haven't wasted any of your time.'

'No, no, no, not at all. And I am interested, I really am. It's just it was all a lot to take in. And then an old case came up—I thought there may have been a link. Just a theory. And the thing with all these theories is that none of them can be proven, of course. What happened in the office? What kind of illness was this and where did it come from? Are the colleagues in any way complicit? What happened to him? Where did he go? Isabella?'

'Yes?'

'Aren't you scared? Isn't it terrifying?'

'What?'

'What you were describing, with the reports? That he may no longer have been himself. That a minor physical change might do that to someone.'

Isabella paused. 'You've seen your share of beatings. You've seen the head struck, haven't you? The head on the ground? Do you think the same person gets up from that?'

'It is easily changed, then. Easily affected. I don't know how it can go on.'

'Inspector, if you have any specific worries you should tell me, in strict confidence. I'm here.'

'Yes.'

Silence.

He breathed slowly, audibly, controlling it. 'Sometimes I wish,' he said, 'I could get out of this city. Not right now, that's not practical with the case ongoing, but still. From here, I can't even see outside it. I can't even see the sky at night.'

'What's so good about the night sky, Inspector?' She sounded suspicious.

'Well . . . the stars, I guess—'

'Ugh!'

'Isabella?' He wondered if something had happened, if something weren't wrong; she would be talking to someone else now, someone present in her room.

'We spend too much time looking at the fucking stars! I'm sorry and I don't mean to shout, but I just hate it, I do. I hate it. That urge to look to the transcendent. This idea that life is suddenly magical and incredible because of astronomy, the story of where the matter has travelled. Honestly, give me grandeur, give me my feet. Look at your feet, Inspector, at what you stand on. No, really. Forgive me, I'm being serious. I am. Yes, yes, you can laugh. We are generally, I think, so prejudiced when it comes to scale. There is enough in a simple glimpse of the ground. More than enough. The earth surface is an infinite mesh of bio-trails. You work on it, too, at a slightly different scale—of course you do, you inspect it. The mesh of lines is constantly renewing, but so are we. If it were up to me I would spend my whole life digging up the lost civilization of a single vanished person. There would be no end to the project, Inspector. No end to what may be discovered.'

Several seconds passed. When he didn't know what to say, and when something was expected, he undermined himself. He hated this. Why couldn't he just stay quiet? 'You're a scientist, Isabella. Of course, your perspective is limited to substance. Sometimes the rest of us need something . . . more.'

'Can I be direct with you, Inspector? You know what else I hate? I hate it when people give me my perspective. When they describe my perspective for me. Apparently, I believe we are just this. Human beings, I mean. That we are merely this. All the time the emphasis is negative. We should be ashamed for being only a collection of materials. What we are is not enough. Et cetera, et cetera. But it's nothing but a verbal trick. Listen, I am not saying we are merely this, in the pejorative sense. I am saying we are exclusively made from this and that there is nothing more extraordinary. Believe me, I am the last person to set limits on what we are capable of. But I am stunned, routinely, in my work, to discover again and again how precarious this life is. It does not take much, Inspector, to knock this balance. And yet . . .'

She trailed off. This time he kept his silence.

'I grew up in a small fishing community in the south, Inspector. People used to wait on the beach the morning after a boat was lost. It wasn't uncommon. But they weren't just waiting for the boat: they were waiting for their loved ones to be remade. Children would gather slop from the edge of the shore, keep it in a pail, inspect it every morning to see what had grown. Weird thing is, it's more than just madness and consolation, isn't it? Because the information that expressed those lost came originally from the sea, where it was now deposited. It is still there. That is a fact. And I am amazed, still, every day. I am amazed and I just don't know what to do.'

XIII

It is well known that animals see a different light, plants too. No one in the community would believe that because they cannot see their loved ones they are gone. Hunting dogs bark in bursts for no apparent reason and ants gather on patches of land as if they had a focus. All of the missing, it is believed, are present in different sizes, densities, and at different points in the light spectrum. The missing continue to be involved in essential processes such as breathing and eating, living simply on a different scale.

TRIBES OF THE SOUTHERN INTERIOR, P. 201

THE PROBLEM WAS THAT he had lost the name of the hospital, and although he had approximate directions, he didn't know the exact address. It was a private medical practice and, according to what he had heard, it didn't look like a hospital exactly, at least from the outside; it was a modern construction similar in appearance to any of the dozens of corporate buildings in the area. He would never have been able to park at this time of day, so he had taken public transport and was walking what was supposed to have been the last part of the journey. It felt, if anything, even warmer, although he didn't see how that was possible. He had just got out; already his shirt was damp, the air felt blocked, something against him.

His interview with Carlos's doctor was for 3.30. There wasn't time to go back to his apartment, retrieve the address and make his way to the hospital, and he didn't have his phone. He couldn't miss the appointment; the doctor might have significant information. Some insight into Carlos's condition. He felt, or imagined that he did, his own brain, as he walked, scraping against the dry grooves of his skull, as if it were no longer insulated by the necessary concentration of fluids.

He had thought he recognized the street, but when he turned north—what he assumed was north (the tall buildings blocked sight of the sun)—he was confronted with another scene, not at all the one he was expecting. Looking back on the apparently familiar street, he realized he hadn't recognized it at all—it was modelled on the one he had been thinking of, a duplication; although the street he did know—the one he had been thinking of and that he had thought, just a moment ago, he was actually standing in—was itself a duplication of a marginally older one in the same area. The superstructures were all alike: shimmering light columns, generic and difficult to identify. They didn't brand themselves with names and they seemed particularly inaccessible; literally so, as in many of them there was no obvious entrance, people getting in, he assumed, underground, through high-security parking lots.

He stopped, closed his eyes a few seconds. The only place he could identify with any certainty was the building immediately behind him, which, according to the text embossed on the glass front, was a regional embassy. The region it represented being distant, he was, of course, no closer to working out where he was presently.

Several of the adjacent buildings were also embassies. When he stopped to ask someone where he was, they looked suspicious— wasn't it obvious? He smiled, to reassure the stranger he was perfectly aware of this, but that that wasn't exactly what he meant. He wanted to know where they were physically, he supposed—what this place was. He couldn't say it like that, but it was closer to what he meant. He went out of the shadow and the high sun made everything more difficult. Already he wanted to be done with the day, to be home.

He always had a problem admitting he was lost. Generally, he would keep walking, as if the unfamiliarity of the environment was an illusion and the real place, the place he knew, was bound to come out from under it eventually. To get lost in your own city was something a child did. It certainly wasn't acceptable for someone in his position. So he invariably coasted on, attempting to allay the raising heartbeat and void the ridiculous images in his mind: bewildered conversations with doormen and shopkeepers; non-meetings with pedestrians and office workers on lunch breaks, moving briskly past him as he asked them for a moment of their time.

There was something dreamlike about the isolation. He remembered Maria's phrase—or was it the actor's?—about feeling as if you were in a foreign country, surrounded by a language you couldn't hope to understand. He was tired. His sleep had been interrupted ever since the night at the hotel. Not insomnia exactly, sometimes quite the opposite. At times he felt he had never been so far away, he was in the midst of such a great comfort that he never wanted to leave. Other times the sleep was shallow and he almost reached out, as if swimming just under the surface of a crystalline sea. In these latter spells he was aware of something ongoing in the room. People moving freely about all around him—he could hear their footsteps, their words, even their breath—and he would finally see to it just as soon as he was fully awake. He would just sleep a little more first. Then he would stand up, discover what was going on and banish the strangers from the room.

He was dazzled sometimes, stopped completely in his tracks, by the sense that he was letting everything pass without apprehension, and it hurt him. He would wake, suddenly alert, poised and set to go, aware of an inordinate amount of time having passed and with the sense of being released. Then there would be a small interval of conscious activity and he would be asleep again. The periods of time he was not aware of, the time he didn't consciously experience, seemed to be longer than the time he was awake. Opportunities were brief and quickly passing. Life raged past, a great and inconceivable expiration he faced with nothing but a yawn. He had to be getting on with things, if he could just put his finger on what they were.

He walked for several minutes in one direction and turned back. The uniformity of the buildings and his impatient attitude in retaliation to the hard sun made it difficult to establish whether he wasn't, in fact, heading back towards where he had come from. The embassies had disappeared. The traffic moved fluently and quietly, interchangeable dark cars, not a single bus or a taxi he could flag to bring him back to a place that he could name. He had missed his appointment, the day wasted, and still he was walking.

Circumstances were dragging him further into despondency. He was out of his depth in a case he couldn't understand and would never resolve. This aimless walking was the most honest thing he'd done in a long time. He didn't know where to go or what to do.

There was something there at the end of the street, something different, incongruous. Getting closer, he saw that a crowd had gathered; he lifted a hand to shield his eyes and see. No doubt a feud, some escalating disagreement. He needed to intervene. There must have been forty, fifty people huddled together, spiralling round towards the dead end. Approaching the outer edge of the crowd, he excused himself and tried to push in, but they were so focused on whatever it was they were watching that no one paid him the least attention. Eventually he had to push quite firmly past the middle-aged woman next to him just to make any kind of inroad at all.

It was exhausting. The crowd was jeering now, some yelling in encouragement—there was no doubt that what they were watching at the centre was a fight. He had already begun sweating, even before he had tried pushing in, and now things were getting worse. He had obviously settled on the worst possible point of entry—he had tried several and somehow alighted on the least favourable. But he was in now, he supposed, and it would be more trouble than it was worth trying to get out.

He continued apologizing, redundantly excusing himself—he was yet to receive so much as a glance from any of these people, and it was not as if they were all of one demographic, some crowd of youngsters, say, that he could dismiss as ignorant. He had noted all types of people still resisting him, unconsciously, a tide of people repelling him: old women and infants, the finely dressed and the scruffy, bankers breaking from nearby offices and maintenance workers in high-vis vests.

Soon enough he would know for himself what it was they were all staring at, which must really be something marvellous, he thought, the eagerness in their eyes, the concentration of their posture, their apparent obliviousness to anything other than whatever it was that was going on at the centre, and that he must—it was imperative—find out now for himself. There was more, he thought, riding on this than the satisfaction of curiosity—he had the feeling, now, that something significant was at the centre, a revelation or at least a clue that would lead him closer, for what was going on there was no ordinary scrap, drawing in all these different groups of people, mesmerized by whatever it was that was going on at the centre. Not even the best kind of street fight could result in that.

Please, I just need to get past, he said, in spite of all that he had so far learned. I just need to get a little closer, you see, he said, even laughing a little despite his discomfort. I haven't been able to see what it is yet, would you believe! I can't see anything, he said—would you tell me whatever it is there, at the centre? Honestly, I'm not joking. I just haven't been able to see yet. It must be my eyesight. It's been deteriorating steadily, most noticeably so in the last few months. I swear it's true. It's my sight failing me, that must be what's going on, that's it.

He barely muttered these words, in fact he may not have uttered them at all, spoken them only to himself. Certainly they weren't audible, not that anyone in this strange crowd would have listened to him anyway; he doubted it would even have registered to them what it was that he was doing—speaking, that is.

Finally, he was getting close to the centre, sweating profusely now in the struggle, and all this contact with so many people, strangers too. Still he hadn't seen or heard anything that could be said to be going on at the centre, despite the fact that he was so close now that it should be obvious what it was, and the thought struck him that children were at the centre, that was why he hadn't seen anything, they were small; but before he had even had any time to enjoy the relief of having come up with a rational explanation for this whole strange business, he was overcome instead with disgust for the fact that they were all, himself included—he had to admit he was party to it, despite his ignorance and his innocent intentions—they were all essentially exploiting children, that's what they were doing. It was disgusting, appalling, and he had to put a stop to it now, right now, just as soon as he could finally, and it wasn't far now, arrive at the precise centre.

He had to stop, and that was difficult now, for he was almost flowing with the people. He had to stop now, because—and he knew this was impossible, but it appeared to be true—he had passed over on to the other side, gone, that is, past the centre, which he hadn't even noticed, hadn't seen a thing, and now he was actually moving against people that were facing him, coming, as he was now, some-how out from the centre, and if he didn't stop, if he continued just as he was—although he wasn't willing anything, it was just happen-ing by itself—then he would soon find himself on the opposite limit, the edge, and then he would be outside, gone, and he would never be able to muster the energy to get back in, the idea impossible and hardly worth thinking about; he would be gone forever. He hadn't even noticed he was in the middle of it, that was the thing. He had not recognized the centre, had passed right through it and missed his chance, seeing and learning nothing, drifting through it, car-ried on the momentum of other people, people he didn't even know, and now what was he to do?

He walked away and took a taxi. Before entering he looked back and nothing appeared to have changed, the same excited jostling and commotion was ongoing, and he was none the wiser. What's going on over there? the driver asked him. Oh that, he said. That's nothing, nothing important really, and he gave the driver his address.

XIV

Skilled mimics simulate the sound the missing made. They blow into their cupped hands to make a distant percussion like the footsteps coming closer. It is a consolation for loved ones in the evening and seems to go some way to maintaining order and continuity in the community. It is also designed as a provocation, an appeal that might tempt the missing back.

TRIBES OF THE SOUTHERN INTERIOR, P. 223

THERE WAS A PROBLEM in the production of where he lived—specifically his apartment, but other things had been corrupted too, including his thinking, his skin and the wider area surrounding him. He didn't like to leave the apartment now, not since the confusion with Carlos's doctor. He remembered the crowd packed around him and it made him shudder. Although he could work, for the moment, largely from home, he still had to go out for supplies. And when he came back, he wouldn't recognize half the stuff. Sometimes he felt sure there was someone else living there, some transient waiting for him to exit before taking his place, living as himself. Those weren't his cups of coffee. He didn't make them. Didn't know whose food that was. The air was heavy and there wasn't enough oxygen, which made it difficult to breathe. There were smudges on his fingertips, soft blurring patches that felt strange to the touch, one on the other, that sunk in whenever they were pressed, much deeper than they should have, really. The sensitive parts of his fingers were slipping off and the identifying marks became fainter every day. He imagined the process developing across the surface of his body from the tips in, so that the rest of him became less real, not marked skin any longer so much as neutral flesh.

There were no photographs in his apartment; he hadn't had a camera in twenty years. He didn't like the frame. He was uncomfortable with paintings that had people inside—small, bent under skies, fields and mountains.

The air abraded him. And as he diminished, the sky fattened. The sun disappeared behind banks of thick black and purple cloud, heavier every day. The glare, the brightness had gone, but if anything the heat was worse, even more oppressive, a vegetal heat. Waking each morning he found his nostrils filled with hard black blood. The sunsets were sudden and irregular. The night had never been so close; without a hint of starlight the sky came lower, black vapour that soaked his hair, his back, his groin. He was waiting.

Where was the cloud coming from? Rolling westward every day. He gazed at the dark amassing in the sky and realized, of course, that it had drifted from the forest, an effect of breath.

A report on the radio, as he swirled a small spoon through his coffee: all schools in the district were to close for the week, in light of the weather. Problems with breath. Unprecedented. Official advice was conflicting: stay indoors, use fans and AC; conserve the use of AC to avoid a surge of the grid.

He didn't feel well. He could pick up the phone, call Isabella. Just a precaution. It couldn't do any harm. Unless she then brought him in . . . Diagnosis wouldn't help anyway, would it? Besides, he doubted it was anything as serious as that—it might even have been common, related to the weather—and he wouldn't want to waste her time.

He sat at the monitor on his desk, tried to refocus on the investigation. He searched online: 'holdings', 'Pérez', 'microbiome', 'Carlos', 'weather'. He picked up folders, went again through the notes, the clippings, the testimonies. It was useless. He put down his papers, shut off his computer.

He picked up a book, sat on his most comfortable chair and prepared to be relaxed. A free evening, now, the street quiet, his living room nicely, encouragingly lit. Then he opened the book, a paperback, and winced. It was happening again; he thought he was rid of it. Whenever he opened a book, now, he couldn't help shiver at the fabric, the feel of the pressed paper and glued spine, the fluttering concertina of the open pages held upside down. He had an impulse to eat it. He felt the shivering irritation of chalk on gums, a cold, squealing unease across his shoulders and at the back of his neck. He heard the creak of the spine, felt the bend of the heft carried by his fingers, and knew it was impossible for him to enjoy it any more, holding a book like that and simply reading. Instead he was fixated on the idea of consuming the book, putting its dry paper inside his mouth and eventually forcing the thing down, his gums lined with reams, his teeth stained with ink.

That's enough, he said, clapping the book closed. Even if he didn't know where he was going, he still had to get out. He laced up his shoes, turned off the lights and thumped the door closed behind him. It was thin and the lock gave a little when you pulled on the handle. He tested it again, watched what his hands were doing. The key had turned; it was as locked as it was going to be. He had to get on with things. He lifted his nose—it was evening, why weren't his neighbours cooking? They never cooked any more. He never smelled them. Whenever he was coming up or down the staircase he would go slowly past their doors, especially between seven and ten in the evening, when he could expect at least some of them to be preparing food, but always the same—no evidence of lives.

He wanted distance. He took the first subway he saw and got off several minutes later. He set off walking in an unfamiliar area. He was enjoying walking with speed, tricking himself into the suggestion of purpose. Now he stopped and waited for the lights. On one side of the junction, to his left, the traffic continued. To his right the vehicles paused; several feet away a truck driver leaned forward in his cab, pressing his chest down on the wheel. The inspector waited, along with two dozen or so other pedestrians, more arriving every second. The crossing was technically clear, with little traffic turning in. Normally in these situations you could sense a frustration building; then one person walks onto the road and then another, until finally something breaks and a mass of pedestrians illegally crosses.

For the moment he seemed the only one affected. Those around him looked contentedly ahead, as if focusing on something further away. Composed, arms clasped or held to the side. He made a sound somewhere between a click and a sigh. The lights were taking an age. Nothing caught on. Stuck on red at least 120 seconds, almost certainly longer, given he could only count from his arrival. He wasn't sure what the procedure was should the lights actually be locked, how to begin to deal with it, a potentially volatile situation.

Three minutes now. He turned around, trying to establish eye contact, but no one responded. He scoffed, gestured at the lights, the traffic, the road. It was now absurd. The path was clear and no one took it. The day got hotter and hotter. He didn't see how patience could hold in a situation like this. It was quite clear that no one shared his concern. What he should do, he knew, was walk blindly onto the road.

A huge thunderclap and, at last, the rain.

The light turned green, the people dissipated and he crossed the road.

Tarpaulins were rushed out to cover the fruit laid at the front of the smaller stores. The streets seemed to clear and even the traffic was less intrusive. He didn't cover his head—already he couldn't get any wetter. Water ran in lines from pedestrians to the sewers. He had always enjoyed the rains at the beginning of the season, the celebratory effect of the new sensation and the blurred air. This was the beginning of the change. The streets were dark under the clouds, but new pools of light shifted in the intermittent traffic. His short-sleeved shirt clung to his thin chest and his jaw streamed hanging water.

He felt refreshed, newly determined. He stared at the people around him. There was something odd in the way they were behaving. All you had to do, he thought, to witness it was to stop and look at nothing in particular—it would just happen. Like the people at the pedestrian crossing. Or when he had gone to pick up dinner one time from Celeste Imperio and seen children running, stopping, then practising shaking hands for several minutes, trying to tell each other that they were expected to be doing this kind of thing for the rest of their lives, and so they should be getting used to it, and getting on with getting it right. They were laughing. Everything was done as if it were not quite real, some joke; and without even realizing it, at first, he had begun to play along, too, to walk a little less securely, pause an extra beat before opening a door, drag his words out just a fraction of a second longer than necessary.

He must look like one of those actors too, he now thought; it must be obvious just by looking at him that he was trying hard to do what he was supposed to be doing; that he wasn't quite at ease with it, any of it; that he was suspicious, deeply sceptical.

This kind of thing had been going on for quite a while. It was a problem of perception and it was linked to the dreams he had been having recently, the most vivid and affecting of his life, that left him sweating and shattered when he woke, more tired than when he had lain down—he couldn't believe the idea that this was to be the beginning of the day, the recuperation over. Every time he was running, struggling through what appeared to be an identical forest, furiously unvarying, never letting him feel as if he were getting anywhere, and precluding the possibility of an ending. This forest became a fixture in his life, a consistent passage between the thin and insubstantial days of his eating and working. The intensity of his exertions in the forest seemed to explain, retrospectively, the spectacular fatigue of the sleeps. He returned to the piles of sticks in Carlos's office, wondered if he had had the same dreams.

The surpassing experiences of the forest might explain the oddness of everything else. He played with the old childish idea that the relationship between dreaming and waking life should be inverted, the experience of the former comprising the more significant, purposeful and major period. It felt like his journeys in the forest really had happened, and that as he ran or stumbled he had lost consciousness and been brought back to his room in his apartment. He surveyed the room silently each morning, sniffing the odd, neutral air inside, listening to the weight of his breath, examining the place for other signs of activity. He studied the walls of the rooms, tapping them, anticipating the sounds of a hollow. The more he examined the place the surer he was that it was unreal, not his original place at all. It had a smell of nothing, had no trace of life or matter. Somehow, and he knew it sounded ridiculous, he suspected the real place he lived in had been measured and rebuilt somewhere else, in a remarkable feat of craftsmanship. It was a marvellous reproduction of his apartment, he had thought, casting his eyes about the bedroom, walking in his bare feet through to the kitchen where he would pour a coffee. Everything was in its right place; you could spend almost a whole lifetime believing it was real. For whatever purpose, someone had engineered a thorough and comprehensive duplication of his living space, rebuilding the same foundations into the hole dug out of the earth, erecting a similarly sized and sourced tenement building filled with people looking and behaving approximately as those did whom he had previously lived among, at a more settled period in his life, and further had made out of the surrounding area outside, at least as far as the eye could see, a simulacrum of urban life, with all its rhythmic motions, its traffic and mercantile undulations and manic community.

Quickly he had opened his books, sure that they were just copies, holding only blank pages underneath their covers, but the few he happened to choose had been so thoroughly duplicated that it would have been difficult to tell they weren't real. In a cookery book, he even found marginalia in a perfect forgery of his wife's handwriting.

He thought it through again, watching the rain. The links failed. Still he was certain that this whole area surrounding him, with its neutral, dead air, its insubstantiality and transience, had been constructed over part of a much wider region of wild land. The forest remained on every side, around and even underneath this temporary place. The area he was presently living in was a stage and this was a passing performance. Somehow—it must be due to subconscious drives he had little control over—he was breaking out of the artifice, thrashing through the wild undergrowth in expectation of some other kind of encounter, but each time he was brought back to his room, where he lived, waking up suddenly and with a start.

The figures moving in his room at night, talking over him as if he were entirely passive, must be linked to this duplication. They would have been measuring the place, recording all the detail for the construction of the duplication, the place he lived now. He had been moved from a real world to an inauthentic and virtual location. He maintained at the same time the understanding that this couldn't be happening, that the duplication was an insane and impossible idea and that everything was, of course, normal, as it had always been, day to day, and likely always would be until it ended. And yet he still believed it.

It rained so hard he could barely see.

He took the conviction that this new, insubstantial world couldn't be happening as proof in fact that it was. Feeling that the unreal world didn't or couldn't exist was quite consistent with its properties, he thought. It simply made the experience stranger, more disturbing. He didn't know where he was or how it had been done. His sensible understanding that the substitution of this unreal world was impossible—it could never have been done, no one would ever have those kinds of resources, and even if they did, then what was their motive?—revealed a truth, he thought. Because everything had always been impossible, that's just the way it was, and he had got used to it. And now, for some reason, he had lost that easy relationship and was no longer accustomed to the place at all. He saw it as inauthentic, marvellous, unreal. The worktop in his kitchen, the railings on the fence outside, the wet tar in the too-warm air, all of it was fascinating, suspicious and strange. Somehow all of it had been built to replace the real. He sensed the industry as he slept and came near to consciousness and fell back down again. The figures moving and talking urgently, preparing the great duplication of the world. It was likely there were some sort of officials, men in suits, guards, perhaps, monitoring the inspector as he went about his life in the small area permitted him. The guard, drawing on a cigarette, pulling away in some anonymous vehicle, was like a ranger delineating the perimeter of a national park, maintaining its borders and ensuring that none of the animals crossed the invisible line.

He could not help imagining the continued journey of the vehicle, its movement through all of the other built things and its arrival, at some point, on the threshold of the real, a place where all the sets came down. His brain swarmed. He was filled, he knew, with the craziest ideas, the kind of ideas that, if he admitted them, would have his friends haul him off to hospital.

The rain fell endlessly, determined to push in further to the earth, break the surface, flood more. He let out a short laugh as he closed his eyes, still walking, enjoying the different awareness of his body. He was sketched in water and sound. He heard and felt with the rain his shape and size come back at him. If it rained forever and he kept his eyes closed, then soon enough he would see by it, would feel and know what was around him.

Opening his eyes, he saw parallel lights over the pool rising in the road and he had to jump backwards so the car didn't hit him. Only after it passed did he register the sound.

He tired; he had been walking an incline for some time. He was far from his own district and unfamiliar with the street. The identifying details of individual streets had, anyway, he noted, been sheared off. It didn't matter what the name was. He had enjoyed the feeling of the rain and the exertion of the climb enough, and he felt, maybe, that he had got somewhere in his analysis of his dreams—he was due a stop, a drink even, time to relax and dry off a bit. There was a reasonably large building ahead, lit up and apparently open to the public. He shook his head vigorously, ran his hands redundantly through his hair and stepped into the entrance of La Cueva.

He hadn't intended visiting the restaurant, although it was hardly a surprise that he had ended up here, he supposed, given the amount of time he had spent in it recently.

They recognized him at the door, handed him a towel, a fresh shirt, asked if he would be taking his usual drink. 'A meal,' he said. 'Steamed fish.'

Both floors were full; he sat for the moment by the bar on the second. He closed his eyes and dried his face again; the ongoing sound of successful parties continued around him. The percussion of cutlery on plates seemed louder than usual, so too the chorus made from the many conversations.

He and his wife had always eaten together in the evenings. They established early on how important it was that they made time for each other, despite their irregular work hours. Dropping in, one of them would leave a note, a suggestion or prediction, something they might eat, a time they might be expected home. The notes developed and she would shame him into acknowledging his own lack of talent by the things she drew: individual pasta shells, shaded into depth; sprouting asparagus plants; herds of moving animals; big-eyed fish.

They'd both liked to cook. He would have the radio on and, although he claimed to barely listen, he'd always find himself surprised by her sudden touch on his hips, her hand on his shoulder. She seemed always to come from nowhere, walk right in through the walls. He maintained, to her loud protests, that she was as light as air; she would roll her eyes, hunt for the corkscrew, put on a record.

The height of La Cueva, and the spectacular bay windows, had a dramatic effect on a storm night such as this. The festival aura of the rains encouraged people to drink, talk, feast. Quite discreetly, he turned around, so that he could face the diners and the windows. As usual, almost as a reflex now, his eyes settled on the long table by the east-facing window. This was where the family had dined on the night in question.

The rains were fading for the moment, the sky clearing.

Although it was surely not long until darkness, the evening was peculiarly, almost artificially lit in the electric charge. Looking out, you could see, tonight, a distance of many miles. He wasn't familiar with the long perspective, despite having visited the restaurant several times in the past few weeks. Perhaps it was because of his now slightly elevated position, seated by the bar, in combination with the storm-light.

He left his stool and walked towards the long table. Would you mind a moment? he said quietly, as he ushered the middle-aged woman out of Carlos's seat. He looked straight ahead, over the meals and conversations, the half-empty glasses and the cooling meat, towards the window. Quite clearly, framed almost geometrically by the light, was a forest patch. It didn't belong to the scene, next to the reflected interior and the many painted faces. He assumed, at first, it was a picture, a reflection of a painting held inside La Cueva, only it wasn't. It was an image beyond the city normally too distant to see. But post-storm, and presumably momentarily, the forest was clear and sublime.

Carlos had sat here. He would have to confirm the details of the weather on the 24th, but he knew what he would find—a storm, earlier that night, an odd, late light scattered across the city. Carlos had stared straight at it. It was hypnotic—he was seeing it for himself. This is what had been disturbing him recently, affecting his sleep and his mental firmness. He had sensed a significance, a correlation between La Cueva and this forest, and he had been playing it over and over in his subconscious. It was why he had left his apartment this evening, the reason for arriving at the entrance to La Cueva. Leaving the subway, winding through the streets by unknown design. He had been waiting, night after night, for the exact meteorological conditions present on the night of the disappearance, and now he had seen why. Was there any reason, any reason at all, why a man, upon washing his hands in the bathroom, would not walk directly out of the building, past his family, and aim straight for that image, beyond the glass and the artificial frame—into the forest itself?

A SECOND THUNDERCLAP, THE breakthrough he needed, the release of all this tension at last. His mind stilled, the noise stopped and he could focus. He relished the air, a verdure he could taste. He enjoyed what seemed like his first full inhalations in a month. He was calmer; he knew what he needed to do. He cleared his apartment, organized all notes and testimonies in his office room. He arranged immediately for an initial forensic survey of the forest perimeter, convinced that Carlos had gone this way. This was no great forest, rather a suburban reserve, but the perspective from the seat, looking through the window in La Cueva, post-storm, was dramatic, alluring. The reserve was only seventeen miles away. On foot, Carlos would have reached it before the morning.

He supposed he had been hoping to find evidence of some recently abandoned, makeshift camp. Assuming Carlos had been here—he still hoped Isabella, once she arrived back from her current project, would be able to confirm—he must have seen quickly that it wouldn't do; the place was trimmed and neat, the trees planted at an unnaturally regular distance from each other. More than a forest, it was a garden—with a car lot, a small perimeter wall, a pond. Carlos would have felt embarrassed leaving unannounced like that, disappearing and making a scene, hiking in his formal clothes towards what was really a picturesque and sentimental destination. Why would he have stayed? Nothing would have kept him in that place. If what had changed him, that night at La Cueva, had been the picture of the forest as seen in the frame of the restaurant window, then the real forest lay behind the image and he would have had to keep on walking. He would have had to go on further.

The inspector turned, scuffed loose gravel. That way, south-east, that's where the forest was, two million square miles of it. It would take him longer than a night to get there.

HE WAS RECEIVING POTENTIALLY useful information, but was having trouble identifying and validating the sources. Broadening out his search, hunting a pattern, he found several allusions over the past two years to sightings of distressed individuals in formal attire, incongruously placed in the rural interior. A middle-aged woman, both shoes clasped in one hand, bent over a river edge, lapping at the water. A locked briefcase spotted near a forest track leading the farmer who had spotted it further in: in the valley beyond, emerging out of a stream, a man stood, dripping, in red braces. To the inspector's frustration, but hardly his surprise, he found no one had pulled these sightings together. Nothing, beyond a curt transcription of the initial calls, had even been written up. The calls had come in from anonymous individuals: small-hold tenant farmers, long-haul truck drivers taking timber. If they had approached the disconnected individual, whose clothes were invariably described as faded, stained and cut, then they didn't get far. The individual, making his or her way through the trees, did not want to be contacted; the reports described an expression of panic, the sound, after an attempt at calling, of branches crashing, a river splashing, thick leaves falling.

Games, his colleagues said. Corporate initiation rites, pre-wedding penalties, that kind of thing. They had a point, he conceded; if there were anything to these reports, really, then wouldn't the relevant families have reported the individuals gone?

Things started to make sense with the new information from the forest. His intoxicating dreams the past few weeks became instructive, as did his inability to concentrate on anything except the suspicion that none of it was real. His devastating, wholly frustrating sense of loss and opportunities not taken, the maddening certainty that he was failing to wake up to something utterly clear and surpassingly important all around him, could now be explained in reasonable and cogent terms. He was, as it happened, and to his great relief, not lost. He hadn't been infected. He wasn't ill. He still had his mind. The events of the past few weeks were simply mechanisms used by his subconscious, which had picked up, from somewhere, the key to Carlos's disappearance. The key was the forest, and time spent in the city was wasted.

Isabella had named the gut and brain habitats, said it as if it were nothing. He went back to his dreams, some of which he had noted down, placed among the other documents relating to the case. The office worker, the heart attack. A parasite escalating in species, a fat and eyeless grub growing. Momentum, propulsion. One leaf and a forest; a single cell and a human being. Rampant expression, complexity through local repetition, and there it was, all that life made. He thought of the dun colour of the missing office worker's eyes and the piles of sticks reported on the floor the morning following the disappearance. The small forest framed by the window of La Cueva, and the bigger place beyond, the greatest concentration of extant life there is.

Carlos, openly expiring in his chair, was missing that life, even as it exploded across him. What could he do? He could walk, the inspector thought, and breathe, and needed nothing more to take him to the forest.

By remaining here, in the city, he was postponing a necessary confrontation, and he had struggled to live with that. He had woken guiltily and gone through his days hazily, apparently constantly hungover, prone to isolation and to long spells when he failed to recognize anything around him, and to other brief, stunning moments of transparency.

He wasn't sure what he expected to find there, but the obvious thing was to follow the corporation's trail. The contingency sites, from the start—he had been right. He went over everything. São Vicente, he read, had been totally abandoned. No road, no means of transport at all, no buildings, no population. But Santa Lucía remained active; he might even get a place on the monthly flight. He speculated again on possible links between the flora rife in Carlos's body and the great wildernesses and biological eruptions in the continental centre. He had no conception of what bacteria looked like, instead picturing their shadows while great, vast herds of them stomped and grazed in the forest. The two zones matched in a way that intuitively pleased him—it felt right to go there. Where better, he thought, to disappear?

FLYING TO THE INTERIOR

Case Notes on the Forest

1. Amateur ornithological associations tagged carrion birds as a means of tracking their feeding and mating behaviours. In the project's ten-year span several spikes were noted—short periods when unusually high numbers of birds congregated in the same area. Many of these events were found to correlate with the timings of unexplained disappearances of light aircraft.

2. Balloonists prepared a cross-Pacific journey, documenting every step of the process online until the official launch date. A period of silence followed, lasting between two and three months, after which it was announced that the flight had not yet begun. Adjustments were made to the original reports, explaining the delays to the expedition launch. In the drafts of the documentary record, discrepancies emerged relating to the number of people believed to be taking part in the ascent—first six, then three, then finally one. The record continued to be revised over the next several years as further, more ambitious expeditions with new balloonists were planned and then deleted. Each time, in the run-up to the scheduled launch date, all reports confidently stated that the balloon would now ascend. Numerous blog posts

were posted along with media interviews, photographic journals and short films explaining the technical operation of the flight. Doctors and dieticians described what would happen to the body at each respective height, how it would be replenished and stabilized against the changing pressure and temperature of the atmosphere. Marine geographers explained in detail the nature of the water crossed and experts in rainforest ecology described the life present in the canopy terrain of South America and Asia, which comprised the planned launch and landing sites. As every new launch date approached, the problems affecting previously scheduled balloon flights, forcing multiple postponements, were laid out in some detail, and hired actors read confidently from scripts prepared by technical staff stating clearly why now, finally—this time—the balloon could be airborne, the crossing would take place.

3. Rumours were spread on in-house message boards by coders in Guyana and encrypted into economic predictions by financiers in Brasília, relating to the practice of 'urban marches'. Administrative workers in middle age walked alone out of the office at midday, carrying only basic supplies—sandwiches, pasta, sliced fruit, half-litre bottle of water, suit jacket. They were to walk as far as was possible into the interior of the country, avoiding all use of public transport and organized accommodation and eschewing any human communication. Men and women known as exiles modelled their journeys on sixth-century monks who drifted for thousands of miles on rafts, directed by ephemeral voices, whale song and atmospheric pressures, possibly discovering archipelagos and whole continents hundreds of years before any government missions did. They drank river water and ate fruit, insects

and birds' nests, walking further into forest and marshland. Sedentary colleagues alluded to their journeys in impenetrable legalese and in long financial reports that would never be read. Large sums of company money were invested betting which individual would achieve the greatest distance and who would be the first to make it out the other side, past the interior, rather than ultimately retracing their outward steps on the long homeward journey. In-house, these extended leave periods were referred to as 'performance improvement sabbaticals' or 'stress-related time away'. Returning exiles quickly ascended to senior corporate positions and generally established a family, including a stay-at-home wife and at least one mistress.

4. Over six days and ten thousand square miles of rainforest, forty-six reports were made to emergency services, local media outlets and churches regarding visitations of saints and angels in trees. The epicentre was established as an agrarian commune, and a quarantine was put up. The previous day all associated livestock had died, having shown no prior signs of disease. The surrounding flora began to dry, degrade, fold and collapse; epidemiology experts discovered that all insect life in the commune had disappeared, the vegetation dying as a direct result.

   All twenty-three members of the commune were imprisoned and interrogated, suspected of collusion in a pre-terrorist plot. The site was meticulously searched for evidence of the toxins responsible. The commune members maintained innocence, until their respective pain thresholds were met, at which point they invented what they hoped would be a plausible story. The stories were mutually incompatible, bearing no coherent thread. Flashes of white light were reported near the upper canopy around the time the livestock died. Noting the absence of birdlife from the area, government advisors rerouted the flight paths of all aircraft due to fly within a three-hundred-mile radius. In a four-hundred-page report, subsequent to a spontaneous wildfire destroying the entire commune, administrators avoided using the words 'non-terrestrial pathogens' and 'site of awe'.

5. NASA-sourced heat-imaging technology floating on balloons over the forest revealed inexplicable concentrations of unknown mammalian forms. Given the nature of the recording equipment it was impossible to identify the beginning and ending of bodies, and so the warm life-cloud, moving in an approximately homogenous manner along the ground, could not be identified by species. It was estimated that if the bodies were human, then the number was two hundred. Tracking body heat, the movement was seen to be regularly slow with infrequent bouts of extreme speed. No communities were recognized as existing in the area. Government-sponsored 'tribal reconciliation' missions had previously charted the adjacent land to significant distances in every direction. Trusted cartel representatives assured ministers of their ignorance—products were harvested and hostages maintained in clearly defined and officially sanctioned areas. Such was the density of the canopy, satellite and drone-supplied images were rendered redundant; nevertheless, all footage was exhaustively examined.

Tracking all records of activity in the area, a technician noted a missile launch centre abandoned 120 miles northeast of the heat cloud's present location. The site had trialled experimental, non-petroleum fuel sources and innovative propulsion technology, but the results had been insignificant and any equipment worth less than the cost of extraction was left to melt into the roots, vines and animals of the forest floor.

In the sole survey of the site, biologists had noted moderately unusual rates of floral growth, as well as several newly discovered and endemic symbiotic relationships. The identity of the mammalian forms was never established.

6. Automated checks on flights missing, believed crashed, over the forest in the past two decades brought up statistically unlikely repetitions. Of the nineteen flights still unaccounted for, sixteen carried men and women flying on return tickets that chronologically contradicted their journey. The return journey, in the case of one person on each of these flights, was scheduled to take place while the outward flight remained in progress. The age of these passengers ranged from twenty-seven to forty-two, origin was local and ethnicity Caucasian, and the stated purpose of travel, every time, was 'business'. They all worked for a series of small corporations linked to a larger umbrella unit whose remit remained unknown. It was proved, in thirteen of the sixteen cases, that the passenger in question had at least some experience of piloting small aircraft.

Independent enthusiasts investigated these figures and the circumstances of each missing flight. Rumours spread and people became suspicious of briefcases carried on small planes scheduled to fly over the interior. It was advised to dress in informal clothes. Increasingly elaborate and outrageous rumours circulated. Online forums proliferated; for every one taken down another three sprang up. It was claimed that a mechanized belt, eleven miles long, was built into the forest and covered in inauthentic, permanently preserved flora. When activated, the belt moved backwards, revealing a long strip of runway. The figure—the affiliated employee—on each flight allegedly forced command of the aircraft and landed on the artificial strip. Possible reasons for bringing the flights in were various and disputed: it was the material contained in the suitcase; it was the identity, rather, of another of the passengers, who worked as a foreign operative and possessed valuable information relating to a new technology, which would itself then be built in the forest, using the materials of the dismantled aircraft, under the supervision of the interrogated and re-educated foreign operative; it was the aircraft itself, kept hidden under the forest belt, used to spray experimental poisons over small and unsuspecting indigenous communities; it was the passenger cargo, freely incarcerated deep in the vast forest, monitored remotely as they attempted to come to terms with their situation, remaining sedentary or planning a long escape, isolating themselves or forging alliances, making peace with the strangely impassive captors or waging futile war—they were placed, members of the passenger cargo, into artificial situations, put into uncomfortable domestic and dramatic arrangements, offered rewards or punishment according to how naturally they played along. The more aircraft that were taken, and the greater the number of conditioned passenger cargo, the quicker the newly landed adapted to forest life. Some of the first to be captured, who had reacted violently and rebelled for years, became among the most valuable of those present at the base, playing a key role in convincing the newcomers how fortunate they were to be there, how exciting the project was. Generations of people were born in the sprawling campsite, raised with only specific, planted knowledge about the 'outside world'. Many situations were run, in the camp buildings, constructed from flat-pack materials contained in the suitcases and from everything that had previously composed the aircraft, from the wings to the head-rests, the toilet seats to the trays the reheated food had been presented on. The idea was that the camp would in time run organically, autonomously, as the younger generations, those who had been born in the environment, grew to maturation and learned to command. New arrivals came periodically—the rolling out of the eleven-mile belt and the landing of the unfamiliar object were built into the community's mythology. The reality behind the situation—that this was an artificially constructed community illegally planted in the forest, that none of them belonged there and that the scenes of their lives were scripted simulations—became only one among many of the fantasies popular with the younger and idler camp members. Other fantasies entertained included that each member of the camp had come there via water, swimming a period of approximately 4.58 billion years, this being only the second leg of an even longer journey largely involving darkness, sudden rapid and inexplicable inflations and the serial arrival of massive, spinning light bodies. They were very tired after that journey, but at the same time exhilarated, both jaded and anxious to begin, and in the tension between these states they each lived for approximately sixty-seven years.

New languages were developed, old ones filtered out, and on each new landing the incomers, when they opened their mouths, were treated with righteous, furious disgust: their words were a disease and their mouths would be broken and reset.

Speculations over the ultimate purpose behind it all—the corporate involvement from the very beginning, the bringing down of the aircrafts, the willingness of sixteen men and women at least to overhaul their lives, leaving families and friends behind, and taking more than a thousand individuals forcibly captive in the forest, the huge expenditure involved in the operation, the meticulous planning and the enormous energy invested from the start—were similarly various. Many of the theories centred on the commercial advantages likely to be gained by the company ultimately responsible, the usefulness of the vast amounts of anthropological data gathered in watching how these people lived, day in, day out, in situations that were prompted and invented by those ultimately in control. The commercial benefit of insights gained would be incalculable— in research and development, in marketing strategy, in product design—and in one sense, this may have been deemed enough for establishing the simulated society with all that it entailed.

A closely related group of theories claimed a religio-corporate remit for the establishing of the artificial world, the compound being prepared as a new beginning, ready to step in after the inevitable implosion of larger, linked urban areas. After running for a thousand years, having utilized materials collected from increasingly sophisticated aircraft, and after a sufficient period of silence, the corporate compound would move outwards to the coast, build satellite communities, cross water, establish an increased rate of reproduction and ultimately colonize the world.

Those in positions of authority dictated domestic arrange-ments, work routines and available leisure activities. Apparently indiscriminately, people were removed from their everyday life and transplanted into another building where they lived with a new family, worked a different job and were called by an alter-native name. Children were raised according to alternating philosophies, a firstborn being told that they were a frail organ-ism decaying at an increasing rate, and a second believing that experience, folded into memory, is endless. People tried to escape in new ways. Smoke balloons, their fabric stitched from tens of thousands of small patches torn from clothing, lifted children no more than seventeen miles from camp, at which point they returned for food. Several generations of a single family, some of whom had never met, worked together on a narrow tunnel leading east from beneath the front room in their home building. In order to reach a significant distance, a single individual was required to live underground, tunnelling, for extended periods, which involved considerable practical difficulties. To provide food and drink, one male and one female white mouse were tethered together on the end of a two-foot stick—the tunneller utilized their high reproductive yield as a source of milk and meat, consuming many generations of a direct familial line. The generations became increasingly tame and docile, living with limited freedom and in the dark, subsisting on black beetles and ants. In eleven generations the rope used to tether the mice became redundant, as they were now programmed to move in line with the human tunneller and to provide them with the necessary meat and milk. Their brains reduced in size accordingly, unnecessary energy expended on maintaining obsolete functions deemed too costly. Relatives of the tunneller currently chosen would take turns, on the surface, impersonating the missing, so that the extended period of absence would not be noted. Each tunneller would typically spend one year digging east, before crawling backwards through blood, faeces, urine and expired mice, and exchanging places. After forty years' tunnelling, when it was finally decided to dig upwards and emerge, the twenty-nine-year-old man currently occupying the role looked around him in some surprise. He had been confident, as he rose, that they had built a route going so far from home captivity that he had reached some kind of edge—perhaps the ocean. In the tunnel aural hallucination was common, but he was certain the concussion heard above was really waves. He would fell a tree, use vines as twine and sail to a port to contact the world, the real world, the bigger world, and the whole artificial construct that he and his family and everybody he had known were brought up in would collapse.

As he broke the surface his vision fizzed. The light slowly drifted back into sense, form and specificity and he saw his family sitting together at the table and apparently enjoying a meal. They looked at him in some confusion. He was struck by the details of the objects in the room. Plastic white cutlery separated neatly into Tupperware containers. Foam-backed seats set directly onto the earthen floor. A table made from differently coloured fabric stitched together, supporting his family's heads and elbows. He had seen every one of these objects uncountable times before, but as they had been the last things he expected to see, hundreds if not thousands of miles from home, they were amazing. Somehow all of this—the family scene—had been extracted, lifted and transported to the land edge. They were there to meet him as he emerged, and it was the last thing he expected. There was a knock on the door and a community leader entered. She explained that the family, over generations, had charted a significant area of forest, but that rather than leading due east, as they had intended and as they had started out and believed they were continuing, they had actually traced what had become a perfect circle, unconsciously following the apparent direction of the sun and inevitably returning home. What is more, the community leader informed them: 'There is no reason for you to do this underground. You are more than welcome to attempt such an escape on the surface. It will be safer that way. None of us will stop you. Rest assured, you will not be watched or hunted. Nevertheless, we are confident that you will ultimately choose to return here, the place where you belong.'

ANOTHER EXPLANATION FOR WHAT happened to the missing aircraft was that the corporate identities taking hold of the controls deliberately crash-landed over particularly dense coverage. The cruising speed, altitude and fuel levels were calculated to optimally facilitate a 'soft crash'—a particular form of mechanical free-falling in which the aircraft and its cargo are not immolated or otherwise entirely obliterated on contact with the ground.

Typically less than a third of the cargo survives and the injuries are substantial. For months individuals may subsist high in the trees on leaves, insect larvae and rainwater. Others suffer multiple fractures and amputations on impact with the ground. Significant trauma-induced amnesia, combined with dramatic physical injuries, at times recasting the whole anatomy of the living human, puts the identity in a state supremely suggestive to environmental and imaginative cues—anatomical displacements enabling increased flexibility, lesions on the brain causing curiously adaptive psychological disturbances. Ex-academy anthropologists were quoted stating heterodox opinions on the viability, under such extreme conditions, of a 'reversion' to prelinguistic modes of living: shifts in diurnal settings leading to the development of nocturnal hunting behaviour; landing impacts on hip and spinal areas forcing quadruped locomotion, arboreal sleeping and increased communion with animals; loss of medium- and long-term memory causing disintegration of selfhood and abandonment of narrative and time. Pictures were drawn of survivor communities existing in a state of flux, pre-cultural, rapacious, successful. There were stories of these people, formidable hunters, working less and less in tandem with each other, favouring a voiceless, pre-cooperative method of society, meeting only periodically, seasonally, to copulate in mass events. Men began experimenting with other organisms. Some emerged as 'guest' members of smaller primate troops, accommodated for the advantages of their unusual dexterity, but ejected, usually killed and eaten, because of the severe, warlike and proprietary elements structured deep within their behaviour. The ex-humans also, occasionally, activated the larynx and diaphragm and made strange, loud, prolonged nasal expressions, which frightened the other animals and disrupted their hunts; these episodes occurring exclusively in the night, when they were forced down and the salted emissions were licked from their faces.

PART TWO

THE FOREST

I.

THE TOURISTS SWAPPED STORIES of permits and inoculations, the many weeks of waiting while the paperwork was processed, the rigorous interviews and thorough (some claimed intrusive) medical examinations, the injections producing temporary lesions on the upper arms and a thankfully passing state of nausea and lightheadedness. He nodded repeatedly, doing his best to move the conversation along.

He'd been horrified when he identified the travel party. The T-shirts and baseball caps, the loud voices and English words. Immediately, he thought, the pedlars would appear with their Amerindian crafts and wares, and the previously sleepy community would light up, touting for business. But things had actually worked in his favour. It was proving disarmingly simple. Of course he could go upriver. Of course he could meet remote communities. He was welcome to join them, so long as he paid. He told Knut, the group's tall, red-faced, blond leader, about what he had read in the book at the hotel, the anthropologist and the tribe. Knut hadn't heard any of this; it must have been a long time ago. These aren't the people we're meeting, he said. This isn't the tribe.

'How do you know?' the inspector asked.

'Because these people are original. They have not met us before, any of us. They have not met anyone from outside. This will be a real experience, a genuine first contact.'

He did not like it that the guides carried guns.

'A precaution,' Knut said.

He imagined they weren't loaded, that it was a detail added by the tour company to ratchet up excitement. From the way the local guides carried theirs, they certainly believed it was real.

They had a busy few days planned, one activity after another. On the first excursions, even though they weren't going far, they should still, Knut stressed, remain vigilant: it was an area of wildness. They should be mindful of snakes, stinging insects. It would be unusual for cats to be active during daylight hours, but it's not unknown, he said.

Whistles, approving sighs.

First stop: a crash site. Eleven miles upriver, followed by a three-mile hike. A sixteen-seater Cessna carrying missionaries came down nine years ago with no survivors. Authorities collected and extracted what they could. The crash was of particular interest to the inspector, as one of the fatalities listed on the manifest had sat, at the time, on the corporation's board of directors.

The tourists nodded gravely, lowered their voices. What had happened was tragic, it was agreed. They would respect the dead as they entered the site. Still, they might as well be useful while they were there, Charlie said. There was no good reason why they couldn't have a look around. Perhaps they would even find objects, possessions they could take back with them when they left the forest.

Knut gave them gloves and plastic bags.

They would return any objects to the authorities, who would then distribute the material to the families.

Naturally, someone affirmed.

The inspector said nothing. The motor caught and the boat took off.

From the river to the site they didn't hack at bushes once. It had all been trimmed. Clearly they weren't the first group to visit. The hike barely stretched two miles. Still, in the humidity, he was finding things difficult.

The site itself had all grown over. They would have to use their imaginations, Knut declared.

Reconstructions suggested the aircraft had ignited and partially broken up before hitting the canopy. It was likely some passengers had jumped.

'Is this really it, here?' The inspector noted an almost embarrassed air of anticlimax. They continued looking around for something.

'The noise, the light, the heat . . .' Knut's voice trailed off.

'Maybe we'll find a wedding ring.'

'From a plane of nuns?'

'The pilot?'

The inspector began to feel a little ill.

Some of the things they were meant to be looking for, he supposed, included black habits, simple shoes, eyeglasses with cords, photographic magazines, pages from paperback thrillers, toilet paper, waste, intact teeth, mercury fillings, inflatable headrests, flesh-coloured tights, strings of matted hair, half-filled notepads, rosaries, pictures of relatives, modest nightwear, sheet sleeping bags, nets, Plexiglas, milk-moons at the bottom of fingernails, axions and dendrites, low-reaching thin white socks, hand-fans, earplugs, return tickets, around $900, hymn books, the deceptive floor, a shattered roof.

They went off alone, prodded and pushed through branches, pulled back vines and looked up in hope. There appeared to be competition over who would be the first to mention the possibility of survivors.

'But how would they know? How could they have been certain none remained?'

None of it existed any more—it had been unmade. Glimmering things—reinforced glass from windows and mirrors, alloy wheels—were used by birds for display, internal wiring from the engines and communications systems swallowed and regurgitated as glue for nests, food for young.

He pictured analysts in the forest sampling the leaves, the ants, the birds and mammals of the area, reading matter and blood and fibre, scanning for toxicity in altered mineral levels, identifying in the spread of the new life exactly where the plane came down. Leaked heavy metals in the soil were absorbed in plants, then escalated via insects, fish, mammals and the people who ate them. Lithium, from the downed plane, now producing ecstatic visions, dreams of suicide. A sketch of the plane and the cargo drawn finely over the area, invisible but still, for the moment, recoverable. Rapid generations reproducing the information, in body and behaviour, the sketch drifting further away as the effects of the crash levelled out and the event, in time, disappeared.

What was this cloud, he thought, that they walked through?

He imagined, as he pushed past branches, suddenly seeing an intact torso, amber preserved. Even if what they were doing was fictional—say, this wasn't an authentic crash site, that they all knew that, really—the exercise, nonetheless, induced nausea. He didn't want to be there. He couldn't for the moment hear any of the others. Who knew what they might claim to have found? He wanted to be back in the settlement, around voices, other faces again, reading, enjoying a beer.

They ate lunch together at Santa Lucía. The tourists had been nearly everywhere, they boasted. Right to the top and right to the bottom. He had made the mistake of introducing himself in English and had expected brightness in the eyes, a flurry of questions, routine requests for useful information as they tried to exploit any opportunity, but, strangely, it hadn't happened; they had all but ignored him.

They walked in a group very uniformly, all together with their red caps and jackets bobbing up and down. They didn't have the shrill buoyancy he'd seen in other tourist groups. This one was quiet, solemn even, and there was something mechanical in the way they jerked their limbs up and down to make them walk.

Later they swam in a natural pool. Knut had judged the air and pleased the men by declaring he 'wasn't certain' how safe the water was. Flesh-eating fish, deceptively enormous constrictors, near invisible insects that would enter any orifice and tear you up inside. They went slowly through swamp water, thick, green liquid up to the level of their chests and chins. Waded slowly, suspiciously, looking around for something that was surely bound to happen. Each had their left hand extended up into the hanging vines, carrying aloft a small leather bag or purse, additionally wrapped in plastic, containing passport, ID card, permits, money.

They came out disappointingly intact, dried at the side on cleared land they knew better, by now, than to ask about. 'Most likely formerly used by the tribe'—it was becoming a refrain.

The inspector, watching, continued to ask about corporate compounds, ruins in the forest.

'There's nothing,' Knut said, more irritated every time. 'Anyway, tomorrow we leave on our first contact expedition.'

'WHERE'S CHARLIE? WHAT HAPPENED to Charlie?'

'Right here!'

Finally they were off. The boat was filled at one end with bags of rice, tinned fish, nuts, salted meat, dried biscuits, black bread, water skins. The motor made a distressingly loud noise. He couldn't help feeling a little embarrassed, aware of how incongruous they were. Still he attempted excitement, leaning forward from the front of the boat, willing on adrenalin.

From an initial burst, they moved at a gentler speed, at times cutting the motor and paddling through thick river. He lay against a rolled tarpaulin, too tired for English.

He brought out *Tribes of the Southern Interior*, which he'd picked up at the hotel. Despite the title, the book focused on a single community, population around two hundred, based at an unspecified point south-east in the forest. There seemed pieces missing, whole chapters ripped out. Even he could see it was short on data. Relations with other communities, analysis of language, diet—simple, foundational areas had been omitted from the book. Instead he read prolonged interpretations of mythology, confidently rendered in grand, formal prose.

He let himself be amused by some of the claims, even copied out passages into his notebooks. He'd draw from them later. A chapter on the dietary habits of the community was the biggest omission. He wanted to learn about their health and medicine. The mythology, at least in the translation he read, was fixated on the idea of missing persons. He read this as a suggestion of poor health in the community—perhaps the writer had been present not long after a period of disease. Therefore knowing of their diet would be instructive. The rhetoric on departures acted as a form of consolation, an accommodation of unbearable hurt, a system set up to formalize something chaotic and inexplicable. He wondered, naturally, how much of this was the invention of either the writer or translator. Many of the stranger parts of the book could be explained by simple, ordinary grief. He imagined the bereaved European making, from observations of the community, a whole system to complement his internal crisis. The period spent 'in the field' could even have been planned—an exile, a physical escape from loss. The material in the book he read, then, would be interesting primarily biographically, but revealing, as was usually the case, very little about the lives of those it purported to represent.

The pace of the boat was pleasant. Most were occupied with binoculars and cameras clamped to their faces and pointed high up. He fingered the leather pouch attached to his waist, which contained his own set of optical lenses. A gift from his wife, several years ago. He didn't take it out. From the river, the trees seemed too high. He didn't see anything, he never did. That was the thing about forests, Knut was now telling them: it's very difficult to see big life. That wasn't on the brochure, Charlie said.

THEY CAMPED NEAR A stream. Essential, Knut said. Various reasons. They had a lot still to do before the dark.

It looked cleared, as if used regularly.

'That will be a tribe using it,' Knut said, uncertainly.

Around them the guides were hacking bush. They had the use of a clearing already, and in relatively flat land; the inspector watched to see why they were cutting more. What they came away with, after hacking and splitting, was a series of thin poles, each several feet high. Without needing to say anything the three guides began posting them into the ground, marking out corners and midpoints along the perimeter of the clearing, several feet or so in from the beginning of the bush. Knut told them, explicitly, what was already clear: they shouldn't step beyond the border. Rope-lines were put up, linking the poles and sealing the space they were to sleep inside. Nothing was above them except the distant canopy thatch. They would cook and eat here, lay down their mats and single-sheet sleeping bags and hang their insect nets.

They would not go outside the rope space. Someone was laughing. Charlie was asked to speak up.

'Yes,' Knut confirmed. 'Obviously you will have to leave the space when you need to use the facilities, but that is the only time.'

They heard noise continuously around them. The inspector saw a couple—the Belgians, he thought, who always appeared as if they'd only just put on their clothes—approach the rope border. The man, Leo, in shirt, high socks and a broad hat, was slowly pushing his hand out past the line, as if gently, cautiously, testing water temperature. Leo suddenly whipped back his hand, his wife putting her arms around him, scolding him. He stared. The guides looked concerned and consulted with Knut, who stressed, again, the dangers of moving outside camp bounds.

Charlie was continuing to ask questions, offering unsolicited commentary on any topic. The inspector was careful to delay laying out his own mat, waiting for Charlie to make his move, so he could then position himself the furthest distance away. He was frustrated. Nothing at all had got started, and despite, as it seemed, being in a reasonably remote forest area, their group maintained a loud and festive air. It was reminding him of a coach party and it didn't have to be like this. They couldn't, it seemed, be subdued. The difference, he thought, the marked change in behaviour, had really begun with the setting up of the rope-lines. Everything was a game, anything happening beyond the camp just a distant source of entertainment, as indirect as television. Soon enough, he had to hope, they would be done for the night. They were scheduled to resume travelling before dawn. He winced. Any attempt to see this as legitimate investigative activity, an 'expedition', fieldwork into the corporation, something that may even help him establish further information relating to the disappearance of Carlos, was undermined by the gossipy tones, the vulgar sight of money belts and spat-out tooth-paste froth staining the mud white.

He sat up—people were moving about more purposefully. Tin mugs and paper plates: dinner was being served. The tourists unfolded their trek-chairs, while he sat directly on the ground.

Charlie was next to him; he prodded the inspector on the arm and asked if everything was okay.

He hadn't realized how hungry he was. He tore into the fish, mixed with vegetables and rice. 'Fresh,' the guide sitting to his other side commented, pleased at his evident relish, 'fresh from the river.'

A bottle of hooch was passed discreetly; Charlie winked. The liquid burned and, gradually, began to settle him. Despite his frustrations, despite the people around him, he began to relax. He felt good and old in the forest. He loved the sweep of the sudden dark coming over him here, a sound as much as a disappearance. They gave themselves over at dark. The air was heavy, thick with millions of blood-filled points of light that somehow flew. Occasionally he sensed something greater, a different order of life above them in the trees or even many miles horizontal, and he felt a leap in the emptiness inside him, a thrill, a voicelessness and a wonder.

Occasionally he became conscious of how loud they were, but the amazing thing was just how easy it was to lose all sense of location. The paraffin lamps arranged in a row on the long, low table—the inspector, now, was propped up on a box—lit only their faces, their upper bodies and the food they ate. The lamp created, as if intended, a very limited and discrete area. Nothing, you could almost believe, was beyond it. The inspector set down his plastic fork and pushed himself up. 'Excuse me a moment,' he said. Knut passed him a candle and a guide absently pointed past the rope. He waited a moment, almost expecting to be accompanied—was this, he thought, what had become of him? He couldn't even do this alone? Given the warnings about the dangers past the rope-lines it was a little strange that no one had showed him exactly where to go. Presumably he had missed something earlier, while he dozed. He stood several feet back from the group, the table, the lights, and realized how ridiculous he would appear if he asked for clarification. Even worse, what would almost certainly happen is that a guide would insist on escorting him, the whole business mortifying. When he got there, the guide standing by, he would have to mimic the action and then come back later, illicitly, alone. He turned away from the table, light in one hand, paper in the other, and ducked out under the rope-line into the dark.

He walked and the artificial sounds died away almost instantly. A rough path had been cut and he located the pit latrine without difficulty. He found the business easier in a squatting position.

There was a shovel, a bucket of lime to throw. Walking back up to camp he reminded himself how quickly he had moved out of the range of voices. There was something a little unnerving about it, even with his light and the delineated path. He couldn't hear the group, couldn't see them. They would be back soon enough. He should appreciate the momentary isolation, enjoy the forest sounds.

He remained on the path, but was dully aware of the longer length of the return walk. It made sense, given he had marched out in something of a hurry, returning more calmly and with an awareness that he should at least try to appreciate his surroundings. The trouble with the candlelight was that it offered no distance, its reality had no depth. He saw little more than the immediate air, heavy with moisture, antic with mosquitoes and outsize moths, burying into his forehead and his exposed hands. Snuffing the light he would see more. He had stopped, stood still. Why hadn't he seen the camp yet? The path led directly, so nothing should have obstructed the image. Again, he put it down to the parochial effect of the light he carried, which he had been too afraid to put out. The danger, of course, was that if he did so he would see nothing. Darkness, the faint blues and greens of vegetal drift.

The path leading in one direction to the latrine may have branched off somewhere else, not merely leading the one way back to the camp. How much could the forest cover over? He was dimly aware of some of the measures taken in urban planning—unusually verdant median strips, say; a minimum number of city parks, however small—one of the benefits of which was apparently in noise reduction. As well as absorbing pollution, the green areas had the effect of storing sound. If a simple park could do that, then it shouldn't surprise him that he sensed no evidence of the party, even so close by in the forest. The forest would be loud with itself, beyond them. The light absence could be explained by a simple turn in the path he had been too preoccupied to notice, meaning that when he looked up, back towards where the camp doubtless was, it was hidden by the trees. He had solved the problem, but still he hadn't moved. He then asked himself if it were not possible that, in thinking this, in going over the possible explanations, he had turned himself around. He could not be certain either way. The moment he considered this, he lost confidence in the way forward. It was so easily done.

Something crashed into him, causing the inspector to lose his footing and drop the light, which immediately went out.

'Whoa, easy!' a male voice said, as he was helped up. 'You okay there?' It was Charlie. 'I've been sent to find you.'

Quickly enough his eyes adjusted; the camp was less than thirty metres ahead. He had been walking the right way and would have arrived there any moment.

THEY HAD BEEN TOLD that, all being well, they could expect a meeting today. With a significant hike ahead, they should eat well at breakfast, but many of them had trouble keeping anything down. Nerves, Knut said. That's all. 'Aren't you excited?'

The inspector was wholly uncomfortable, a sensation compounded by the fact that nobody seemed to share this feeling. They had been told at the start, as they set off, that they would ride for three days and hike for two. But there was no momentum. They started later and finished earlier on each day's sailing. The previous day, the first of the great 'hike' days, had seen fitful walking at best, prolonged mealtimes, extended rests. He didn't understand. Although the party was middle-aged, they all seemed in good health, and as Charlie had stressed they'd each passed medical tests confirming their fitness. So why weren't they doing it? Why weren't they going in? Why was everything still mitigated, compromised, deferred?

THE GUN FIRED. THERE were cries, branches breaking, leaves thrashing. Flashes of light, which he had taken to be further shots, somehow preceding their own noise, but which he later realized were cameras adjusted to the low light.

He couldn't construct a face. Everything had been a blur. He couldn't state how many of them there were or even how close they had come. He frantically tried to reconstruct everything—already passed. They had been tracked, Knut told them. Hunted.

The tribesmen had followed them for a long time, perhaps hours, and were preparing an ambush. The shot wasn't intended to harm anyone—the group needed to be certain of this. It was a warning and had dispersed the attackers, who had dissolved back into the forest. They wouldn't make another approach, he stressed, but the guns would be readied as a precaution until they had made it safely back to the boat.

'How will we sleep? How can we make camp, knowing they're right there?'

'We will keep watch during the night. You will be looked over. You are safe.'

They resumed their walk quietly, intensely, still stunned by the experience. Within fifteen minutes, however, they grew animated again, talking loudly and making gestures. Several people remained quiet with their heads stooped. He was impressed, interested. It took the inspector some time to realize they were studying the footage on their cameras, walking in time to the footstep in front. He stepped back and watched them more. From his perspective the forest grew bigger the further out they got, made the figures small and thin under the weight of it. But they wouldn't see it like that. The camera light attached to each face looked like a charm, a preventative measure or superstition, insulating them from or holding back the pressure above; it contracted the world.

Later they passed cameras around as they ate, ravenous. Several seconds of electric noise and bright light each.

'You can see one, here, from the back—'

'Here, look, he's leaping—'

'Oh my God, she's naked—'

'I think that one's carrying a child!'

'Did anyone get a good shot of a face? Anyone?'

They discussed how they could combine the footage, the various angles, the different time periods, into a single comprehensive document. It seemed to him they were adding new things, affirming additional details.

Again, in the evening, they ate hungrily and talked over each other in rushes. They camped in the same clearing, and long into the darkness, long after they had been told it was no longer safe to talk, the inspector could see the faint blue light of their films playing privately, over and over again, held inches from the face.

II

MARIA'S CAFÉ WAS SET directly opposite the hotel; a small space, he thought, with a surprising capacity and terrific coffee and eggs. Maria wore an apron and her hair up, and she cooked and served. She seemed to mock all of them equally and none of them minded. He couldn't find out what she was doing there. A family to support? She didn't give much away. He had been humiliated by his complicity in the expedition episode and he could fool himself a while into believing it was the reason he stayed so quiet.

He wasn't sure what had happened, how much of it was real and how much invention. They had been theatrically guided, the adventure artificially framed. After all the anticipation, the weeks of investigation seemingly leading here, the forest, he was experiencing a shattering anticlimax. What did any of this have to do with Carlos, with the corporation? What had he expected to find in the interior? If something significant had indeed been there, what would it have looked like and would he have recognized it, would he have seen it for what it was? Preparing the trip upriver he had imagined picking up a trail, breaking off from the group, moving further in.

When he went for coffee in the morning he had found the tourists gone. Knut, Charlie, all of them, left on a flight before dawn to a famous trail.

165

'Did you enjoy your adventure?' Maria asked, bringing him his order.

'Why are you smirking?'

'How much did you pay?'

'Too much.'

'You went eleven miles.'

'No . . .'

'You took a tributary and looped yourself. We heard your gun!'

'Why? Surely you'd make just as much, if not more, from real excursions?'

'Too complicated. Too much effort, and the reality would be uncomfortable for them, for you. The real experience would be sickness and disappointment. You'd never see anyone. Really, it's much better for everyone this way. And you know,' she said, smiling, 'I quite enjoy playing the role of a young tribal mother.'

He couldn't believe he'd been there ten days already. Time was different in Santa Lucía, that was the only explanation. His flight had been delayed, landing past midnight at the tiny riverside settlement—all rotting, temporary wooden buildings and rusted motorboats—and he'd walked, eagerly, with his suitcase and his hat, dramatized by the thick velvet dark and the binary transmission of the cicadas, to the Terminación reception.

Three children, no more than eight or nine years old, played at the counter, picking up and dropping receipts and laughing, exchanging nonsense words. He waited to be acknowledged.

'I would like to speak to the proprietor,' he said eventually. The children continued playing so he spoke again, louder and more insistent. 'Excuse me. Is there an adult present?'

One of the kids looked at him, a boy in shorts with long black hair.

'You would like a room,' the boy said.

'Yes, but may I speak to the manager?'

'How many nights? He's not here.'

'I don't know yet. Not many, I shouldn't think.'

'Fill these in and I'll give you your key. Welcome to the Terminación.'

THE FIRST THING TO establish was that none of the population, at any point in their lives, had had any dealings with Carlos. The name meant nothing to them. The photographs were substandard and he knew he was asking a difficult, even impossible question; distorted in transit, the colours running and smudging despite his determination to keep them sealed. He dried them out in his room. No one would ever recognize Carlos from these, he was sure. The image could have been anyone. He tried describing Carlos—height, weight, features—but soon gave up.

He brought out the maps he'd sourced from the district head-quarters, huge sheets representing barely differentiated tracts. They spread them at the small, dank hotel bar—local gins, warm beer bottles and boiled eggs—pointing, disputing and resolving nothing. People crowded around. Fishermen could take him upriver, but where exactly did he want to go? He would have to be specific. They didn't need to tell him how huge the area was; he should bear in mind the amount of food and water necessary, and for two people, of course, there and back.

It would cost him. His guide would be with him the whole time—given the fuel premium, going out twice wasn't an option. They would require full payment in advance. And there was the matter of insurance: not only must he waive any right to compensation himself, he would have to assume responsibility for the guide and for the guide's family, as well as for the vessel. All of this had to be agreed in advance and put in writing.

Officially the settlement capacity was four hundred, although it wasn't possible to say, at any one point, exactly how many people lived in Santa Lucía. Some, including the missionaries, would be further inland; others would be temporarily back in the city, arranging supplies. The settlement's buildings were elegant and functional, although in a faded state. The Hotel Terminación was the only two-storey structure.

Even the residents admitted there was little reason for it being there. Not any more. Dug out thirty years ago, it was initially conceived of as a temporary base in the construction of a timber route. But the road had never been extended and Santa Lucía remained cut off. It profited from tourism, from religious missions, from fish farming—until recently, river fish had been harvested in pools just to the south.

NOBODY REALLY STAYED HERE for long, Miguel explained. Miguel—wire-thin, frizzy hair sometimes tied back in a band, shorts, colourful long shirt, cheap plastic sandals—ran the Terminación. He did not, the inspector thought, seem particularly reliable. Well meaning, affable enough. Rarely at reception, Miguel instead spent his days in a hut of oil and parts. He played old cassettes, smoked and worked on boat engines, there from the start of the bright still mornings till the sudden temper preceding night, sleeping for the most part in the hammock strung from his hut to a tree.

He could tell immediately that Miguel was happier occupied, when he could focus on something else while they talked. He built and rebuilt engines and took them apart. He asked the hotelier about it: I thought you were fixing that up. I thought you had it. I thought it worked.

Miguel appeared to have dismantled an entire functioning engine, spread it flat and separate, atomized over his workbench surface.

Everybody in Santa Lucía, Miguel said—down to the cleaners and the fishermen—held a residency permit allowing a maximum stay of two years. The population was in flux. Miguel had been granted dispensation, but he didn't particularly like the arrangement. The permits were a deliberate ploy, he claimed, prohibiting the development of a real community. There was no hospital, no school. You weren't supposed to live here, not really. He admitted his children were there unofficially—a long story, he sighed. The point was that they didn't want anyone to be born. Equally, there were no provisions for the dead.

'They? Who, the government, you mean?'

Miguel shrugged.

'Say I want the bigger history: business interests, trading relationships, general comings and goings. You're the man to ask, right? You'll have the records, the accounts? I'd like to see them, when you have a moment.'

'Whatever you want. How far back? And you're in luck: I record every guest.'

'Businesses, particularly the larger operations, whose representatives have visited the site. I want to know what goes on here. I mean, I don't see tracks, logging routes . . .'

Miguel nodded. 'There were delays—I'm not quite sure what the problem was. Much of the land around was taken, bought up, but then there were legal challenges, which led to more delays in constructing the rest of the route. I'm not sure exactly what happened, but operations were suspended, anyway.'

Miguel had a low focus, always looking down, close, whether as a consequence of living so long in what could seem a depthless forest or from years adjusting parts, working on leads, batteries, boards.

'What about recently—anything happening? Commercial research, representatives passing through. I don't know, people collecting samples?'

'Timber samples?'

'Timber, plants, anything really.'

'It's been quiet for some time.'

'So no one working in any kind of commercial capacity has been through recently?'

'Well, when you put it like that, I mean . . . Of course, there's business going on locally, small-scale stuff. There's the tourist groups, for instance. A lucrative business. The boats are always ready for them. Some filmmakers, working on documentaries—it's not unusual to see them, either. The abandoned fishery involved a bit of work.'

'Nothing else?'

'Not to my knowledge. Well, there were the two individuals, but they weren't here on business, I don't think, that's why I didn't say.'

'Who?'

'Their names are here somewhere. I'll dig them out, along with the rest of the records. Bear in mind we can only take cash here, so . . .'

'When was this? You didn't mention it earlier.'

'Five, six weeks ago, I think. Though it's difficult to tell sometimes. Stayed six, seven nights. Unfortunately, Marcelo is no longer with us. He took them by boat.'

'The man is dead?'

'What? No, no. He left. He works seasonally.'

'What were they doing? Where did they go?'

'I can give you Marcelo's details. Track him later, he has all the information. I don't know anything about them.'

'Nothing?'

'Well, they were young, I guess, a bit sullen. I don't think they really wanted to be here. And I mean, I know you don't like them either, but they really didn't take to the kids. Dressed oddly, too.'

'How?'

'I don't know. Just not quite right. Didn't fit.'

'Miguel, this might sound silly, but the names—Mengano, Beltrano? Mean anything to you?'

'What? No, nothing at all.'

'What did they have with them, what did they bring?'

'Nothing really. Just the usual, suitcases. And there was the crate. Marcelo, I remember, mentioned something about a crate. I don't know what it was for. It wasn't made up in the end. Maybe I heard him wrong. They didn't leave with a crate.'

'You're sure? They didn't leave with anything other than their original luggage?'

'I don't think so. I can't say for sure.'

'This crate: I want it clarified. They didn't arrive with a crate?'

'No, I didn't say that. I didn't see anything. Marcelo only, he said something about a request, building a crate. Look, I'm pretty busy here, we can do this later?'

'Just a moment more. So the crate was not built; they didn't take it in or out?'

'I guess not.'

'Nothing else you remember? Nothing at all unusual?'

'There was one thing at the hotel, not particularly unusual.'

'Well?'

'Sometimes people, they'll book an additional room. The rooms aren't expensive, I'm sure you'll agree: good rates. They do it for privacy. I do what I can, but I can't stop people making a bit of noise, coming in late from the bar, fumbling with the lock on their door, that kind of thing. And the walls aren't the thickest, I'll admit. You might hear people walking around, pouring water down the toilet, coughing or whatever. So people do it to help them sleep, I guess: they buy up additional rooms.'

'How many rooms did they book?'

'Three.'

'Three rooms together.'

'No. I didn't say that. That's what was a little odd. They stayed in adjacent rooms, but the other room, the third room booked, that was on the other end of the hotel, facing the forest. Actually, if you look at the plans, you'll see the third room couldn't have been any further from theirs.'

'Well, what for? What was the room used for?'

'Nothing. No one came in or out, as far as I know. When the cleaner went in after they checked out, she said it hadn't been touched.'

'Isn't that strange?'

'Yes, it's strange. But there's nothing illegal in it, is there?'

'Miguel, I'll need as full a physical description of these two men as possible. I'll need their names, their bills, receipts. Every piece of information that they left. Additionally, I want you to show me to the other room, the empty one.'

'That won't be necessary.'

'Why won't it?'

'The third room, the additional room, Inspector. It's yours.'

III

HE WAS STILL WAITING for the records. When he needed him, Miguel seemed to go missing. He didn't see how it was possible in a place this size, this cut off, with nowhere else to go. The settlement was like a ship, an island, a theatre. You passed seemingly the same people always, in the same limited space.

He eventually found Miguel, who claimed to have been in the hut all along. Miguel threaded wires while he talked, his words small and conservative next to the fluency of the hands. The inspector was unable to identify either the different machine parts or their condition. He couldn't tell if one half of the room, for instance, represented a different state of progress compared to the other. It may have been the case that the room moved into order, that Miguel had separated out the parts that way, according to progress. He couldn't tell what was being built. The inspector was not so adept with machines and repairs. It had been a frequent source of gentle teasing. It still amazed him, really, that anything could go. That these lidless boards and lead-acid batteries could be fitted into a boat shape and you could step on it and trust and it would take you. He was careful not to ask any more questions about the work.

'I'm afraid I have some bad news,' Miguel said. 'They're gone. All records, gone.'

'What do you mean—you lost them? They've been stolen? There's been a fire, what?'

'They've gone through all my ledgers. You can see for yourself. It's all ruined. This is bad news for me. How am I to explain this to the authorities? For tax, and what have you?'

'Who did? Who went through everything? Bring them to me. I want to interview them immediately.'

'What? No. The insects.'

OFTEN, IN AFTERNOONS, THE inspector retreated to his room. The draining light, the feasting insects, the manifest frustration of life on this tiny, blank outpost. The children took to laughing at him, parodying his gait and walk, a slow and high-kneed stride, pointless and mechanical, like a puppet, they said. He hadn't been the least aware. They laughed, called at him, threw pebbles at his room, disturbing him as he tried to read back through his case notes or dictated notes on the little progress he had made.

His room was small. Noise from the bar filtered through the shutters. Doors rattled, laughter broke. He was certain someone knocked, but it must have been another door. Guests came in and out—they'd nod when they saw each other, without making introductions. His net wouldn't attach securely to the ceiling, so he woke tangled. The mattress was damp and grey. Something smelled.

Shortly after settling down for the night, he'd spent twenty minutes debating whether his bladder could hold, but it had now become painful. He scrambled out of the net, untucking a corner from under the end of the mattress, crawled to the floor. With the shutters closed, the only light came through the door. The bathroom was ruinous—mirror stained and cracked, broken pipes exposed, holes in the floor and walls. A pair of bright blue flip-flops had been helpfully provided. A thick, fuzzy ant line emerged from a fissure; it looked like hair shaved from a face. He squatted over the drop hole, just in case. As he returned to bed, he checked the lock on the door. It held, barely. For some reason he then opened it. The corridor was empty. He could go back to sleep. An object caught his eye. It had been deposited between his room and the next on his left. It was dark. He shouldn't leave his room as he wasn't dressed and didn't want an embarrassing encounter, a trader stumbling back from the bar. It might have been an item of clothing, perhaps a hat. He leaned closer and it seemed to move. But it was just a gathering of dirt, a pile that had been brushed there for some reason. Mud, stones, mainly small sticks, trailed in by someone who hadn't wiped down.

The doors rattled with the barest movement—a breeze, another door being opened or closed, someone coming in or out. A few more times he thought he heard someone and, once or twice, voices and even footsteps running away—the kids, he guessed.

He determined, the following morning, to put a stop to the incidents during the night, the banging on his door, the laughing. He couldn't get any work done in these conditions.

He found Miguel returning to his hut and explained the situation. It wasn't acceptable; the man really had to keep a tighter leash on his children. The conditions in the room were far from satisfactory. 'And why is it only me, Miguel? Why do they bang on my door?'

'I don't know. Some foolishness—I apologize profusely. It won't happen again.'

But it did. A pattern repeated. He'd finally, after some delay, get off to sleep, when he'd hear the banging, the laughter, the footsteps running away. So close, especially the voices, he could have believed they were right there in his room. He'd scramble out of bed, dismantling the net, run to his door as quickly as he could, but find, on throwing it open, that the corridor was empty. Then he'd wait. He knew they'd come back. Only somehow they anticipated him. They waited not only until he'd left his vigil, but for him actually, and miraculously, to fall asleep again. Then the knock. Another. Repeating until he gave in, jumped up from the bed, ran to the door, saw nothing in the half-light.

He sealed the open office window as soon as he noticed. He tested the lock three times, then traced the edges of the further two windows, checking for any airflow. The atmosphere had turned over. It didn't seem possible that somebody could have been so blithe, so ignorant as to have done this. Carlos, he thought, had been lost anew, all remaining evidence gone.

He left the office, closing the door behind him. The employees appeared oblivious, habitually absorbed in work. He wasn't sure who to approach. Nobody would admit culpability. He would be passed from one department to another, simply wasting his time.

He returned to the empty office. The keyboard was meaningless now. The carpet, the chair, the windows and the desk. Whatever had been left in the vacant office was gone. For the first time he sat directly on Carlos's chair. The rings from the coffee mug were just perceptible on the desk. He wondered how long the window had been open. Although it hadn't rained, the corners of the carpet were damp. Detritus had blown in. Something was present on the edge of the desk, too far to reach.

A bloom, soft, blue, no bigger than the nail on his smallest finger. Rather than pick it up, he leaned in to smell. It should have been dead, neutral, but the odour was as strong as the colour was bright. Carlos's desk was narrower than the model used in the other offices, only just wider than his extended elbows. Carlos had requested it, perhaps brought it in himself, requiring the assistance of a friend or colleague. He would ask Vasquez. A horizontal board weighed it down, doubling as a footrest. The desktop little more than a slab, a butcher's block. Standing over the table, bearing the instrument down and splitting the animal carcass.

Now the evidence had gone, he was clear to run his hands over the table. He was surprised at how uneven it was. Damp patches. The midday shadow cast by the open computer screen only just failed to hit the flower on the edge.

He blew onto the desk. The bloom reacted, but remained in position. He looked closely and saw that it was rooted there. A single wildflower blooming in the damp desk.

He woke up. A weak sun lit the room; the dream receded. Mosquitoes had stripped his back in the night, leaving blood on the sheets. It had hardened into crust, but when he washed his back fell fresh open. He sat on the edge of the low bed, his feet on the soft wooden floor, his hands on his knees. He was too warm. The fan barely moved. He tried to slow things down. He had to decide on a course of action.

The thick odour of the flower in the dream was fixed to the back of his throat. The pungent smell he had noted earlier was now much worse. An awful smell. It was there on the blood-stained sheets. Was it him? He left the room and went to investigate outside. He saw the lights of a labourers' camp down by the river. They were constructing a new bridge. He could smell burned incense from their tents. They were trying to isolate themselves, ward off the source of that same stench.

It wasn't excrement. He went around the back of the building. The wall beneath faced the forest, away from the settlement. Vines climbed it, smeared in thin dark splashes. Was this where dead animals went? So close to the community, the hotel?

He went back to his room and closed the shutters, sealing them with tape. Somehow it got worse. It was the smell of holes opened in the ground. Endings. He pressed his hands to the top of his head. Unbroken. He wiped sweat away. He had imagined a blade put against him, planing down his head, shavings like sawdust around him on his shoulders. Pulped tissue and nerve. The smell of his own brain. Scent and sense, matter and memory.

IV

HE RELAXED AT THE small hotel bar, continuing with *Tribes of the Southern Interior*. He found himself reading the same few pages several times, losing the thread, unable to make much progress. He put the book aside.

There was a new, rather conspicuous group at the bar, youngish and particularly thin, the men with three-day beard growth, clothes uniformly dark and torn. He nodded and waited. When one went to order, he introduced himself. Alberto—tall, pale, red-headed—cut an unusual figure in the forest.

'Bad timing,' Alberto explained. 'We're just back. Five weeks' filming. We had our own boat, but it was arranged back home.'

'I've been here nearly two weeks already. I should explain—I'm with the police. I'm looking for information relating to a particular identity, an individual reported missing seven weeks ago. I believe he may be in the area somewhere to the east of here.'

'What, kidnapped?'

'I can't say, for the moment. But I need to see if I can pick up the trail.'

'Like I said, bad timing. Wish you all the best.'

Alberto turned to go. The inspector saw the knuckles of the man's spine through the loose shirt.

He kept to the periphery of the conversation. The team had worked on nature documentary films, gathering footage from the forest. They set up twenty-four-hour recording stations and planted motion-sensitive photographic triggers next to samples of rotting meat. Having gathered sufficient material they were leaving Santa Lucía in three days' time, the next scheduled flight out. In the interim they'd trawl through digital footage and develop analogue in darkrooms. 'And drink,' Alberto said. 'We intend to drink.'

HE WANTED TO SEE how the darkroom was built. They let him come along the following morning. He heard them mention 'la cueva' and thought he was hallucinating, when someone clarified, said that's what they called these places—caves. They tried various spots: vacant hotel rooms, the café and a back room in the bar. Each environment seemed too unstable and unpredictable—people kept coming in and out, doors opening and closing. They couldn't rely on this dark, so they had to make their own. They found a level spot by the river to the south of the hotel. In eight minutes the tent was up. Then they lined it, on the outside, twice in thick black tarp. It held. Inside there was real dark. They split the space in two—one half dry, one wet. Attached wire hangers to the roof poles, set up a fold-out counter and a two-foot-wide plastic tub. Marguerite monitored ambient temperature; one of the biggest challenges developing in the tropics, she said, was the heat. 'Changes conditions. Develops quicker than we'd like, emulsion gets softer, more susceptible to abrasion.'

'How does it affect the film?'

'More likely the images will come out scratched. Rougher. With less developing time it's harder to judge how much agitation to apply—too much and we destroy it, not enough and we'll have silver bromide streaks all the way across.'

The scale effect was strange when a light crept in to what had seemed a darkness, the line on the still-imperfect seam spreading over the fabric, appearing just for a few moments like the sky at the transition stage of an eclipse.

They had piles of stock. He hadn't anticipated so much. He was disappointed by the images, which they found amusing. 'What do you expect, action? Animals leaping out in focus?' Unfortunately, explained Luis, the youngest of the crew, the camera was not perfect. Sometimes it was too sensitive—things like a falling branch or even a wind-blown leaf could trigger it. But they had got some life.

They hung the drying sheets on wire lines between the trees and watched the monochrome forms come out with the afternoon. The atmosphere was drowsy and he dozed on a hammock. He imagined them drawing Carlos up and back from the few things found remaining in the ground. The pools of his blood collected in the insect clouds, the fractionally altered consistency of the groundwater on the spot where he had fallen. Concentrating very hard, as if what was required was partly or even primarily an act of imagination.

He got up, walked indoors and poured some water. Miguel, emerging from his hut, stopped him, asked what was going on, what the crew was doing.

The confusion was partly the inspector's fault; he couldn't have been clear enough. Immediately he had mentioned the caves, Miguel warned against them and against the journey inside. The inspector eventually explained that they were referring to photography, hoping to gain an image. Miguel mentioned real places, cave formations he had visited a couple of times. 'Years ago,' he said. 'Even tourist groups went.' It had since become unstable, too dangerous to visit, and access anyway, he said, had likely become impossible simply due to the vegetation. It wasn't the caves themselves, he said; bats flew out in clouds at day's end; there were strange hidden pools inside, walls and roofs spectacularly carved by erosion and minerals; and there were the paintings. He had seen only the ones closest to the entrances; he hadn't in any of his journeys witnessed what was said to be the more spectacular art further and lower in. He had no idea of the age. Animals still used the sites; he remembered beaming his torch onto a strange scene, dozens of large peccaries in a sequence on the wall, flowing into each other according to the broken lines, and seeing, when he went to shut off his torch and continue with just his headlamp, a mass of two-toed prints on the ground, around him, all but fresh. A guano smell and mammal faeces.

Alberto interrupted, walking urgently towards them. 'Inspector, there is something I think you should see.'

THE PHOTOGRAPH WAS MONOCHROME on a landscape A4 sheet. At first it was difficult to make it out—a thick mesh of dark strokes, little light. It wasn't easy to establish depth. The area had not been cleared; it appeared relatively untouched. Examining the scene further, he saw the camera faced an embankment. High up in the trees was a patch of white artificial fabric.

He looked at the second photograph. This image was close, blurred, white. From this perspective, despite the distortion, it was clear the fabric was inhabited. There appeared to be a human crown slashed several times and dripping black ink. A light fuzz of hair only. The face looked down, remaining unclear, but suggesting shame, resignation, perhaps death, he thought. The shirt was soaked, torn, partly stripped. Some of the liquid would be blood. The limbs seemed splayed awkwardly, as if the figure had fallen into position. But something about the pose, the relation of the man to the surrounding forest, made him think he had been put there.

They split into three separate teams to develop the rest of the film in caves. They hadn't the time, he insisted, to wait for night. 'Couldn't do it then, anyway,' Marguerite said. 'Insects are attracted to the chemicals and torchlight.'

He asked if he could help, but they declined the offer and so he watched them building. Across the terrain of Santa Lucía south multiple caves went up. They used black sheets borrowed from the Terminación to drape around tents. Inside them was to be the appearance of nothing, so they could then develop something. He saw the chemicals blend and swirl like smoke, imagined Carlos, as an image, a form, briefly coming together before breaking apart. The process was primitive, ritualistic. He imagined murmurs inside, low, focused chanting; Carlos called up from the air, from the ground, and disappearing. The ground turning over, rising in layers, the mountains lowering, the water levels rising. Each discovery seemed to reverse the progress it suggested: building up a picture, they saw someone in a state of decay, shapeless and disordered, hurt. He felt the same combination of excitement and dread that he'd had on the verge of the forest—any one of these photographs could, in theory, present an unobstructed image of the face.

Luis was almost certain that another photograph had been taken later of the same spot; in this one the figure was absent.

'Meaning,' the inspector said, 'he is alive.'

'Or has been taken.'

While they worked on exposure, the inspector pressed for all the information they had. They'd covered a wide area, setting up two dozen filming posts, and no one was certain of the exact coordinates of the shot. Alberto drew a map, marking each of the posts— the nearest eleven days out by boat.

'We put rotting meat on site. The idea was to attract animals. A man wouldn't come to this.'

'I don't know. Say he had been walking a considerable time, six weeks or so, and for most of that had been without substantial food. He wasn't himself, he was desperate. It's not inconceivable. Was the camera completely concealed? Maybe he noticed it. Maybe that's what he was aiming for. Contact.'

HE WAS AWARE OF time and opportunity expiring, the force of the pressure. Things were moving too quickly, he felt a little passive, swept along. There was a chance he was missing something, a piece of information that might have been integral to the success or otherwise of the case. The crew was leaving in days and there was still so much to do. They had more to uncover. He was frustrated: he couldn't achieve the necessary speculative distance.

He went over, again, the photographs discovered so far. Each time he took them out he expected resolution, proof, this time, that it was Carlos beyond doubt. But the turn of the face and the position of the body were perfectly arranged, engineered as if to evade personal identification. Initially, thinking the position looked artificial, he had posited the involvement of a second person. A standing figure, tall behind the automatic camera focus. Did the figure appear to be turning from someone, deliberately facing away? The inspector willed some evidence in the picture, anything to increase the likelihood that he was still alive.

Something remained in the figure's arrangement across the seven photographs, something he hadn't yet identified. A significance related to the contrived nature of the stance. He read it again, again. He was always drawn to the face, although it had turned and said nothing. A fragment of the open mouth was revealed in two of the pictures, but he couldn't make it out. What call it made. The words were mute, like the hummed melodies remaining in the ground surfaces of nightmare-weathered teeth.

He watched the fingers, visible on the left hand only and which he saw, for the first time, were held in a loose grip. He noted a slightly unusual and, hopefully, unnatural proportion in the distance between each of the fingers. He then studied the neck, the violent stretch and sideward twist of the bowed head. Proportions, relationships. Holding a body, artificially and in front of a lens, was an opportunity to communicate information. The figure, he thought, may even have been wittingly expressive in the photographs. The significance almost floored him, almost distracted him. Assuming for the moment that the individual wanted to be found, then the most likely content of his information regarded his location. What could he say, through the fingers, the empty clasp of a hand, the wrenched neck?

The inspector sketched angles and proportions. Drawing out all available spatial information, he mapped the body every way he could. He was flooded by possibilities, theories relating to the language intended in the figure. Morse, a binary communication— slow, heavy, expensive—at most speaking a single word, and what? His distinction between major and minor, regarding the angles of the expressed body was, he knew, fairly arbitrary, and the message he drew out contained nothing intelligible.

Perhaps he had the wrong scale. Did the body contain coordinates? Did Carlos—the anonymous figure, he corrected—have knowledge of his precise position and the ingenious ability (suggesting prolonged captivity, the resources of tedium) to express his coordinates through digits, the angles created by the gaps across his body?

He spent twenty minutes trying multiple ways of extracting numbers from what the body did, but again got nothing intelligible. He needed assistance, a second professional opinion; he was certain then that he would unscramble the body's expression. He put the photographs back into the sealed plastic folder and went to return to his room. In the alteration of his blood movement, his airflow, his heart rate, and his moving perspective of the forest, he noticed something. Environment, landscape. The body as environment itself, he thought, not encoding one, not charting it in numbers, but being a landscape. He needed only to confirm with the photographs, but he knew it: the body drew a picture of a particular location. The figure, Carlos, mimicked the arrangement of the rocks, the precise bend of an adjacent river. He was communicating in his apparently unconscious expression his exact location in the forest.

V

THE DECISION WAS MADE: he would leave with them on the flight the day after tomorrow. Enough had been found to justify a comprehensive and fully funded search of the whole area. Alberto struck the inspector as a dependable, capable man, consistently responding to enquiries helpfully and succinctly. He appeared sympathetic to the case, willing to help in any way he could. They would come back together. He and Alberto would lead a specialist team, bringing adequate transport—a helicopter, perhaps—substantial supplies, a variety of professionals, hunting dogs. Forensics, even. Isabella's help would be invaluable and she was hardly likely to turn down a chance to visit the forest. It was the sensible option.

He felt himself relaxing. He ordered at the bar that evening and joined Alberto and the team at their table. 'The nature of this work is very solitary,' he said. 'I can't tell you how grateful I am to have your help. All of you. Even talking is a relief. These weeks have been difficult. When I'm back,' he said, 'I'll need to make some changes.'

They smiled and nodded politely, except for Luis, who was frowning in front of his open laptop. Luis, an intern, wasn't being paid. A couple of days ago he had described his digital recordings to the inspector, the 'making of' featurettes which would appear at the end of the film. This was his own project. The inspector felt uneasy when Luis had shown him. What he saw was surely obtrusive optical and audio equipment along with their operators (young men and women in faux-military fatigues) as they filmed their footage, at times closely interacting with animals. It looked dangerous, reckless.

But such scenes, far from being casually taken from actual feature-filming, Luis said, were scripted pieces produced afterwards, on revisiting the site. They were popular because of the flowing, unrealistic nature of the dialogue—viewers were supposed to enjoy 'behind the scenes' access while maintaining the uncanny suspicion that the featurettes were just as worked at as the main productions (and that the real authority might remain inaccessible). According to Luis the featurettes were an ingenious way of exploiting suspicion, extending the intrigue of creation. By appearing to offer full transparency over the means of making them, but actually only deferring the truth, the films, he explained, became more popular.

If he were to believe Luis, then 20–30 per cent of any one production was 'stock'; that is, taken from archives of classically satisfying general material. This stock, used to varying degrees from one film to another, was not original to any one film, but worked rather like cliché in language and in art. Just as a painter applied certain background styles to frame the focus, producers and directors filled out natural history films with stock dynamic waterfalls, hazy canopies and wide deserts. Whole features—series even—might be composed entirely of recycled footage, old material reapplied in new arrangements. Identical animals had been located in features thirty years apart or more, apparently unchanged in time, as if cloned without a single copying error.

From features—new narratives—made entirely of old and unrelated things, the inspector reasoned, it wasn't such a leap to producing so-called documentaries made up of scenes animated artificially from the start, pixels generated that bore no real relationship to what they purported to represent. A script could be written without restraint—anything could be said to happen, as anything could be produced. Some of the nature scenes might never have happened, being computer generations from the start, dreamed whimsy of isolated, burdened, overworked producers in offices.

'Are you looking for the thin man?' Luis now said, interrupting the conversation at the bar table.

'Thin man?'

'Yes. You'd see him at night, in silhouette. Preparing food in his room, standing by the window.'

'Who, sorry? What room is this? Do you mean—?'

'In your room. The room you're in now, I mean.'

Alberto stepped in. 'Luis, you're mistaken. The inspector's staying on the other side of the hotel. What you were seeing was Miguel.'

Luis looked steadily at Alberto for a moment, then shrugged. 'Sure, right.' He turned his attention back to the screen and began typing. He stopped again. 'But the photographs, Inspector. What if it's not what you think? Did you consider that? What if this person doesn't want to be found?'

'Why would he not—?' The inspector broke off. He couldn't be distracted any more by philosophical questions. He had a job to do. He instead finalized a few details about departure times and then went to settle up at the bar. As nothing could be left to chance, he reserved rooms throughout the whole of the Terminación, anticipating the arrival of a large investigating party. Miguel required a deposit to be paid—no problem, he said. They would most likely be arriving on the evening of the 24th, departing early the following morning, and they would require provisions.

He looked forward to the occasion, the feast they would hold. He wanted Miguel's and Maria's help coordinating everything. They would eat well, lavishly, making the most of the opportunity, before going further on into the forest. They would gather up their strength and enjoy themselves. Eat and drink till late, fill themselves all the way up, their laughter drifting out into the sounds gaining on them around and above the settlement buildings.

ON HIS LAST AFTERNOON, he went for one more coffee at Maria's. For the first time, really, in all of this—apart perhaps from the forensic work with Isabella—he felt he had support. They had evidence, in physical form—Carlos's image recorded, a range of approximate coordinates within which he could be found. The time had come to step back, change perspective, call on wider resources. The department could mount a comprehensive search of the area, after which there was no doubt that Carlos would be found.

He had earned time off, he thought, now that resolution was in sight. This, he decided, would be his final investigation. Surveying the last thirty years, this would count as one of the great restitutions. Missing persons cases were like fissures, breaks in the earth, and there was no greater feeling than a resolution, correcting the error, restoring the identity back to its place. The family could eat again, one day, at La Cueva. Whatever strangeness had caused this could be settled, the old order restored.

He made a note of all the things he would need to do once he was back home, the friendships he had neglected, the upkeep of his apartment. He would sort out his diet, eat with a greater focus on his health. There were many opportunities. He had been meaning to look up some old friends. He looked forward to resuming his regular life.

He continued thinking ahead. Once they had recovered Carlos, he would personally make the call to the mother. Although it wasn't advisable, or even feasible, that the family would come to Santa Lucía, he imagined it that way—Carlos being led out of the boat on the jetty, the relatives there, waiting. There would be hysteria, disbelief. They would want to touch him. They would admit that they had thought him gone, dead. Despite their claims, they'd believed there was no hope. But there he would be, helped out of the boat, dazed, thin, concussed, alive. They would tend to him on the flight back out, supply him with water and salt, maybe feed him through an intravenous drip. Arriving back in the city, he would be brought directly to the hospital, where they would thoroughly examine him, check for internal damage, any indication of possible long-term trauma caused by a blow to the head. The question of what exactly had happened to him, how he had come to be there in the forest, thousands of miles from home, wouldn't be raised until later. Not until his convalescence was complete and he could walk, digest food on his own, speak for himself.

The first person to hear the full story would be himself, the inspector. Everything would be confirmed to him privately, before being put on the record. All of the suspicions, rumours and the links would be settled.

He took another sip of coffee and looked briefly on to the settlement's facing edge. The huge ferns dipped and swayed; they were colossal, but each one also looked like a single leaf, diminishing him and the meagre buildings around. Not for the first time he wondered about scale, an error of perception. There was a lightness in his head and a turning, lifting sensation in his stomach. The coffee, the eggs—Maria brought him a glass of water at room temperature, quicker to digest. Composed, he looked again to the edge. If anything it appeared marginally closer—he must have shifted position slightly in his chair, leaned forward a little.

He reconfirmed, with both Alberto and Miguel, the schedule for the flight departing the following morning. He considered his experience on the outward journey, his almost manic state, and was amused by the difference. He had felt, coming in, a tremendous sense of excitement, a feeling, he had to admit, that he had never quite experienced before. It wasn't knowledge. Everything, at that stage, was being done in hope, in promise. But there had been, as he flew out over the grids of his home city, out past the part-constructed industrial estates of the suburbs and into the surrounding mountains, an extended sense of extraordinary anticipatory pleasure. And, he told himself, his instinct had been right. They had found Carlos. This was it, he said. This was the end of the investigation.

WHAT HAPPENED TO CARLOS
Suspicions, Rumours, Links

1. A cargo of chemical supplies—carbon, antimony, ruthenium, lithium, oxygen, silicon—stored on a vessel. The crew unaware of the purpose of the shipment or the nature of the organization listed to collect. A thirty-five-day crossing. Individual birds sometimes seen at dawn perched on the bow. A line of vast green turtles moving east below the translucent sea surface. The nearest shore—a single tiny, all but barren volcanic island—1,800 miles from the current position.

2. CARLOS: A sharp rise and dip, a venture just beginning, eagerly and with high expectations, before dissolving into failure and regret. The shape of the mouth opening widely, as if in astonishment, contracting into the low O shape, sound and silence.

3. A free man. A man at liberty. A man who has come free of his moorings.

4. A temporary euphemism hung upon a large amalgamation of disparate biological material, memory and feeling. The name attached as a country is assigned to a stretch of land and water—nobody is expected to believe that it is real.

5. THE INVESTIGATION: An indulgent and morbid fantasy created by a man in middle age in grief for his dead wife.

6. The playing out of the investigation, beginning with the first interview conducted by the inspector in La Cueva, was an elaborate production performed by an experimental theatre company, the large cast frequently changing, the performers aware to differing degrees of the artifice, ranging from the inspector, who knew of some of the fraud but was beginning to suspect more, to the workers in the office, fully aware, and terminating in Carlos, who had never existed.

7. Carlos was collected in a box in La Cueva on the 24th by two company representatives. He was taken out of the building via the emergency exit. The box was placed in the rear of a company car, driven eleven hours to port and loaded on to a container ship. The terminus was a mid-ocean island rich in minerals but having no resident population; quarry workers present three months a year. The box was placed inside the quarry. Rain was due in twelve hours and would degrade the lock on the box, allowing Carlos finally to get out. And it would fill the lower third of the quarry.

8. Among the products funded by the corporation was a partly synthetic bacterium that produced in its host an overwhelming desire for escape. This may or may not simply be a symbol representing the crushing effects of corporate life. Carlos killed himself in the bathroom of La Cueva; everything since is mythic sublimation and fantasy.

9. Due to an unknown personal catastrophe only retrospectively implied in analysis of his daily behaviour and performance in the workplace, Carlos decided to leave his family, his work, his city and embark on a pedestrian march to the centre of the continent.

10. The gastrointestinal infection implied in analysis of material found on his keyboard seized Carlos suddenly as he approached the bathroom door, arresting his heart and causing a fatal attack. The decision was made by the family, chiefly the mother, Maria, to refute the finality of his ending. Carlos's sudden vanishing was deemed temporary and an investigation launched with the express purpose of bringing him back. The mother did not believe that what was described in the initial survey of the scene—the death of her son—was credible, even possible, and so she challenged it. It was hoped, in the forest, that some sort of answer would be found.

11. Carlos shaved off his hair in a La Cueva cubicle with a razor and a handheld mirror. He hit his face repeatedly, puffing the eyes, nose and mouth to become unrecognizable, and walked away from his life.

12. Carlos remained sitting in his chair at the table in La Cueva, having never got up to leave for the bathroom. He was tied securely to the heavy chair, while everybody else—all members of his family, the entire staff, all other diners—left the premises, walking the short distance to a separate property owned by the Rodriguez family. The reproductions were already in place and all that remained was for the diners to carry their plates, glasses and knives. The sign was removed

from the original La Cueva and placed in the new restaurant. Carlos remained sitting in his chair at the table in La Cueva.

13. Carlos never, in fact, disappeared. The disappearance existed only on paper. In reality he returned from the bathroom and was present at the table when the first officer arrived to begin interviews. It being assumed that the disappeared person was not currently present and in full view, even cooperating with the enquiries, the issue was never explicitly addressed.

14. Carlos had been poisoned by the food prepared by an inexperienced member of the restaurant's kitchen team. Noticing him holding his stomach en route to the bathroom, the cook followed, retrieved the corpse and incinerated it on-site.

15. Carlos never entered La Cueva, sending instead a male of approximately similar age, height, weight and complexion. The replacement took care not to hold eye contact for more than three seconds, generally keeping his head bowed. The replacement, leaving the bathroom, shook off the mannerisms he had so far affected, walking differently, holding his head to a new height. Appearing to everyone present as a different person, the counterfeit walked out of the front door.

16. Carlos was never born to Maria, the foetus being miscarried seven months into term. The night in question at La Cueva had been created by Maria, in development with members of her family, as well as with several councillors and her parish priest. Maria publicly acknowledged the tragedy and mystery of what had happened to Carlos, collaborating with police, media and other institutions in an investigation into his absence.

17. The disappearance of Carlos was a simple matter of the earth swallowing his identity whole, overcoming in one moment the whole person, making him nothing.

18. A funny thing happened as Carlos closed the bathroom door. When he made a movement, instead of carrying on into the new present, he preserved his whole body—kept it frozen in one place—and made another, very slightly different one. When the new body moved it did so by halting, preserving itself, building another. This went on. It wasn't just large, macroscopic moves such as footsteps that resulted in preservation and re-creation; even small, infinitesimal frames like the twitch of a lip were copied, changed.

    A footstep was made of 4,000 small frames. There were 4,000 new creations when he moved his foot. He realized all this must have been taking up a lot of room and that there must also be a vast amount of resources fuelling all the new versions that were built.

    He was becoming aware of the building process in increasingly fine detail. It took longer and longer to do things. When he turned his head, neck and part of his left shoulder to look behind him, the process occupied around nine years. So many constructions had been made in that turn; he saw, in the corridor, a collection of mildly different identities each assuming a slightly changed shape.

    There was little space for air and light—between all the bodies were only thin drags of different colour. Above the height of them was an ordinary layer of upper-corridor. It made him think of being in a low-roofed swimming pool or an aquarium—though this wasn't water, at least not any more. From a greater distance it might have looked like a museum or a slaughterhouse. This was all going to take a very long time; the planning, supply and construction of movement was so great it barely seemed possible. It was very unlikely he would be able to see a person again.

19. Carlos—his domestic life, family relations, work, relationships, temperament and interests—was the result of a series of deep suggestions planted in the mind of a permanently incarcerated man undergoing experimental consolation therapy. The disappearance of Carlos was coincident with the prisoner waking up, the ongoing investigation into his whereabouts the grieving of the prisoner for the life he thought he had.

20. Carlos's official disappearance at La Cueva, aged twenty-nine, was the culmination of a long wish granted finally to him by a loving mother, who constructed the evening with the express purpose of allowing him the pleasure of a vanishing. As he saw it, the action of walking anonymously out of the building was only a long-delayed fulfilment of an agreement drawn up at birth—namely, that he didn't exist—and pretending otherwise, for the sake of appearances and certain administrative customs, had been a great strain on him.

21. Carlos suffered a sudden and giant molecular distortion. He became more fluid, loose, less detailed or recognizable. His hands were paddles, his eyes sewn up. He couldn't see anything, and gradually the part of him prone to reflection drifted further towards nothing, back inside the tree, deeper into the forest.

22. Carlos resumed his place at the table in La Cueva upon returning from the bathroom, and it was only after several minutes

that he realized none of the people around him were the same. He had become disoriented as he opened the bathroom door and, despite the fact that La Cueva was a smallish restaurant, he had turned the wrong way, leaving his family out of his line of vision, so that even when he realized he had sat down at the wrong place he couldn't initially see where his family was. Not wanting to make a scene, he stayed calm, slowly looked to his immediate surroundings. The number of people in the current party was approximately the same as his own, the meals, he noted—even the drinks—seemed to be in accordance with what he could remember of his family. The clothes worn by the people around him were quite familiar, just a little bit different. There seemed to be the same number of adults and children, male and female. He surveyed their faces. This was confirmation that his instinct was correct and that none of the people were the same; he didn't know any of them, their faces were all unreadable and blank and he hadn't set eyes on any of them before. Soon enough he would remember how to get to his own group, but until then, he thought, the safest thing was to carry on acting naturally, as if nothing were wrong.

Before long, the cicadas and the bullfrogs bellowed and he realized it had got dark. All the food had been eaten, the wine drunk, and people were preparing to go home. Most people, in fact, had already left, he saw, craning his neck, surveying the tables of La Cueva. He had begun to feel at ease in the company of the strangers. He didn't mind spending the major part of the evening with them. There had been a lot of drink, at his own party as well as in the strange one, and obviously that had played a part in proceedings—his family, evidently, had forgotten about him, and not for the first time. He wondered what had happened to the real occupant of his current seat, the person who was supposed to be there and who had originally ordered food and wine and begun the meal.

23. Attending to an urgent phone message received while Carlos was in the bathroom, the party left mid-meal, gathering all their things and exiting the building. As it was a busy night the restaurant staff wasted no time in clearing away all trace of the party, removing the plates, glasses, cutlery and half-empty wine bottles and in so doing knocking Carlos's jacket from the back of his chair onto the floor, where it lay unnoticed under the table. By the time Carlos had returned to his seat—seven minutes after he had first got up—a new party had not only been ushered in but had ordered their starters and begun drinking. Assuming he had become disoriented, slightly sheepish at doing something so childish, the kind of thing that would never have happened to any of the other men in his family, he made his way to the broad, front-facing window and turned back, inwards, hoping to gain a perspective on the whole of the restaurant floor.

    He saw nothing, no one, just a sea of unknown figures making their way through their meals.

    If he had turned the other way, however, and looked out of the windows of La Cueva, he would have seen, on the adjoining street, all the present members of his family leaving, walking away and carrying all of their things, talking animatedly. Past them—La Cueva was on a hill and offered interesting views over the city and on clear days beyond—he would have seen a suggestion of the surrounding mountains and thought how small and vulnerable his family looked in that landscape, and he would have run after them, calling 'I'm here! I'm here!'

24. It took him some time, adjusting his eyes to the dense light of the room, but Carlos, having exited the bathroom, finally realized what he was seeing. Everything had been petrified.

The interior of the food had collapsed; coats of fungi had generated and attracted blowflies. The red wine had dissolved into a thick, organic cake, writhing with moulting worms. The floor hummed with insects. Nothing could be seen through the broad front windows, meshed in larvae and web.

Dust fell in a slow, amber haze. The cloths draped over each of the tables had come apart, the material regurgitated.

Lastly, incredibly, were the bodies, to which he felt no kin at all.

25. When Carlos exited the bathroom he was stopped before he could find his seat. He had wandered absent-mindedly towards his table, only looking up when he noticed someone reaching out a hand. 'Excuse me,' the voice said, 'but you bear an extraordinary resemblance to a relative of ours.'

Carlos assumed his uncle was playing some odd joke on him, which was strange because the two had never enjoyed that kind of a relationship. But as he looked closer at his uncle, he realized that wasn't exactly who it was. In fact, he looked rather a lot like Carlos's cousin, Bernal, only considerably aged.

Looking out across the long table, he had the same feeling: these people were like decayed reproductions of his own family.

He obviously appeared confused, because the man smiled and gestured in an effort to demonstrate that the atmosphere should be light, there was nothing to worry about here. The man went on: 'My cousin, Carlos, disappeared in a similar restaurant, in an occasion just like this, twenty-two years ago. You look a lot like he did then. Maria,' he went on, 'I don't want to alarm you, but doesn't this young man look approximately as Carlos did, the last time we saw him?'

Maria, a very old woman, didn't seem to have heard. She wore thick glasses and was dressed in black.

'My name is Carlos,' he said. 'I was having a meal with my family, just like you said. I know you. I know your names.'

'You've been watching us, listening to our conversations. I don't know who's put you up to this, what kind of strange joke you think you're playing, but it's got to stop.'

'No, you don't understand: I'm your cousin, Carlos. I really am. I left for the bathroom five minutes ago, that's all. Look, here's my identification.'

He reached for his trouser pocket and remembered that his wallet was in his jacket. But his jacket was not on the seat where he had hung it. The seat was occupied by a woman he almost recognized—she had a name he couldn't quite place—and on the back of her chair was a grey cardigan.

He obviously gave the impression of being wounded, because the man, the one who looked like an older version of Bernal, but not quite Bernal's father, Andreas, said, 'Okay, tell me about myself. Tell me things you would only know if you really were Carlos, and not things that just anyone could have found out by eavesdropping or by interviewing friends and colleagues, researching my history.'

'I . . .' Carlos stumbled. 'We never really knew each other very well. We were never particularly close. We only really saw each other at weddings. But you are my mother's brother's son, Andreas's son, Bernal!'

Bernal, or the one who looked like Bernal, waited a couple of seconds before turning around, fixing the position of his chair again, straightening his napkin and resuming his meal, clearly disappointed. Something in his actions suggested it was not the first time this had happened; many people, perhaps dozens, hundreds, over the years and decades now, had pretended at one time or another to be Carlos. Now that he was finally here, really here, Carlos, it was too late and none of them would believe him.

26. Carlos returned six weeks after the disappearance, dizzy, gaunt, confused, walking back to his table at La Cueva, where the staff recognized him at once. There were jubilant scenes as the police and then the family descended on the restaurant. The matter of what exactly had happened was temporarily brushed aside— Carlos, for the moment, remembered nothing—and the family, newly resident in the suspended operations of the restaurant, celebrated. Carlos was taken under guard to the hospital, where his health would be restored, the story emerging in tandem with his convalescence.

The following evening, at precisely the same hour, Carlos walked through the double doors of La Cueva. The staff alerted the authorities at once, the owner a little irritated. Nobody was blaming Carlos, he said, to his head waiter, it is the police who can't be relied on to do anything. They can't find him, the owner went on, they continually disrupt our business, and then, miraculously, when he offers himself back they go and lose him again. It was incredible, but then, he said, they should hardly be surprised.

The police clerk still had him on hold. Eventually an officer's voice came on the line. 'There seems to be a misunderstanding,' she said. 'Carlos is under guard in the hospital. I've just had it confirmed.'

The second Carlos remained at the restaurant, and the following evening, on cue, Carlos returned through the double doors of La Cueva. The subsequent evening a space was reserved at the table for Carlos to inevitably come home to. The evening after that, the entire table was cleared, the word 'Carlos' written in concise script on a folded piece of magnolia card.

Carlos returned, again and again, filling up the restaurant. There were too many, soon enough, to know what to do with. La Cueva closed for business. The restaurant became a temporary shelter for many Carloses, who lived alone, suspicious of each other, but reliant on cooperation to survive. Each of them appeared identical, wearing a torn, folded white shirt, their faces thin and cut and smeared. They prepared food and cooked together in La Cueva, emptying the larder and the fridges and moving on to the carcasses stored in the basement freezer. Every evening, at the same time, they had to accommodate the presence of a further Carlos. They were not unaware of the problem. Soon enough there would be no space. They would run out of food. And then there would be nothing left but Carlos.

27. On 14 April 1832 the party rode on from Socêgo to a further estate on the Rio Macaé. The following morning they left the cultivated ground for uncut, Atlantic forest. Don Carlos noted the curvature of the fronds on the tree ferns. In the evening it rained and, despite the evidence of the thermometer, he was very cold.

Their party picked at a meal of rice, fish and coffee, while the rain hammered on the fronds above them.

After the rains, Don Carlos watched the spectacle of the rising evaporation. From the valleys the vapour rose up to the hills. The forest became obscured. Patches of the land floated in the general mist cover. He saw the white clouds rolling at speed, coming in to them. Soon, neither he nor his companions would be visible at all.

28. An atomic detonation, on the evening, locally, of the 24th, removed the Earth of its larger species. A fifty-six-year-old, semi-retired inspector was eating a meal alone in a hilltop restaurant when the explosion occurred. His body mass, along with that of his fellow diners, the waiting and kitchen staff, the parking attendant doing his rounds outside, the local population and everybody beyond was vaporized.

    His last external sight caught an anonymous male, mid-twenties, he thought, in the process of getting up from his seat, excusing himself as he left his party. His back was arched and he was pushing his chair in, tucked beneath the table to aid others walking by, when everything stopped. But the inspector did not see it that way. He found himself at home, in his apartment, with no recall of the restaurant, the meal, the other diners. He received a call from his immediate superior urging him to take a case, a current investigation that required his help. A male, twenty-nine, working in the corporate sector, had disappeared suddenly from a restaurant during a family meal.

    The inspector struggled in his work. There was something, he believed, not quite right. He felt a growing sound and pain inside him. The city was warmer than he had ever remembered it, with periods of extravagantly dense light, especially in early evenings. He had the suspicion something was going to burst. Although his wife had died some years previously, he had never felt alone like this. He came up, in the course of his investigation, against a series of dead ends, false leads, apparently pertinent discoveries that led nowhere, to nothing.

Nothing had ever been so enticing, so delicious, and yet so maddening and frightening, as the certainty that something momentous was pressing in on him and he was bound to discover it. In the meantime he was cautious, wary. He thought he heard voices and suspected that neither the people nor the fluid sets around him were real.

At a table directly across from the inspector, at 18.45 on the evening of the 24th, a thirty-four-year-old pharmacologist browsed the wine list, turning around an inch or two to converse with her partner, when the bomb detonated. She found herself at home, in her apartment, with no recall of the restaurant, the meal, the other diners . . .

29. Carlos isn't here. Carlos isn't gone. This isn't everything. This is a brief light.

VII

HE LAY IN THE dark a while longer, the sounds louder than he remembered. He didn't move and couldn't make out a thing. For the moment he didn't seem specifically located, just general in the sounds of the birds calling, water dropping, twigs breaking and the branches falling.

He was absorbed in his room, in a dark forest nest. The walls were thin, the exterior boards beginning to rot. Beyond that, circling the Terminación, covering it, was untouched forest.

The smell, he had learned, was fish. The farm had rotted and had not been cleared. Thousands of fish had bled into the mud. A tremendous waste. The stench drifted to the nearside of the Terminación, and, despite his acclimatizing, he remained conscious every morning of waking up inside it.

Miguel, reluctant as ever, almost seeming pained, had claimed it wasn't a simple matter. He sat on his stool, in the hut, drew on his cigarette again, said there had been a dispute about rent, tenancy and commission. The farmers in the end, in protest, had drained the pools dry and the fish writhed. It was unfortunate, he agreed.

'But this smell,' the inspector said. 'Don't you mind this smell?'

He hoisted himself up and felt for the lamp, then watched the room assemble. He walked to the toilet, came back, lit the canister and heated some water. He had risen early, had some time still before the flight out. While the water boiled, he cleared the small desk by the bed and positioned the upturned bucket as a chair. He poured the water into a tin mug and mixed in powdered soup, then prepared some tea. He unwrapped his half-packet of dried biscuits, preserved by newspaper tied with an elastic band. Sitting down in the dim room and facing the wall, low against the desk, he ate slowly, every crunch of the biscuit amplified, every slurp of his tea and soup louder.

He brushed crumbs off his thighs, grey in the lamp. His singlet was slack on his chest. His arms were as thin as a child's. He tensed and felt the discs protruding from his back. He imagined a warmth expanding into heat and agony as the head and the neck were bent, the back pressed too far, the spine snapped.

He wiped the desk clean and rinsed the containers. He remembered enjoying simple, basic actions such as this on the first days of convalescence after fever as a child. Those were the longed-for days when he didn't want anything else, just this, his health. In all the days before the convalescence, he'd gazed, stunned, at the prospect of a blank morning. Just the ability to move, see, listen. He was light from lack of food, uncertain, curious. His thinking was slow, wide and lavish, every word a new colour, and he was grateful, a kind of happiness.

THE RECEPTION WAS VACANT. Miguel was rarely at his desk, but you could normally count on one or more of the children playing, sitting momentarily, leaping from place to place, and, after enough prompting, one of them would eventually fetch the man. He wanted to reconfirm arrangements, just one more time. It was imperative that sufficient accommodation and provisions be arranged.

He waited.

The desk drawers were ajar, the calendars and accounts laid out for anyone to see. Someone was in trouble—the place had been left quite insecure. The door was propped open, all the shutters too. Light flooded in. Miguel would angrily chase the children when he found them. He was always having to sweep the floor of leaves, sticks, extract the moths from the walls and sluice a bucket of water through the ant columns. The children, several days ago, had told him what the ants would do. With typical exaggeration, Miguel's son informed him they would spread throughout the building and go under all the doors. They would go through his things: his boots, his rucksack, but they would not stop at the floor. They would climb the legs of the furniture, a live stream of several hundred thousand animals. Moving in lines, the ants looked like autonomous stitching, only they were working backwards, taking things apart. The girl added that he should check under his bedsheets before he lay down at night. They had run off, Miguel appearing, cursing them, and the inspector had laughed.

It was quite unlike Miguel to leave everything open like this. Still no sign of the children. He trailed back up the stairs, into the corridor. He knocked on the filmmakers' doors. 'Alberto? Luis?' No matter how much they drank, the filmmakers were always up and working early. Must have gone especially early this morning. They would be out recording one last time, filming final footage, gathering establishing shots, continuity.

The reason, he thought, he could hear the birds particularly clearly this morning was because of an absence of the thoughtless sounds typically made by the other guests rising: chairs loudly dragging on the old wooden floors, gumboots clomping back and forth, insistent voices calling to one another with no regard for those who might still be asleep. He had always cursed them, muttered to himself in his own room as he tried to doze. But it was strange, now, without them. He would have liked to have known what was going on.

He walked back to his room and opened the door. His case stood up on the floor, where he had left it, his coat—a stupid idea, of course—carefully folded across the handle. His folders, his change of footwear, the underwear and spare shirts that he had washed with suds in a bucket in his bathroom and hung out the front on a hammock, it was all there, in his single leather case, neatly packed. He was surprised suddenly by how little he carried.

As he always did the day of a departure, he wondered whether he'd forgotten anything. He patted his trouser pockets, felt the jangle of his keys, his wallet. Everything was there, it was all in order. Travelling, and especially by air, always unsettled him. It didn't matter how excited he was or the extent of the planning that had gone into it, how sure he was of his actions, he felt a kind of nervous dread. It was illogical. Once he was up in the air everything would be fine. He could enjoy the view of the forest one last time, making notes, directing the order of all the tasks he had to attend to back home. It was good. He had reason to be excited.

He sighed loudly in the hall, as if expecting it to draw comment. He looked about him as he turned the key a final time, his coat over his shoulder, the light case in his left hand. He headed back downstairs, certain that the children would materialize to tease him one last time before he left.

The inspector passed through the front door of the Terminación, propped open with a brick, and walked out into unusual sunlight. It was never clear, in Santa Lucía, where the sun was, but he could even believe it was the middle of the day. That noise. A loud serenity. The river still. And the settlement completely deserted.

He was being dramatic. The place wasn't deserted. Of course not. He had simply come out of the hotel at a time when most of the residents were indoors, eating breakfast or otherwise at work just out of view. On the other side of upturned boats, standing, smoking, concealed in doorways, swimming, even, and momentarily submerged. But the river was unclean, oil-filled. He could see no smoke, hear no motors, no hammering. The labourers' camp was still. He waited just outside the hotel. There was a worrying absence of smell. Coffee, gasoline, baked bread. Nothing.

He walked directly to Miguel's hut. The one person, he thought, that he could count on to be there. He knocked, paced outside, then knocked louder. Miguel had no window on his hut. 'Miguel!' he called out. Was he being ridiculous? There was no answer, so he pushed open the door.

Dust motes circled the air, lit from the doorway. The hut was warm and seemingly unchanged. The worktops, the wooden chairs and boards were still stained by oil and burned by battery acid. The severed connections, the brush copper of broken wire ends and exposed parts, remained laid out, waiting to be put together into a functioning whole. But Miguel was absent. Where, then, was he, if not here or the hotel?

He strode to Maria's, his head down, muttering curses; he had no time for any of this. As he swung past the dust-covered windows, he glimpsed tables laid and filled. The depth of his relief surprised him. He really had been getting worked up.

He walked in and the café was empty. It had been carefully set up that morning, he was sure of it, not long ago at all, but there were no people there. Instead there were half-eaten breakfasts, mugs with coffee lining the bar. Should he, he thought, check under the stained, long white cloths hanging from the tables—impossible to clean, Maria had said, although he hadn't noticed until then—even walk behind the service counter, where people could be crouching?

He paused before entering the kitchen, sure he would find at least

Maria and that he would then have to apologize, really, for trespassing, going behind the service line.

Where was she? He came here every day, same time. She brought him his order, didn't even have to ask.

He'd wait a little longer, just a few minutes, for her to come.

He stood by the counter, tapping the wood, blood pounding in his ears.

He picked up a mug, still warm. The coffee couldn't have been prepared more than twenty minutes earlier. Definitive proof that they were all still there, around him. He was beginning to suspect that Maria had organized this trick, this prank. She enjoyed acting, after all. Perhaps it was some game, a kind of present before he left. It would have been a good sign, really, proof of how well he had integrated into the community. They were doing it all to mark his leaving. A lot of thought had gone into it. But he shouldn't assume just yet that it was all for his benefit. There were plenty of other explanations. Very rarely, he had heard, animals approached the settlement. There may have been a sighting, something spectacular, something to draw them out. He didn't understand why no one had thought to alert him. It didn't seem fair. He would have the point clarified with Maria or Miguel on their return. They were both quite aware of his interest in the natural world; surely they knew how much he would have enjoyed the sighting, how much he missed it now he wasn't there?

The coffee went cold; from lukewarm to cold in the brief time that he had spent waiting. They had to be there, just out of view, even around the settlement's edges.

As he approached the double doors he realized he'd delayed. The longer he spent in the café, the more likely the settlement was to be repopulated. He felt through the soles of his feet and the thin rubber of his boots the impression of dozens of them making their way back in, resuming their familiar places and carrying on with their daily work. There was an all but palpable pressure on the ground, the faintest suggestion of a sway, a gentle tip in the incline as the people landed. He tried not to smile. A momentary appearance of erasure, that was all. People indoors at their desks, bent at work, or standing, heads bowed, arms to the sides, in colours particularly suited to the surrounding vegetation. With their skin concealed, there was nothing to offset them from the forest, there was no reason he should necessarily have seen them, really. He pushed open the doors, smiling.

Santa Lucía remained deserted.

He traced every single building and he knocked on every door. The windows were open, the doors unlocked, and he was surprised to see how unclean the rooms were, how much evidence there was that the outside was encroaching. He was really beginning to worry. Where were the filmmakers? He couldn't miss his flight out. Everything had been arranged, all the plans had been put into place, and they were on the cusp, now, of recovering Carlos. It couldn't fall down now, it couldn't.

He was still reluctant to call out. When he did he felt young, foolish. He was meek and unconvincing, the voice insufficiently urgent. He was suppressing alarm. The area no longer had phone coverage; messages were brought in by traders. And if he did have access to communication, what would he say? He shouldn't risk greater embarrassment—he had detected, already, a creaking in his calling voice. It was too early to panic. Whatever was going on—and there would be a simple, natural explanation—it would be revealed soon enough.

Should he take a boat? Had they moved upstream en masse? Perhaps something innocent had been organized and they had simply forgotten to let him know. He had retired early the previous evening, determined to sleep well before the journey out. He could have missed something. Equally, it was possible the date was significant, a point marked annually or even once a decade. A festival, a celebration or a mourning, something that couldn't be casually explained to an outsider. The community was participating in the festival. Something with costumes, repetitions, a suspension of disbelief.

He still doubted it. But whatever had happened—and he would find out eventually, he had to, and it would almost have been worth it, worth this distress, to know—they had to have gone somewhere.

He had a distinct feeling, over his shoulder, that he was being watched. The only thing stopping him turning around was fear of humiliation. It may yet have been a game. He couldn't give them what they wanted, couldn't have them doubled over with laughter at him. He should do his utmost to remain composed. It was conceivable that, as he entered one building, moved from one zone to another, they coordinated their own movements to remain hidden. They would be pulled, tied by thread, so that his movement produced an opposite force in them. He would never see them. The discipline was remarkable, especially in the children.

He made his progress irregular in an attempt to catch them out. Knowing the area so much better, they were at an advantage. They were around him, he could sense it. Although they kept quiet, they still had to open and close their mouths to breathe, move their limbs to keep out of sight. He felt the cloud of their breath and the swish of their procession. He would wait them out. Nobody was better at it. Eventually, they'd lose discipline and the theatre would fall.

How much food had they brought? Had they planted water and meat stores in pits in preparation? How big was this?

It escalated. He couldn't help himself. He took everything back further, all the way to the beginning. He had been guided here. It had all been set up, right from the start. He was naive in believing he had discovered the route himself, linking Carlos, the corporation and the forest. It had all been planted, mapped out in advance. There had been so many clues—how could he not have noticed it? The laughter, now, at his expense. None of it had been real, none of it authentic. The events were coordinated to bring him here, to this. The interviews inside the corporation, the actors portraying the family. Even the reports. The doctored microbiology, Isabella acting under instruction, reading out confabulated data relating to non-existent flora in a body, Carlos, she had never in reality studied. He had sensed something strange, once or twice, in her manner. The sound of her voice on the telephone. Unusual pauses as she expressed herself. She had wavered. She had almost given in.

But she had held firm, allowing him to make the inevitable discoveries leading to the forest. It didn't seem conceivable, now, that he had been so foolish, so naive as to believe in the authenticity of the investigation and the autonomy of his own role.

He imagined them carrying plants, quick-growing crops, cassavas, peanuts. They could establish another settlement before moving on again, always provisionally. But he was rushing ahead. He had to think carefully, realistically. They had not gone far. Chances were they were all around. There was room under the earth. It wouldn't take long to dig out pits, shafts concealed by surface turf. They could live there, assuming their provisions were in place, as long as the air held. They would be laughing at him now, under the soil.

He looked up to the swaying perimeter trees. A vertical solution, moving either above or below, was more likely than a horizontal one. It would be instant. Without having to travel, they could achieve a sudden and total vanishing.

There was something about the coffee, the meals unfinished on the café tables, that conflicted with the dirt, the evidence of the outside found in the homes. Something artificial in the picture, staged. The suggestion of recent activity in the café seemed contrived. Someone, a single individual, must have set it up, thus allowing all of the other residents to leave earlier, perhaps in the middle of the night.

Hadn't he woken differently, hungrily, and with the feeling of having only just recovered? Perhaps he had slept longer than a night. Some soporific fed into his food, putting him out. The rest of them ferried away, in boats and in several light aircraft, many journeys. The single other person—he wished he could picture them—remaining, maintaining the heat of the half-drunk mugs, the appearance of freshness in the bread and the eggs, waiting for him to wake, before slipping out to join the others, wherever they were, whoever they were.

He intersected the clearing, walking absurdly, stiff joints moving his limbs awkwardly. He returned to Maria's café and took bread and fruit from the kitchen, not wanting to interfere with the meals laid out on the tables. He gulped water, sat at his usual place and tried to be calm. His reaction to the situation, the theories he was generating, proliferating, was not a positive sign. Paranoia, egomania. He would have identified the symptoms instantly in anyone else. Rationally, none of it could be true. He should do his best to ignore the current evacuation and everything would return to normal. When Santa Lucía was repopulated he would be told what had really happened and it would be remarkable, amazing, he could enjoy it. It would have been worth it.

He should continue to walk into the forest, press ahead. Acting as if nothing had changed, he would not be so surprised when he found that was the case. One day he would return and find Santa Lucía active, full of hammering and calling, food, oil and gasoline. Everything would be restored and it would be the most natural thing in the world.

VIII .

HE DID NOT LOOK forward to the night. He concentrated on food preparation and on having sufficient light. He walked cautiously and kept to his own room in the Terminación. Wind picked up after dark and he had forgotten to do his routine checks on the shutters and doors. He heard them whipping in the pre-storm breeze, clattering against the walls. He withdrew further into his own room, pleading, but he knew he couldn't stand it. He struck the lamp, dressed, and left the hotel. In the dark it wasn't clear that Santa Lucía had been created. There was little suggestion of anything having been done. A town here—not even a town, a village, a temporary settlement—required a lot of work. You had to take so many things away first, day after day, making space. And now, in the dark, all the work was gone. He could not make out the clearing. He had no sense of depth. As soon as he left the hotel, he put his hands out in front of him, although he knew the path and should have been quite familiar with it, shouldn't have had to think. He expected at any moment to walk into the trees. The shutters and doors crashed against the wood walls, startling him every time, because he saw nothing, he couldn't establish where they came from.

He wondered if the evacuation would be noticeable to anything else: if animals could detect the new absence of life, the plunder they could have with just him left.

He wanted to return to the hotel, to his room. But he had to close all the shutters and doors. He had barely started. If he were to do it properly, he would be there all night, walking from one empty building to another. But it was important.

He couldn't leave the place to rot. In all likelihood the residents would return soon, any minute now, after the interruption, and the buildings must be ready for them to resume their lives. He had to ensure each of the buildings remained in a fit and habitable state, indefinitely. It didn't matter how impossible it sounded, how meek his efforts seemed; he had to try.

They were important places, really. He still silently apologized on the threshold of each new door he entered, each room he intruded upon. The last thing he wanted was for a child to return and find their room caved in, as if all their time living there had counted for nothing. He didn't want that sort of message to come across, so he continued. Everything exactly as it was, ready indefinitely.

The rain started and things dissolved faster. He chastised himself for not working harder in the day and the early evening. Especially when the wind had started picking up and it had become clear what was blowing in. He had spent too much time waiting, deferring, as if nothing would expire.

The storms these nights were so bad that he could imagine nothing remaining in the morning. When he woke in his room, parted the curtains to the soft light, opened the shutters to the gentler, instructive sounds of birds calling and the forest reshaping, he was amazed. A slow fracture into light. A morning, a simple morning, was not a continuation of anything. It was wholly new and wrought. It stunned him, inexplicable.

The first thing he did daily was inspect the hotel, the largest of the buildings, for damage and infiltration. He had to prioritize. He cleared and fixed what he could, opening out the shutters and the doors to give the dampness a better chance of drying. His original idea had been to leave everything as it was for the repopulation, but then he saw how impractical that was. Food was the biggest problem, the greatest provocation to the wild. The rot, the damp mould, approached like a predator. He had no option but to burn organic things. He dug a pit and piled in what he could and what he thought would be the first to rot (old food, surplus food that he couldn't store with the generator broken, bright cotton clothes still hanging up, rows of fetid shoes arranged in lines by front doors), took matches from the café and set the pit ablaze, sizzling it in river water when he thought enough had been destroyed.

He carefully washed the plates and cups, still turning around, still expecting Maria's dismissive laughter, and positioned them on the café tables exactly as they were, just right for the following morning's meal. He wanted to be there, in the clearing, when they came, see them slip back into position at the tables, ready for food. In their absence, he would have been an adequate custodian.

He was still delaying, deferring. His previous weeks in Santa Lucía had been spent preparing for and investigating the prospects of a journey east, into the approximate region where the figure had been sighted. Though there was nothing now to stop him going, he had, immediately following the evacuation, established a new routine, inspecting and cleaning the buildings, sweeping the clearing of storm-spread bush and floods, preparing his food for the day, collecting and filtering water from the river. He needed to stop.

Standing just outside Maria's he looked around. He was close, so he couldn't be certain, but he thought there was a chance the settlement had changed, in however little time had passed since the evacuation. Living in it so closely, at completely the wrong scale, really, he hadn't noticed anything until now. But it *had* changed. The lines were no longer clear.

His food supply diminished. He should have been better at rationing. If he had really thought about it, what he would have done was eat half-artificially and half-naturally: half, that is, from the community's existing supplies and half collected from the forest. That way he could slowly and imperceptibly change the ratio in favour of wild food gathered directly by himself. The process would have taken a reasonable period of time—years even—giving him plenty of opportunity to adapt.

Now, however—and he was not really certain how long had passed, how much time—he was going to have to make a radical change in food. He needed to go further, spend longer in the forest.

IX

HE COULDN'T MAKE OUT the sun. He hadn't found a compass in any of the buildings and in thirty minutes he was lost. He turned, facing identically bewildering views. There were few flowers in the minimal sunlight. It rained. He examined vines, huge—a foot thick and wide—when he realized it was actually a separate tree, twined around the principal tree, without root in the ground. He would like to have asked Isabella: Was he seeing things? Was this real? He couldn't tell if it was killing the tree and how long the process might take. But it was ruthlessly clawing, desperately shooting upwards; here, barely a mile, he reminded himself, from the settlement.

Each new day he got a little further. He lived in the settlement now only in darkness. He ate berries, roots, any soft fruit. He left earlier and returned later and the only thing limiting his progress was that he kept coming back. His legs convulsed in the night, cramped and buckled from the increasing distances of the marches.

The damp, dim forest, fat and bursting and loud, had its own light. He saw a small bird in the early evening perched upright on a branch thinner than his smallest finger. Its eyes were closed and it remained perfectly still, not reacting to his artificial presence. This was such a different form of sleeping that he wanted to laugh. When he did, the branch perceptibly but gently moved and the bird's eyes opened. He was inches away. He turned, embarrassed.

There was the grey and green melt everywhere, the fungi and the plants. Huge, wild banana fronds amazed him. Patches of low-lying mist in the morning, silver light filament. He loved these. This light was different every day, dependent on the filter of the current canopy, the cloud cover, the temperature and humidity. He saw a pile of thin sticks creating a thatched effect that reminded him of house-building; a coral snake, brilliantly bound in coloured strips, laid coiled with its fingernail-head exposed at the edge; a hole the width of a man and three foot deep, rampant, when he looked in, with black glimmering insects. Most of all he sensed peripheral activity, the sweep of cooler air in a near wing unfolding, the snaps of a mammal ascending a tree.

Verdure changed at the edges. At any one moment he could see no more than a few feet away. He tried to be aware at all times. Trees came down softly, in slowly resisted falls, one small piece at a time like shavings from a carving. He was present in a vast informa-tion exchange and he read what he could in the light. Thorns and spikes snagged at his clothing and his skin as he lost blood passing through the trees.

His instinct was to keep returning to Santa Lucía, even though it was empty and there was less of it every day. The recurrent idea, late each afternoon as he turned west again to the settlement, was that the community would reappear. He couldn't help it. The idea rang in his head like an insistent and irritating refrain.

Even walking short distances, he became infected. He came out in red blotches and at first he thought it was the air until he saw them, the red ants: *las hormigas de fuego*. He itched and burned, but when he went to wipe them, nothing was there, only the feeling of bodies walking all over him. When he broke the bites, he bled. He thought they were weaving him backwards, threading him out into a long line of numbers. Prophylactic oils rolled on to his body had little effect. In the mornings, before setting out, he would tie the lower ends of his trousers in an effort to prohibit the leeches. But when they fasted they could disappear and they penetrated cloth. He forced himself to limit foot checks to one an hour, removing quantities of slugs fattened on his blood. They broke off full, hanging on leaves like ripe bruises.

He was cutting plant stems, getting water to wash the blood from his feet. He attended to a large blister irritating him between two toes. He rubbed at it, rolled a leaf to fit the groove and stop the toes touching. There was something small and white on the ground: a tiny scrap of paper, attached to a dead ant. He studied it: the paper was thin, with a loop like a lowercase, cursive *a*.

He'd brought nothing with him and was sure no one else had been here in some time. Looking closer, he saw it was a natural emission, something that had come from the animal. The fact it was still there suggested it was fresh. He broke it off and tasted fungus. Why hadn't the ant been stripped and eaten? He knew they lived by scent, issued instructions in code, read by antennae. A decaying ant sprayed with the right pheromone would be protected by kin, like primate mothers carrying the flat furstring of a dead infant for weeks until it all but ran to nothing; one in every ten thousand sat up, opened its eyes.

When he turned back he always felt adrenalin. He tried to suppress smiling at the thought of the repopulation. A great welcome, a celebration and a feast. His pace quickened, he pushed on. He couldn't wait to hear what everybody said. However much he was getting to enjoy collecting fruits and establishing paths, he still thrilled at the prospect of the return.

There was a certain point in the forest where the settlement, as a block structure on the edge of a clearing, became visible. He always paused there and deferred his arrival. Building up levels of anticipation until he could face it no more, he ran back to the always empty place. He marked the viewing point, tied a white handkerchief across a thick stem. The next day he stopped there, looked west, saw nothing. Twenty paces further he could see something, not obviously Santa Lucía, certainly not distinctly the flat-roofed Terminación building. He had the sense again of being watched, toyed with. Someone picking up the handkerchief and replanting it every day. He found the handkerchief again. The trees and plants were familiar; he had even, some time ago, hacked into one and the scar remained. This was the spot. Santa Lucía was getting further away.

The buildings themselves and their features—shutters, doors—shrank. The settlement was lowered into the ground. It looked like a cluster of wrecked and sunken cabins. The houses were simple affairs of plywood and woodchip boards, resin-sealed. Corrugated iron sheets and thin concrete. The wood rotted and the nails rusted off. The lime mortar crumbled and the concrete evaporated. The few glass windows cracked and shattered under the stress of the sliding walls and sinking roofs. Lizards and birds nested and chewed holes in the gables, which fell in. Birds and rats infested what was left of the kitchens. He stood in what had been the clearing and tried to see it happen, the live disintegration of this place, but all he saw were the effects. Plants took root in the moist fabric of beds and pillows. He was helpless and fascinated. It wasn't just the buildings—there were boats, stoves, tables, chairs, desks, uncountable other domestic objects. He wanted to see where they would go, couldn't imagine how it would be done.

He came back each day to less. He had given up the Terminación and his room and now slept under a loose sheet hung on branches. His own possessions had been lost. The shutters shivered and disintegrated, the doors fell inwards and the ruin accelerated. Trees sprouted and took root in the walls and floors. These were sketches, outlines of buildings only. The direction of the vegetation moved outwards, from the buildings' interior. He had worried about infiltration, contagion, parasites, but the buildings had erupted from something inherent, burst open from the centre out, blooming in new vegetable cores.

Paint dulled to grey and stripped to nothing. Purple bougainvillea thorn spread throughout the ex-reception of the Terminación. Metal washed out in rain and drifted through the trees and wildflowers. He saw copper tints in new giant ferns, each frond exceeding the height of his body.

He entered what had been the café and stepped through the rotten wooden floor as if into a river. The floor was webbed in larvae, worms and purple-black beetles. He dragged his feet forward without raising them and found he dug long, brief lines through the water-wood. The smell was incredible. He would have said he was in the body of something that was changing state. The lifted roofs were vast and uncertain, stretching out to the trees and the canopy.

He saw identical pieces of cloth several miles apart, torn by plant growth, lifted, carried by birds.

He tried to remember what had happened here, specific events that he could tie to concrete places. He looked for correlations between memories and the colossal wild drifts. Evidence of the people in the places they had been. Sometimes, curled in resistance to a storm night or after a couple of hours' sleep late in the day, he would soften and think that the colour and the glow of the new plants were of course directed by the feelings of the people who had lived there. That something had happened with chemistry. He smiled, amazed and consoled, at the purple and the orange excess.

He was still reacting to the changes in his diet. He suffered flux.

His thoughts seemed to go on for longer, single ideas stretched out. The sound in the new forest was louder without words. There was less of him and he scouted for parts of the new vegetation reminiscent of his character. He hunted for his loyalty, his lurid sentimentalism, irritability, the blind and contradictory optimism he never understood. Those places, if he found them, may have explained the nature of the substitution, the logic of the depopulation. They would show him where he was going. He searched for the chemistry outside, evidence of his family line and all his memories, stained in the leaves, but the little shelter he had improvised, a kind of nest of ferns that he rolled up in, implied only his shape, despite the hours and hours that he had lain there, dreaming.

Nothing distinguished the buildings from the forest. The world continued. He abandoned sheet and cover. His boots had rotted and splashed off. His body was cut and stained and he was uncertain if some parts were clothed.

He had to twist and cut vines above and below just to move. He couldn't see sky. Nothing was familiar. He had no indication of direction. East and west, interior or coastline. It didn't seem to matter. He ought to have been stunned, he thought.

The repopulation would fail. They had waited too long. Wherever they were, whatever had happened, there was no way of ever coming back. And it was his fault.

Now he dreaded the return. The worst thing that could happen was for the community to attempt to come back. He had cut a thin tunnel east, but the forest filled it every day. There was no way for any of them to come back. He lay listening to all the noises of the night, terrified at the suggestion of slow footsteps, at the thought of their return. Branch ends slicing them, tearing up their clothes and skin. Animals gorging on open wounds. The community, only the faintest trace of life left, crawling through the forest floor, their hair alive, their throats stuffed with earth. Arriving finally at the site, the place where they had lived, they would see that everything had gone. Their space had been removed. There was no room, any longer, for any of them to live.

They would look to him.

It was so stupid of me, he would say, you'll never believe this, but I actually thought you were all gone! You really had me convinced! I don't know how you did it. At first I was sceptical, naturally enough, but after enough time I turned. You really did it. You had me convinced, you know—each of you—that you had gone to the forest and I would never see you again. I'm sorry. I'm really sorry. I know how bad it sounds, how quick I was to turn, to give in. I thought it was just me left. I really thought you were gone, that you would never come back.

I should have been faithful. I should not have turned. It's just that so long had passed, so much time, that I thought I had no other option. All I could see around me was the forest. Even your things had gone. Despite my best efforts to preserve everything, to be a custodian, I was inadequate, and in time everything vanished. The forest reclaimed it all.

What I am about to say is the worst thing I have ever been guilty of. But there came a point, in fact, when I did not want you back. When I dreaded nothing more than your coming back. So much time had passed, you see. I wouldn't know what to say, anymore. I wouldn't know what to do. Besides, everything else had gone. The space and the objects. I can't believe I'm saying this.

I used to imagine you coming back, looking for your chair, looking for the table, looking for our bed. And finding nothing was left. Finding there was no room. I would think when I slept under the sheet and heard branches snap that you were coming, looking for space. You were confused, seeing the ruins, seeing how changed and overgrown all this was. I imagined you finally making it through—your face, your skin, your shape all but destroyed by the effort. You approached me. And I was terrified, after all this time.

She put a fingertip to his mouth to quieten him, then turned away, thin blue rags hanging from her last dress. The inspector himself was torn, his hands lapping blood. He was a storm of liquid. His wife crawled away, she did not turn her head back, she moved further into the forest, and he fell.

X

IT WORKED ITSELF OVER, damp and wide with different surfaces, many voices. Came in, came out. Pieces fell off into the
ground, pieces were added. Breathing, nesting.

Singing in the night and in the morning, making more of it,
working itself over, stretching on and webbing out. Breathing, nesting, singing together, falling and being added. Light touching at the
top. Matter feeling broad light and bursting, seeing, becoming eyes.
The sunrise, the steam of breath breaking, the forest emerging.

He came down from the trees and raised his head. He put forelimbs on the ground, pointing forward. His hindlimbs bent at the
midpoint, lifting the posterior slightly. He moved like this and the
loose bones stood. He remained in place. He ate and slept. He saw
light, then colour. He continued sleeping in trees, a new one every
night, as a precaution. He could smell himself, how strong it was.
He wrote this code throughout the forest, for any living thing to
read. He went to water where he could, but was unable to rid himself of the smell.

He enjoyed water. He ate more, still and moving things. He
heard them call: distress, alarm.

He reached with a forelimb for a fruit. The angle and height of
the branch required him to lift his head to take it. His other fore-

limb had naturally raised in a parallel. His spine was close to vertical and, although his calves strained with the weight, he held and stood.

The new height of the head, as he walked, took him away from most of what he ate. He was not so quick and the plane of the world was distorted, but he could see better. He was no longer living from the centre. When he moved he couldn't see his body, only a smear of skin over his nose, some dirt collected near his eyes. It felt like when he cleaned himself in larger pools. It felt like he was weightless, floating on water. He was unsafe, his position less secure. He had to be very careful, especially with his nose weaker and further from the ground, but also because he was less adept at sensing the world behind him. He was vertical where earlier he had been distributed, his head raised, but the bulk of his body extending horizontally. Like that, the hair on his hindlimbs had been sensitive to changes in pressure indicating noise or breath. Like that, he had felt things coming and he'd remained alive.

He got better with forelimbs. He didn't need them to walk, so he carried. He took good plants. Then he carried branches that helped him forge ahead. He still heard things moving by the way the quicker air rose from the ground up through his feet, and he turned in time. He was better at hunting, using his hands, his sticks. He ate larger things and felt less tired. He was starting to think about things that weren't this, here and now. Good things that had happened before, and warnings. He had to focus—smell, taste—so he didn't float away into old things and imagined rewards. Dreams. Everything was bigger, wider and amazing. He saw details and colours clearer. He had to focus to see through excess. When he looked, there was what he saw, but also what it might have been before and could become.

He wanted protein. He wanted more of life.

When he saw things that weren't there he grew hungry. He had a taste for eating life. His shoulders were stronger and broader, helping him look up. He repeated actions that led to pleasure and avoided those that hurt.

When he rested he saw lots of things. He always woke hungry. He understood that he had been hurt. He had lived in trees and moved on all limbs. It had taken a long time. He felt more comfortable floating. Particularly when he rested, he saw things indirectly. He saw lots of pictures he didn't understand. Big things walking slowly, resting with their backs up and legs out in front and singing like birds into each other. He didn't know why they were singing like that, like birds, close into each other. It must have been helping them stay alive, receiving that breath. It looked like reward, pleasure. Not a thing to fear. He saw one of them more than others. Around them were too many things he no longer knew. He sometimes saw the face of one, at night, when he rested. At other times he saw only the arms, held out before the eyes, reaching towards him, a skin that he could almost smell. He put his own arms out, but nothing was there.

HE HEARD LOUD SOUNDS directly over him, thumping, pulsing, vibrations shaking through him. He was in danger. It was better to be still and small in the trees until they passed. They pressed on the ground, moving as he moved, without forelimbs. He saw them: tall things expressing birdsong through their mouths, like the things he saw when he rested, only these ones did not feel safe. They would smell him where he lay. He breathed shallow breaths down into his chest and was calmed by the dark extension of his body into the trees.

They called and called. Their voices and their limbs waved the trees, the branches, the leaves around and covering him.

I thought I saw him. I thought we had him. He was right here.

Hello?

Wait. Let's sit here. We have to wait a while.

You saw him? You're sure?

Yeah, I think so. I saw something, heard something, and then it was gone.

XI

ANTS MOVED IN A line like sound. When there were lots of them together they had been told something. They heard through vibrations above their bodies that felt good or bad, then they moved in reaction. He picked them, had them moving separately over his palm, and listened to lines of them moving on his tongue.

When he woke he felt difference, origin. Light on him, information, warmth on his skin. Something that drifted away with the forest and came back in strange clarity every day. It was not constant. He ate before it went again. He looked for water, drinking what he could and imagining enough of it that it would be all he could see, covering the forest, drowning the trees and everything in them.

He thought of stepping into, then becoming almost weightless in the water. His own head breaking the water surface, covered by thick leaves and painted leaves, water that flooded his ears and his nose and open mouth and which he dreamed of every time he woke, every time it came back. Sometimes when it was getting dark he could watch the forest disappear and look up; he imagined a great and unobstructed distance and knew that he had felt it before.

He was remembering a little more each day. Something had happened and he had almost died. Every day he felt different. He was hungry and there was somewhere he needed to get to, somewhere outside the forest. There was something he needed to do.

HIS SKIN FELT DRY and unhealthy and his gums bled. His teeth were loose. He was grazed by the arms of trees and when he swam he was lit ablaze. He sensed ripples, disturbances in the black pool of stagnant water, so he got out and continued. He had been walking since the morning and the light was fading, the growth around him was dense and renewing, working itself over again and again. He smelled the rot turning, the old life engulfed, converted, raised.

He stopped when it was dark and he couldn't see his hands, and then he lay by an enormous tree and was surprised how quickly he tired despite the sound of the insects' horn and the birds' clamour. In the morning he ate leaves and drank from the river. Again he felt something moving in it, so he left, trying to follow the direction of the first light, the place it came from. He knew this was right, good; he should listen to whatever it was that woke him, follow where it came from.

He walked with a stick held out to point, move straight always in the direction of the light source. But he came against pools he couldn't cross and banks of earth he couldn't climb. He stopped, looked back. Nothing was different, he couldn't see himself anywhere.

He went back, sometimes far, tried for another way through, trying to picture the light source, go on in a new direction. Everything was green. He saw the same places again and stopped, looked back, looked forward. He lay in the sticks; everything would go away. But when he did this he remembered waking, the light source, and felt bad about stopping.

He got up. He smelled something strong and found an animal body. Part of it had been torn off, but it hadn't rotted yet. He looked, watched the direction of the leaves, smelled the air, listened for another's breath, felt for heat. He folded his hands inside the animal and dug in to reach its softer parts. He scooped them and ate, but his head was loud in blood. He didn't have time. He lowered his head and put it inside the animal, pushed his hands against the outside for force. Tore with his teeth until he had no air, drowning in blood, and forced himself out, scent covered. He ran, exposed. Branches breaking, leaves sweeping aside. Footsteps? Breath? All he had to live was fear. He continued running, thought of his own body being torn, longed for the water, the river.

The rain fell. He had no breath to run. The blood and scent came off him. He went as far as he could and collapsed. He closed his eyes and opened his mouth, wide. When he could stand he took leaves and folded them together into a shape like his resting hand and brought it with him.

He stopped frequently, drinking directly from his cup. The rain undrew the land, pools rose on the ground and the animals became more abundant, slow, woken things on the trees springing, uncoiling, oblivious to him. He hurried on, moving slowly against his volume, fearing the languid parade of the cat, the claws that would bring him down, the open mouth vaulting through air towards his face, removing it in one sweep.

He didn't sleep that night. He looked for eye-light in the clumps of solid dark. The rustling of trees, the soft padding of feet on the ground. Other lights, noises. Calling sounds. Something moving right in towards him, exposing him where he lay.

XII

HE WOKE WITH WATER steaming off the land. Light and fog. He was cold, he held himself, watched the land peel open from the haze. He had laid a mark in the ground, a direction to resume, but couldn't find it. Several marks, none he was sure of. He didn't know which way. The light was unclear, not coming from any certain place. He had no route. Not long after setting off, he lost his footing and fell into the humus.

It took a strange effort to get up. Something was wrong. It was dry after the rain, but more water came off him than before. He had to stop again, he drank from his leaf container, but it came back up. All the undigested animal came out and then he opened below in thin gushes. Under the chest the stomach was a small, hard ball with nothing good in it. The rest of him was wire, frame. A ball of sickness under his chest, sick from animal. Each time he expelled, he tried to crawl a little away from it. The smell of him broken and reversed. He saw things move in his pools and didn't know whether they were his or not.

He continued in flux, but the smell disappeared. He was rotting off, losing senses. He didn't know where he was when he woke. How much more could there be, he thought, of him, to give, and of this? He felt so sure it wasn't over. There would be more, itself, himself, all of it left to go, everything gone until he was nothing, and he was very frightened, lying down in the loud dark.

HE EXPELLED EVERYTHING, THE leaves too, but he kept eating them. He realized he must have been hungry again, after all this time, and also that he had a voice. The next day he lost nothing, ate more. He dug up roots and bit into water. He pushed himself to a gap he had spotted, a place where something big must have fallen, and he woke in it, in clear light. He saw the direction of the light. The early sounds went with it, other life. Routine after chaos, shape out the dark. He looked around and saw detail, a radiance in the patterns of the leaves and the colours of the insects.

He managed to stand, leaning on a vine-wrapped tree. He could easily fall, but he was careful. He walked as something strange and new coming forward. The head was an odd size against the neck and the shoulders. He rolled it round. The other things he'd seen had a different proportion. He found berries, ants, water, and felt more substantial.

He set himself a clear routine. Identify the light as it came, fix it in memory and slowly track the place, as directly as he could. He couldn't be misled by the way the light was passing while moving. He was clear on the importance of the direction of the place it came from. He knew he was not restored. He was thin and weak, the blood of animals hung from him, he had to be careful. He had to make things, like the cup he had used and lost. Make something he could carry and put over him when he rested, to hide him, even block a little of the smell. Keep the morning direction and its detail, follow it. Mark it in the ground before it disappeared. The place it came from, the place, he realized, he was going, was the first to vanish every day. The last place visible should face where it was he went to. Mark the direction in the night, and if the morning confirmed it, then it gave him something, it meant he was moving. Build finer shelters in the last light, places deeper between the trees, spaces he could burrow inside.

He began counting, separating one day after another, but soon gave up. He drifted as he walked, and enjoyed it. A slow, natural continuation. He realized halfway between morning and night that sometimes he was just walking, and other times he was walking and asking things. Questions and walking encouraged each other. He got out further and asked more about what this was, what had happened. He wasn't sure. Little things came back—sounds, faces, shelters. At first he drove it off, but he slowly took on the information, day after day, week after week of walking. He must, he realized, have been going for months. What was he walking out from? A place that had disappeared.

XIII

HE WOKE UP THINKING of Santa Lucía; first the words, the name, then the place, the people. He stopped, weak from the information, and settled on the ground, better supported. He spoke aloud, all the names, kept turning around, made marks with a stick into the ground. He tried to draw, he thought, Santa Lucía, which had been lost. But as it was so ridiculous he threw the stick. He couldn't believe this, any of this. He laughed. Where would he start?

He was some kind of an official, he supposed. An inspector. And he had been working on a long investigation. He was tired. But he had to continue, because everyone had disappeared.

HE BECAME EXTREMELY SENSITIVE to light. He knew how scarce it was, how little it could be counted on. The vast trees, looped and tangled, bent into strange and impossible shapes, wanted only the light, were sculpted out of competition for the light. He disciplined himself to wake in the dark and observe the faintest scrap of falling dawn. He collected it. Occasionally there were temporary light columns, strange, passing images with no substance. He fooled himself, thinking on three separate occasions that the precise area he stood in belonged to the past. He knew this ground. He was aware how unlikely it was; that he would know this place, of all places. That in the infinite forest ground he should go over something familiar, somewhere he had been before. It had all grown over, so it wasn't anything particular in the presentation that was the same, the thing he recognized. But it was definitely here, he thought. It didn't matter how illogical it sounded, he knew he was right, this was it, this ground.

It was one of the few weeks each year they'd managed to get the same time off work. They didn't need to go far. They stayed in three hotels, each carefully picked out. Distant enough from the over-populated coast, still accessible in a couple of hours by car. 'I've salt on my back,' she said. They wanted to run. They'd walked in the hills just out of town, brought coffee, wine, oranges, bread, thick ham, sardines. Finding a level spot they laid out their things, ate in the breeze. Drowsy, they slept, curled together on the ground. He woke, vague, initially confused, stumbled some speech, impressions, and she laughed, pushed at his shoulder. He heard the breeze louder, their things rippling.

They were holding their possessions down in the wind, gathering in, packing up. Driving home. The present rolling on, the year gone already.

This wasn't it, he thought. This wasn't the same place.

The trees moved in the breeze and the light passed and he didn't recognize it any more.

The light did stranger things, especially near the end of the day. It climbed away like smoke; he could never reach it. It was getting dark, he was looking for a place to rest, make an interior of leaves, when he saw a fire glow ahead of him. Just a glimpse, not far away. He tried to walk towards it. When he realized it wasn't spreading, that it must have been inside something, he noticed a building around it made of stone. He couldn't get an absolutely clear view, barred by the trees, but the building was small, perhaps a single room. The roof was domed. Someone inside enjoying the hearth, maintaining the fire.

He put his stick out before him, determined to travel in as straight a line as possible to the building and the fire. It should have appeared closer by now, but the building had exactly the same dimensions. The image was constant, as if either he was static or the building, the dome, the fire was moving in tandem. He could get no clear perspective inside the trees. He was no longer surprised when he grabbed for things that weren't there. He had thrilled one morning, spotting through the mist several hogs grunting in the distance. His stomach cramped, flooded with associations and possibilities. He had marched forward and, as a line of beetles strung on a silver web met his nose, he had realized his error.

He turned from the building. Another trick, an illusion. There could be nobody living here; no built things, no fire. He was adapting the objects in front of him and inventing scenarios. It was a rare bright flower, a bird, a frog in warning display.

He saw the building again several days later. He wondered if he was shutting down, generating new temptations for going backwards and giving up, lying in the leaves, into some consolation of forever.

He called out when he found, suddenly, the river again.

He waded into the river, eyes closed, mouth wide and head bent back to touch his shoulder. Just the sound of the water could sustain him for years. The sudden change in temperature and state tightened every muscle of his body, sending a pleasure shock along each nerve, an electric wave ballooning in his head. It felt so good. He tried to be alert, but the water was extravagant and it lit him and he could stay like this. There was so much water, unlimited quantities under the earth. He could drop it all over him, down the fixture of his hair and his hurt shoulders. He took slow pleasure in drying by heat. He could smell it now—abundant life and where it came from, the sluice of minerals, the cold, faraway mountain heights. And the other way, the flow, a discharge down into something vast and inconceivable, the sea.

Climbing out, he saw marks on the river mud. Prints of a large animal leading from the water to the thicket. He measured his feet by them; they were only just larger, a similar shape. They weren't so different that they couldn't have been his. He wasn't surprised at mistakes any longer. He could have left the water earlier and forgotten. The prints running, extending slightly as the moisture filled them.

A small fish, still wet, lay on a stone on the river mud. It was unnatural. Something, he was sure, had taken it there, discarding it. He looked around again. It seemed contrived, too fortunate. No toothmarks visible on the side. He collected it carefully, turning it in his hands, and then held it up to his nose, the memory of the abandoned carcass making him wary. The stench was over him. He flung it back to the ground and he saw the rot where it fell. Fresh, gleaming, tantalizing, what he had seen laid on the rocks wasn't real, the fish had been surface. Small animals, a kind of micro-circuitry, organized themselves inside it. Soon there would be nothing left, no animal.

He was surviving well enough. He trailed the river for a mile or so, a safe distance, retaining the sound of it and making forays in at the half-point, daily. He was feeling better, stronger. Days later the river dwindled into streams, marshes he couldn't pass, and he had no option but to cut back, wait for morning, find a new route out on harder ground.

XIV.

HE TRIED TO RECALL the breadth of the continent. He judged the time past as conservatively as he could, but even then, he estimated he couldn't have much further to go. He thought he was beginning to see signals, stopped, studied them for hours, read the information every way he could. Although he was very careful, when he pushed away the last of the mushroom body it was still possible he destroyed something inside it, covered. He'd thought he had found cloth—he even thought the shape indicated a shoe, something discarded and now wrapped in thick fungal coats. But he couldn't get at it. Whatever was there had split, crumbled into powder in his hands.

He practiced his story; there was pressure to get it right. But as soon as he started on it, he tired, looked for distractions. Although he was getting better, his diet had been so poor, he reasoned, for so long, that it would take him some time to function properly. He was too weak to enjoy thinking of the beginning of his story. All of the details necessary to fill out the scenes he might imagine—starting with the setting, the levelling of the trees around the perimeter of the coastal village where his audience would be; the strange, suspicious looks of the first people to see him; the structure of the homes these people lived in; the physique and facial appearance of the first person he talked to; the drinks they gave him on a tray when they heard how hoarse his voice was; the clarifications they demanded almost as soon as he began, requests for earlier, 'missing' scenes, repeated expressions of incredulity, pity—were an enormous drain on his reserves, when he needed all his energy just to maintain himself.

The quantity of information he would have to tell them, once he reached the village, was getting to be a burden. There was too much of it. Instead of being pleased, excited at the thought, he started to picture it in volume, the amount of space it would occupy. He looked at strips of his story, its information. He did not see how there would be room for it. It was harder for him to breathe. He imagined laying out even a brief description of a scene from near the beginning, after the evacuation, telling, broadly, how it happened. He was immediately overwhelmed. He felt new pressure on his gut and in his head. Just one frame of memory had led to this excess. By tricking himself, admitting memory only in flashes, he had been able to walk, travel a significant distance through the forest. But now he was thinking of presenting them, the memories became real, solid, a fibre in his head.

He hadn't been able to imagine the village where the story would happen. There was the light, the details of the surrounding environment. He would have to conceive of how people would react. There would be a meal, that was important. They would all eat together. He would have to imagine what type of food they prepared and at what point his story would be set aside for it. He wondered whether he would then, later, when he got back to it, have to start all over again, or whether a recap would do and where he would start with that. At the same time he had to consider the food's preparation, the length of time it would take to boil the fish stew and whether it took place outside, perhaps in a covered but open domestic area, or inside, in a distinct and furnished room. He had to imagine how high the roof was and what it was constructed from. Was there smoke in the room? Was the fish preserved and prepared this way, blackened over coals? The fabric of each person's clothing would have to be imagined as well as their hair, their eye colour, the way they moved their head and what it was that had distracted them, some worry, some anticipation, some long-held doubt. Were they all sitting on the ground? Directly or on mats? He had to think of the source of the water used to thin out the juice of the tomatoes, whether it had come from a well or a river—most likely the village would have been founded on a river. He wondered how long the whole process of preparing the food had taken, and during it what and whom the women had discussed, how many children had got in the way, how healthy they were, what was the nature of the relationship between the siblings, who protected whom, who was the leader, the adventurer, and who hung back, stayed closer to home?

The bigger problem was where to begin. In choosing one particular event he would appear to be prioritizing it above all others, saying this was the source of it, even when that wasn't the case at all. It was all equally important, every detail. If there was some way to present it all indiscriminately, simultaneously, he would do that. That was the only way the presentation would be sufficient.

He had a large investigation to present. He wanted to leap to his feet. He could barely comprehend the idea that he was on the cusp of giving it all over. It was even possible—although he had been gone a long time, and admittedly it had all happened quite a distance away— that at least one person in the village would have some knowledge of the disappearance. There had undoubtedly been several expeditions in the preceding months—years?—of parties sent to the site. Enquiries had been made, surely, after the loss of Santa Lucía, in every settlement around the interior. Chances were that someone in the village would recall his own disappearance, visits made by his colleagues, friends from the department flying in.

For the moment, despite all this excess of time, he didn't think in any detail about his resettlement. The construction of all the possible scenarios was ludicrously unfeasible. To imagine meeting his friends, relatives, colleagues again, after all this time, after everything that had happened, required many worlds to be built. He couldn't just cut directly to a celebratory reunion in a bar, dark, full of people whose faces were lacking in detail; it had been some time since he had seen any of them and they would have aged, naturally, every day counting. He would need some idea, first, of the steps that led down to the basement, the distance from the bar to the street, how close it was to the nearest metro station, whether parking was available, what kind of clothing the attendee wore and whether it was issued as standard or adapted to suit, where the fabric had originally been produced and under what kind of working conditions, the duration of any breaks . . .

Once he got out onto the street, then there were obviously many more details to take into account. An unknown number of people working, commuting, entering and exiting shops, cafés, offices, apartments, moving at various speeds, smoking, talking into phones. Some would be wearing lipstick, lip balm, depending on the humidity, the levels of pollution affected by the time of day and the correlating traffic intensity.

He did not feel prepared for this. The regularity of the peopled world would not come back easily. Even fundamental details were stark and shocked him. He could not move forward from one thing to the next. A single physical detail was excessive, it contained too much.

He tried to picture something that should have been simple, typical—a vendor at a news stand. Begin, move on. He aimed at a clear outline, but faltered, seeing newsprint on the tip of the man's right index finger and thumb; he thought of childbirth, of cupboard drawers in the poorer districts, lined with near germ-free print.

He didn't know where to look on the street. A single street. A bank of space. An overwhelming series of objects reflecting, refracting, obstructing light. He tried to imagine the sunlight, which meant first he would have to fix on a certain time of day for the reunion to take place, dictated by the schedules of the people most important to him, who would by now, it was only fair to imagine, have moved on with their lives; it may be, in fact, that his returning, specifically the reunion evening he was in the process of creating, was greeted with something other than unreserved joy. He tried to make it real, picture the roads, the pavements, the models and manufacturers of cars, the distances the parts had travelled, the nature of the automated machinery used to guide their larger construction, the litter on the ground, the footwear worn by pedestrians, the sounds of the surrounding city travelling as many as six miles or more.

Even then, it wasn't as if he could cut directly to that day, straight from the forest, all the details of the reunion celebration spontaneously willed into being. He would have to travel there, move his body along in a series of different vehicles; even when he had exited the forest and the interior there would be a long time spent with medical experts, physical and mental, evaluating his condition, judging his state and suitability for reintegration. As he was very ill, with all manner of infections, parasites, there would be a long time, weeks at least, he should think, spent in transit, in medical quarters. He realized, in addition, that even just procedurally, as a technicality, he might have to prove to them, the officials handling the case, that he was indeed the person he claimed to be; they would have to verify his identity either biologically or through an extensive series of questions.

He could not imagine what it would be like at the airport. Had he passed national frontiers already, in the forest? Would the embassy have to assign him a passport before travel, and what would that entail? Again there was the long, difficult question of verification, of meeting the stringent demands the officials would place on him. He couldn't think of the word denoting the material passports were made of. It seemed a laborious process manufacturing it, printing on it, laminating the pages, linking up all the details to other profiles on vast digital databases. That was the problem he was facing now, trying to distract himself from the flies on his nose, his cheeks, his eyelids and his lips. Whenever he tried to anticipate something different, something from the future, a new scene, anything ongoing, anything, in other words, that was not this, he felt he had to establish the smallest part, every feature of the hypothetical scene, or else it would fall apart. The effort seemed impossible. How could it be done? How could it continue?

XV

SOMETHING DIFFERENT, HE THOUGHT, around him in or through the trees, but he didn't name it. He went slowly, thinking more about his resettlement, about what might happen to him when he made it out of the forest. His seniors, the department, the friends and even before that, local officials, police authorities, representatives of the council . . . They were all going to expect something from him, weren't they? Then, of course, there were the relatives of the people involved in the disappearance—what was he going to say to them? He had not enough time, yet. He was anxious the more the light filtered through the trees behind him, late in the day. He had to think hard. Could he go back? Spend longer going over the forest, furthering his work on the investigation? Perhaps all the way back to Santa Lucía—to the place, he corrected himself, where Santa Lucía had once stood? Certainly, he wasn't prepared, he hadn't any useful information to give to them when he got clear of the forest, far less any kind of comprehensive dossier relating to the investigation.

The light continued to develop further every morning—there was nothing to accept but that he was getting closer to the end, or at least to a substantial clearing, suggesting a sizeable community. The forest around him now was different, had been harvested, even

251

lived in at some stage, and he was confident, he was almost certain, that people lived not far from here, just a little further on. He didn't know what to do. He could still turn back, make his way into the thicker parts of the forest, which he had lived in, now, for months at least. Perhaps in the couple of days following, a hunter or some playing children from the village would notice his prints, see them as strange, and report on it. There might be an initial, only cursory attempt to locate him, but it wouldn't be anything that could threaten him, really.

He was light-headed, and he kept hearing himself laughing, which was strange. It was all absurd, he thought, the whole thing. But would he not regret turning back, having trusted, up from almost nothing, up from just the ground, the light, moving east and getting there, finally, to the edge? Equally, could he really simply stop, as if it were finished, as if he had completed something, anything, when clearly he hadn't, he hadn't done a thing, hadn't begun any kind of investigation at all?

HE SWORE HE COULD smell it. The salt, the algae, the fish. The forest had changed, there were hints of quicker degradation on the leaves, perhaps from sodium in the air or from parasites, opportunists in the new space. He tried to scan for difference, a greater distance communicated in the bird calls.

He shivered in the cold nights, bundled in thick leaves and branches, wrapped in his rags and arms, looking up at the glimmering networks of ice-points in the terrifying sky.

He found tracks, rough sketches in the topsoil. He tensed his body, stopped and listened. Waited. A hammering, an engine, a calling out. His blood rushed and he seemed to feel, solidly, the entire mass of his head. Was something there? Really there? Had he heard it or not? He looked at the evidence. How old were the tracks? He couldn't see steps, individual prints. He searched for oil, industry, anything artificial through the leaves, then he stopped again. His pulse slowed, he became steadier, told himself to calm, continue forward, same as always.

The forest seemed to grow over again. The thinning might have been temporary, freak, not evidence of habitation at all. The only sounds he heard were birds. In time the birds could mimic everything.

Through the undergrowth ahead he saw a light, a flash. The sun got in. He dug for the source and pulled out steel. A fork. He held it in his left hand, instinctively assuming a mealtime posture.

XVI.

HE WALKED AT A slow pace until he heard it. A low sound, a drift rising in volume to a colossal roar, then a fall, a repetition. The sound so big and wide he was afraid. He was still. The forest ahead, but less of it.

The edge was sudden. He wasn't able to comprehend, at first, that the white through the thin bush ahead was the sky over the Atlantic. He went through easily, not like he'd imagined. Suddenly he had walked out into nothing, all this empty, staggering space and sun.

His first thought was to go the other way, turn back, find shade. His body—cut, thin, swollen in places, with sores across it—burned. Ahead of him was twenty feet or so of level ground, clear, then rocks sharply descending to the sea. He didn't notice much. He thought he'd notice everything. It wasn't supposed to be like this. There was nothing, just this noise, this roar, this heat.

He heard something, like crying, he thought, a long moaning sound coming out from the level ground before the rocks. He thought it must have been himself. Then he heard it again, the sound, strange in the wind, with the waves thick in it, a young, long moaning sound.

A dark shape moved on the edge of his vision. Whatever it was, moving, it wasn't alone. Close enough, he saw the animals, hogs. Seven of them grazing on the thin bushes, wandering freely. He couldn't tell if they were wild, abandoned.

He tried to think, but it was hard. He had almost nothing left. He felt the effort of thoughts building, dissolving in his head. But something went the other way. A shape developed on the slope down, a building coming into form. It didn't seem practical, even possible, on the steep slope, but it was there, it was real. He went closer to look.

More buildings suggested themselves out of the rock, simple, almost cave-like spaces cut into stone. By one he saw bright colours, blue, red, yellow, a line of clothes hung between the building and a bare tree. He heard the fabric move, flapping loud and empty in the sea wind. He saw a path, thin and barely there, a light sketch drawn on the pebbles.

He looked out over the water, stood in the raw air.

He was at a height now, fifty feet or so above the water. Only the loudness of it, against him, kept him upright. He had nothing to hold on to. He focused on the waves, their repeated rise and fall, afraid of looking or thinking any further. He could not comprehend it, the limit of a continent. He was unsure what it meant, now, to be here. His eyes were different in the forest, diverted, set to insects, berries, water signs and tracks. And now, ahead of him, was the vast arc of the horizon, the wide edge of an available world.

The waves shook his thin body. He watched them as a child would, thrilled by their momentum and promise, and stupidly, broadly stunned each time they broke and spilled. He reeled back on the boom of it. A thousand gunshots every time. He imagined the strange and large wooden ships populating the horizon, then saw them disappear.

He looked down at the path, which wound towards the first of the buildings, where the bright clothes hung. But it didn't stop there. It continued, past the building, coming out on the water. He thought he could probably manage the route. There, guarded by the rocks from the waves, he could swim.

ACKNOWLEDGEMENTS

THANKS TO:

Rachel Conway, my agent at Georgina Capel Associates, whose wit, clarity and understanding came as a godsend; James Roxburgh, my editor, for his ferocious intelligence and enthusiasm; Megan McLaren, for giving expert feedback on a chapter; and the brilliant Sarah Ream, for helping immeasurably from an early stage. Thanks, also, to Taylor Sperry and the staff at Melville House, and to the many other people involved in putting the book together, from copy editing to design.

Note: the microbiology featured in several chapters is always speculative, and sometimes wholly invented.

A NOTE ABOUT THE AUTHOR

Martin MacInnes lives in Edinburgh, Scotland. In 2014, he won the Manchester Fiction Prize and a New Writers Award from Scottish Book Trust. *Infinite Ground* is his first novel.